"I guess I don't have a choice." I sighed. "Meet me on The Ramp at lunch on Monday and you can start then. But I'm telling you I don't care what my father says—if I see that you're trying to make me look bad, the deal's off. Got it?"

"Got it," he replied, nibbling away on the black side of the cookie.

"And don't think that this means that all of a sudden we're like friends, or anything," I said. "It's strictly business. Oh, and in case you didn't know, Asher and I are super serious, so if you were thinking of using this documentary thing as a way to, you know, *hit on me* or anything, it's not going to work."

"Don't worry," Geek Boy said. "Like you said, it's strictly business. But who knows—maybe this'll be the start of a long and rewarding working relationship."

Sheesh—*someone* was taking this movie stuff *way* too seriously. "What?" I asked.

"Nothing," he said as he stood up and put out his hand. "So we have a deal?"

I put mine out as well. "I guess so."

As I walked him to what he called the Neilmobile (Hello? Can you *get* cheesier than that?) I tried to look at the bright side of things: helping Geek Boy fulfill his dream of getting into USC film school had to balance out whatever bad karma I may have had.

Not that I had any, of course.

OTHER BOOKS YOU MAY ENJOY

Geek Charming

ROBIN PALMER

speak

An Imprint of Penguin Group (USA) Inc.

SPEAK
Published by the Penguin Group
Penguin Group (USA) Inc., 345 Hudson Street, New York, New York 10014, U.S.A.
Penguin Group (Canada), 90 Eglinton Avenue East, Suite 700,
Toronto, Ontario M4P 2Y3 Canada (a division of Pearson Penguin Canada Inc.)
Penguin Books Ltd, 80 Strand, London WC2R 0RL, England
Penguin Group Ireland, 25 St Stephen's Green, Dublin 2, Ireland
(a division of Penguin Books Ltd)
Penguin Group (Australia), 250 Camberwell Road, Camberwell, Victoria 3124, Australia
(a division of Pearson Australia Group Pty. Ltd)
Penguin Books India Pvt. Ltd., 11 Community Centre,
Panchsheel Park, New Delhi - 110 017, India
Penguin Group (NZ), 67 Apollo Drive, Rosedale, North Shore 0632, New Zealand
(a division of Pearson New Zealand Ltd)
Penguin Books (South Africa) (Pty) Ltd, 24 Sturdee Avenue,
Rosebank, Johannesburg 2196, South Africa

Registered Offices: Penguin Books Ltd, 80 Strand, London WC2R 0RL, England

Published by Speak, an imprint of Penguin Group (USA) Inc., 2009

7 9 10 8 6

LIBRARY OF CONGRESS CATALOGING-IN-PUBLICATION DATA
Palmer, Robin, 1969-
Geek charming / by Robin Palmer.
p. cm.
Summary: Rich, spoiled, and popular high school senior Dylan is coerced into doing a
documentary film with Josh, one of the school's geeks, who leads her
to realize that the world does not revolve around her.
ISBN 978-0-14-241122-3 (pbk.)
[1. Documentary films—Fiction. 2. Popularity—Fiction.
3. Interpersonal relations—Fiction. 4. High schools—Fiction. 5. Schools—Fiction.] I. Title.
PZ7.P1861Ge 2009
[Fic]—dc22   2008025918

SPEAK ISBN 978-0-14-241122-3

Printed in the United States of America

To the real Amy Loubalu,

For restoring my sanity on a daily basis

Acknowledgments

With special thanks to:

Jennifer Bonnell—the world's best editor and midwife—for getting me the way she does, and for always making me laugh through the pain of the contractions.

Eileen Kreit at Puffin for being such an enthusiastic cheerleader.

My agent, Kate Lee, for everything else.

And New York City, which became my new home while writing this.

Geek Charming

chapter one: *dylan*

One day as I was watching *Oprah*, waiting for her to get to her "Favorite Things for Spring" segment (she has *the* cutest taste in accessories), I heard this self-help guru guy say that the word for *crisis* in Chinese is actually two words: *danger* and *opportunity*.

The reason I looked up from *Vogue* when the guru said this is because I have one of those lives where there's always a crisis going on. Like 24/7. My best friend, Lola Leighton, says that I'm just a drama queen and that they're not *real* crises, like, say, the kind she would've had to deal with if her parents hadn't adopted her from the orphanage in China. Okay, yes, when you put it in that context, I guess Lola's right. But since I live in Beverly Hills and not a third-world country, my crises and the crises of nonadopted kids are bound to be different, you know?

Take, for instance, the time I was driving home from the Justin Timberlake concert at the Staples Center and I was all by myself because I had a huge fight with my boy-friend Asher after I caught him staring at Amy Loubalu's boobs like *seven* times that night even though he swears he wasn't, and my BMW conked out on the 405 freeway at midnight and I had to wait an *hour* for Triple A to arrive. Now, that, in my book, is a crisis—especially since I was wearing a miniskirt and tank top because it was a mil-lion degrees out. I mean, if a serial killer who liked girls with long blonde hair and blue eyes had driven by at that moment, I would've been dead meat. The only "opportu-nity" there was the opportunity to be chopped up into a million little pieces.

As far as I'm concerned, sometimes a crisis is just a cri-sis. Like what happened last week with my Serge Sanchez bag. Yet *another* crisis—and the only opportunity there was to see what $1,200 worth of red leather would look like after it dried out. (FYI, it turns out that it doesn't look so bad—sort of a cross between my two favorite nail pol-ishes, OPI's I'm Not Really A Waitress and Essie's Scarlett O'Hara.)

It was Tuesday afternoon and I was at The Dell, which is a huge outdoor mall on the border of Beverly Hills and West Hollywood that my dad happens to own, with Lola and Hannah Mornell, our other best friend. The day before I had seen these absolutely *darling* J.Crew red gingham bal-let flats that I just had to have because I knew they'd look so cute with my black capris and a white shirt I had bought the week before. Very 1960s movie-starlet-ish, which was going to be my new look for fall. So I had gotten the shoes (plus two dresses, some tank tops, a cashmere hoodie, and some lip gloss) and the three of us were hanging out in front of the fountain deciding whether we should go to Urth Caffé for sugar-free iced vanilla lattes or Pinkberry for frozen yogurt when the Crisis-with-a-capital-C occurred.

"Omigod, Dylan," said Hannah as she clipped a tortoiseshell barrette onto her short auburn bob. Hannah is incredibly preppy for L.A. standards. While I may buy something from J.Crew occasionally, like the ballet flats, almost her entire wardrobe is from there. B-o-r-i-n-g, if you ask me, but I do believe in freedom of speech in fashion choices, so whatever. "I can't believe I forgot to tell you who Jennifer Bonnell saw at Pinkberry on Sunday afternoon!"

"Who?" I asked, with my face tipped up to the sun as I tried to get some fall rays.

"Amy Loubalu."

"So?" I said.

"So," said Hannah, "she just *happened* to be talking to Asher."

My head snapped down so fast I'm surprised I didn't break my neck.

This is when the Crisis began.

"She is *so Single White Female*-ing me!" I cried. *Single White Female* was a movie I once saw on HBO about this woman whose roommate starts dressing like her, and gets the same haircut, and then steals her boyfriend and *kills him*.

Lola rolled her brown eyes as she put on some lip gloss. "Um, excuse me but she looks nothing like you. If anything, she looks like me."

"Um, don't take this the wrong way, but if you haven't noticed, you're Asian," I said.

"Yeah, but we both have long dark hair," she replied.

"She has a point," added Hannah.

Okay, so maybe Amy didn't *look* like me, since I'm blonde and she's brunette, but she was obviously trying to copy me by stealing Asher away from me. People like to say that when people copy you, it's supposed to be flattering, but I don't see it that way. Frankly, I find it very lazy. I've worked very hard to be the most popular girl in the senior class at Castle Heights High and it's not fair for some girl to think she can just ride on my coattails.

As I continued going off on Amy in front of the fountain, I was waving my arms a lot, which is what I tend to do when I go into what Lola calls DQM (Drama Queen Mode). Just then my Serge Sanchez bag—which had been hanging on my right arm like it always was because I was terrified of having it stolen—went flying into the fountain. Apparently my arms had gotten really strong from Pilates because it's not like the bag just sort of plopped over the edge so I could easily fish it out. It went soaring all the way into the middle, and since it's such a huge fountain, there was no way I could get it out myself.

After that I did what anyone in my situation would do—I started freaking out and threatening to sue until Hannah pointed out that not only did I not have a reason to sue because the whole thing was my own fault, but since my dad owns The Dell, I'd be suing him and that probably wouldn't go over very well. When I realized Hannah had a point, I did the next best thing that someone in my position would do—I started looking around for a guy to jump into the fountain to fish it out for me. Not to sound full of myself or anything, but getting guys to help me out with stuff is never a problem, whether it be trig homework or opening my locker, which is always getting jammed due to the fact that I like to keep a few different outfits in there at all times in case I have a fashion mood change. The only problem is that most of the guys you find at a mall at 4 P.M. on a weekday are either old or gay, so the chances of one of them agreeing to jump into a fountain fully clothed to fish out a handbag aren't so good, even when you start screaming that there's a reward at stake.

I'm sure I was causing quite a scene, but it's not like you could blame me. I mean, if *you* had put yourself on the wait list at Barneys New York a year earlier for the Serge Sanchez Jaime bag and then used all your Sweet Sixteen booty to buy it, you'd be freaking out, too. Not only was it *the* bag of choice for every celeb who had been on the cover of *US Weekly* or *People* over the last few months, but I—Dylan Frances Schoenfield—was the only nonstarlet high school girl in all of L.A. who had scored one so far.

"Miss. Miss. MISS!" I heard someone say as I sat there on the edge of the fountain with my head between my legs trying to get my breathing back to normal.

My head popped up. "What?!" I snapped.

In front of me was a pimply-faced security guard, dressed in overalls and a straw hat to go along with the whole "Dell" theme. Everyone who worked at The Dell—from the parking-garage people to the bathroom attendants—were forced to dress up like farmers or milkmaids. Ridiculous, I know. You can thank my dad for that. I tried to talk him out of it because not only is it corny, but farming and shopping—unless it's for eggs—don't really go together, but Daddy says that if you want to succeed at something, you have to have a gimmick. He may be a genius when it comes to real estate, but the truth is he's kind of a geek. I mean, I love him to death but he's utterly hopeless when it comes to being creative—especially if it happens to be fashion-related. In fact, after my mom died a few years ago, I had to take over her job of picking out which shirt and tie he should wear with his suit in the morning. I'm not complaining, though. Sharing my incredible talent for color coordinating and accessorizing with the man whose name is on my Amex card is the least I can do.

"Uh, you're gonna have to quiet down or else I'm going to have to remove you from the property," Farmer Security Guard mumbled.

"Excuse me, but my father happens to *own* this property," I shot back.

"He does?"

"Yes. He does. I'm Dylan Schoenfield, daughter of Alan Schoenfield of Schoenfield Properties."

"Oh." He shrugged. "Then I guess it's okay," he said, shuffling away.

I turned toward the fountain to get an update on my bag and saw it bobbing along in time to Christina Aguilera's "What a Girl Wants" that was blasting over the sound system. Another one of Daddy's gimmicks was to have the spray of the fountain synchronized to the music, like you see at the hotels in Las Vegas. I just hoped that it didn't switch to something with a really fast beat or else I'd *never* get my bag back.

"My poor bag!" I cried as Hannah and Lola stood on each side of me and patted my shoulders. I couldn't remember being this devastated since the time Asher blew off my Sweet Sixteen dinner for a Lakers game. "What am I going to do, you guys?" I panicked as a brown-haired guy with thick-framed glasses walked toward us.

"Get your dad to buy you a new one?" asked Lola.

The guy was so busy trying to juggle his knapsack, doughnut, and Coke that he tripped on Lola's Marc Jacobs bag, which she had bought with *her* Sweet Sixteen money, and fell flat on his face right in front of me.

For a few seconds he didn't move.

"Are you all right?" I asked while watching with horror as my bag bobbed around in the fountain.

When I didn't hear a response, I tore my eyes away from the fountain and looked down at him. Because of the glare of the sun, it was hard to see if his body was rising and falling with his breath.

"Um, hello?" I said.

Nothing.

I started to get scared that maybe he had broken his neck and died instantly, which would not have been good because not only would his parents probably sue Lola's parents but they'd probably also try to sue my dad as well. Daddy likes to say that suing is what people do for fun in L.A.

As Hannah ran to the edge of the fountain and reached her arm toward the bag (as if *that* was going to do any-thing), I watched with horror as it got caught on a water jet and started whipping around like it was in a T-ball tour-nament. Extending my foot, I carefully poked the guy with my shoe. Obviously if he was dead it wouldn't matter if I did it carefully or uncarefully, but I was raised to be polite and courteous. "Excuse me, but ARE. YOU. ALL. RIGHT?" I yelled as if he were deaf and non-English-speaking.

Still nothing.

This was now officially terrifying—both the idea that I might be a witness to an accidental murder *and* the fact that my Sweet Sixteen booty was about to go down the drain. Literally. "Omigod! Omigod!" I shrieked. "Someone call an ambulance!" I announced to the mallgoers before turning to Lola. "And you—be a best friend and go help Hannah try and get my bag. *Now*, please."

Lola stopped examining her own bag for scuffs and rolled her eyes before getting off the fountain ledge and slowly walking over to the other side of the fountain. Unfortunately, unlike Hannah, who was being *productive*— she had somehow gotten hold of a pole from one of the mall cart people and was using it like a fishing pole to try to rescue my bag—Lola just stood there and scratched the side of her nose as she watched. I'm not one to talk bad about people, but sometimes I couldn't *believe* how selfish and self-centered Lola could be.

"*Oooofffff*," the maybe-dead guy finally said as he reached up and put his hands over his ears.

"Oh, thank *God*." I sighed. Even though my bag had moved on to being shot up in the air like a cannonball (not a good sign), I was relieved he was alive (good sign).

A moment later the guy struggled to his feet and slowly started bending his arms and legs like one of those puppets with the strings that Marta, our housekeeper, once brought back for me from one of her trips to visit her family in El Salvador.

"Did you break anything?" I asked anxiously as my bag made a graceful arc in the air before plummeting back down.

"I don't think so," he said, wincing as he wiggled his fingers.

Up close I could see that he was around our age, and that he was wearing a T-shirt that said GEEK GANG. I don't mean to be mean or anything, but why someone like him would choose to wear a shirt that announced such a thing to the entire free world when it was obvious just looking at him that he was a geek was beyond me.

I looked back at the fountain. Just as it seemed that Hannah had hooked the strap of the bag with her pseudo fishing pole, the pole slipped out of her hand and started floating away and the bag began to slowly sink.

"If you're okay, then I need you to do me a huge, huge, HUGE favor," I demanded as the guy crouched down on the ground.

"My inhaler! Where's my inhaler?" I heard him mumbling over and over as he rifled through the spilled contents of his knapsack, which included about twenty different pens, some magazine called *Fade In*, and a copy of the *Hollywood Reporter.*

"Your what?" I demanded.

"My inhaler. I have really bad asthma," he replied nervously.

Great. Just what I needed—*another* crisis.

"Here it is," he said. After he took a hit, his shoulders moved down from around his ears to their proper location. "Okay. Much better. Sorry, were you saying something?" he asked as we both stood up.

Was *anyone* other than Hannah able to get out of themselves for just one minute? I pointed at the fountain. "I need you to climb in there and get my bag. Like this *very second.*"

He put his now-crooked glasses back on to get a better look. It took everything in me not to reach over and push his shaggy brown hair off his face. Didn't he realize the whole emo look was *so 2006*?

"You're kidding, right?" he said.

"Hmm . . . let me think about that . . . um, *no!*" I yelled.

"Do you realize what kind of diseases a person could get in there?" he asked. "In addition to leptospirosis, there's shingellosis, and—"

"What are you *talking* about?"

"I read about it on WebMD," he said defensively. He took another hit off the inhaler. "Plus, I'm susceptible to inner-ear infections, so I have to be careful not to get water in my ear."

By this time Lola had decided to be a friend and was putting her flirting skills to good use by going up to all the cart guys to see if they'd help, but from all the head shaking it was obvious that there was no mall community spirit in this bunch. I made a mental note to tell Daddy to send a mallwide memo talking about the importance of coming together in times of crisis to help people out.

"It's only like two feet deep in there!" I exclaimed. "It's not like I'm asking you to go deep-sea diving in the *Bahamas*. Please," I begged. "I'll give you . . . a hundred dollars."

He shook his head. "Sorry. I really can't help you." He crouched back down to put his stuff back in his knapsack. "Just ask them to shut down the fountain until you can get it out," he said.

"I don't have time for that!" I cried. As Christina was replaced by Gwen Stefani singing "I'm Just a Girl," my bag rose from the dead and started a wild modern dance solo in the air. "Can't you see this is an emergency?! What about two hundred?"

He shook his head. "Really, I can't. They canceled our health insurance because my mom didn't pay the bill for the last three months; so I'm trying really hard to not get sick right now. Which is kind of hard, because I don't have a very strong immune system to begin with—my mom thinks it's because I was three weeks premature."

I thought about explaining to him that there were these things called *tanning salons* and maybe if he got some sun and lost the Pillsbury Doughboy look, he wouldn't get sick because the sun is very helpful for colds and diseases, but since I was in the middle of watching my status go from It-Bag Girl to No-Bag Girl, I didn't have time to be giving out advice to strangers.

I turned toward the fountain for an update. The solo was over and my bag was back to sinking. Lola couldn't even get the T-Mobile cart guy—who had a massive crush on her—to come over and help.

I grabbed Geek Boy by the shoulders. *"Please*—you've *got* to help me. I'll do anything. I'll even—" I was about to say *let you take me out on a date*, but then I thought better of it. "Be your friend on Facebook. Please—just tell me what it will take to make you go get my bag!"

As he took another squirt of the inhaler, his eyes bugged out and a huge smile came over his face. "I'll do it if you let me film you and your friends," he said.

"Eww!" I squealed. "What are you—some kind of pervert? That's totally disgusting!"

"No—I mean make a documentary about you! I've been trying to think of something to send in with my essay for my USC film school application and this is perfect. You know, like an 'inner workings of the in crowd at Castle Heights High' type of thing."

My eyes narrowed. "Wait a second—how'd you know I go to Castle Heights?" Maybe this guy didn't just *happen* to walk by me—maybe he was *stalking* me. Not to sound stuck-up or anything, but I have been known to have that effect on guys.

"Because I go there, too."

"You do?"

"Yeah."

"What are you, a junior?" I asked.

13

"No," he scoffed. "I'm a senior. Like you."

"Did you just transfer there or something?"

"No. I've been there all four years. We had Spanish together freshman year."

I couldn't remember ever having seen him before in my life. Which wasn't so surprising, I guess, seeing that none of the geeks ever came within fifty feet of The Ramp in the cafeteria, where my friends and I sat.

Hannah walked up to me, her barrette hanging off the edge of her bob and her shirt soaked. "Okay, I know we're best best friends and all, but I'm done trying to help." She pointed at Lola, who was now twirling a lock of her hair around her finger as she threw back her head and laughed at something the T-Mobile guy was saying to her. "Especially since *she* hasn't helped at all."

I leaned over the fountain as far as I could without falling in, but I couldn't even see the bag anymore. I turned to the geek. "Okay! Okay! It's a deal! Now go," I demanded.

"Really?" he asked.

I yanked the inhaler out of his hand and started pushing him toward the fountain. "Yes. Go! Go!"

Celine Dion started singing "My Heart Will Go On" from *Titanic*, and the bag rose from the dead yet again. Every time Celine hit a high note and sent a jet of water up into the sky, Geek Boy ran for cover behind the marble centerpiece like a duck in one of those amusement-park games. If I hadn't been so worried about my bag, the whole thing would have been hysterical.

14

By this time a huge crowd had gathered behind me to watch. "What a dork. Too bad we don't have a video camera—this would make an awesome YouTube video," said Lola.

"Sure, if you're into making bad karma for yourself, it would be," sniffed Hannah.

"It's amazing how some people *totally* lose their sense of humor when they're PMSing," snapped Lola.

"Um, hi, ladies? This is so not the time for catfights, okay? This is about me and my bag." It was rare that I made it all about me, but if there was ever a time, this was obviously the case. I mean, now that I had experienced how incredible the feeling of the leather from the Serge Sanchez felt against the skin of my arm, it wasn't like I could go back to a regular old Marc Jacobs bag or something like that. That would be like being content with a soft-serve cone from the mall after having tasted Häagen-Dazs. Not that I ever touched the stuff myself.

A huge cheer went up as Geek Boy finally caught the bag like a football and held it over his head in triumph as he walked toward us like an ocean liner sailing on the sea. "Here," he panted as he thrust my waterlogged bag into my arms after stepping out of the fountain. Judging from the way his face resembled a tomato, this seemed to be the biggest workout he had gotten in years. "Where's. My. Inhaler?" he gasped.

"Here it is," I said, picking it up from the ledge of the fountain and exchanging it for the bag. Other than the bag weighing about five extra pounds because of the water, it looked salvageable—especially when the guys at Arturo's Shoe Fix got their hands on it. But once I unzipped it, I could feel my face pale. "Oh no," I whispered. I could care less about whether or not my lip gloss was ruined, or if my wallet was wet, or if my pack of gum was all soggy, but as I pushed the buttons on my Weight Watchers points calculator and the screen remained blank, I could feel my heart start to race to the point where I wished I had my own inhaler.

I looked at him. "My calculator. It's *ruined*."

He took another hit off the inhaler. "So go to Good Buys and buy another one," he replied. "You'll get a great deal—especially with the Just-Because-It's-Wednesday sale going on." Good Buys was this cheesy electronics store in the mall. I kept telling Daddy that it was so *not* in line with The Dell's reputation for excellence, but he just ignored me.

"It's not a regular calculator—it's my *Weight Watchers* points calculator!"

He looked at me like I was crazy. "But you're so skinny. You don't need Weight Watchers. You need to *gain* weight."

I couldn't believe he would say something so rude. "Of course I don't need Weight Watchers," I replied. "And the reason I don't need it is because of this," I said, pointing to the calculator.

"I'll never understand girls. Oh, and you're welcome," he said as he started ringing out his T-shirt, exposing his squishy fish-belly-white gut.

Lola cringed. "Ew, dude—can we watch the nudity, please?"

"Welcome for what?" I asked.

"Getting your bag for you?" he replied.

"Oh. Right. Thank you." I threw in a just-bleached smile. "I very much appreciate it."

Now that the crisis was officially over, everyone went back to shopping.

"So here's what I'm thinking in terms of the documentary," he said.

"The what?"

"The documentary. The one you said I could make in return for getting your bag."

"Oh, that one—right," I replied. "Hey, can we talk about it tomorrow? This whole thing has been super traumatic and I think I need to go home and lie down. Come on, girls," I said to Hannah and Lola, who were now sitting on the edge of the fountain with their faces toward the sun.

As the three of us started walking toward the parking garage, Lola kept trying to edge out Hannah with her hip so that she'd walk just the *teensiest* bit behind us instead of next to me. So rude, I know, but I didn't like to get involved in their drama. While the three of us were BFFs, I was definitely the glue that held us together. Being the person that everyone liked the best could be exhausting at times.

"Okay, but I don't have your e-mail address. Or your phone number!" Geek Boy shouted. "I think we should schedule a preproduction meeting for some time over the weekend to talk about the logistics and how filming is going to work. I mean, obviously we could do more of a guerrilla-style type look and style, but while I was in the fountain I was thinking the look for this should be more polished. I'm thinking how Alek Keshishian did the Madonna documentary *Truth or Dare* back in '91. Even though we don't have a lot of time to prep, I'd like to make the most of the time we do have."

I walked back over to him. "Yeah, let's talk a little more about this documentary thing. Are we talking MTV-reality-series-like?" Maybe I could end up getting a deal there for my show. Maybe even a *talk* show. People were always telling me I was like a younger version of Oprah.

"No. I'm thinking more hard-hitting than that. More in the vein of something Barbara Koppel would do. Or the Maysles brothers."

"Do they go to our school, too?" I asked.

I couldn't imagine anyone would be so rude, but it almost looked like he cringed when I asked that.

"No, they don't go to our school," he replied with a sigh. "They're only two of the most important documentarians in the history of documentaries."

"If it's a pair of brothers and then that Barbara person, that's three," corrected Hannah. It was stuff like that that explained why she was in AP classes and me and Lola weren't.

"I stand corrected," Geek Boy said. "So can I get your number?" he asked, holding out a notepad and one of the dozen pens from his knapsack.

I wrote down my phone number and handed it back to him. "This weekend's kind of jammed but call me and we'll set something up."

"Great," he said with a smile. His hair might have been a lost cause, but he had very straight teeth. He held out his hand, which looked like a waterlogged prune. "I look forward to working with you."

I tried not to cringe as I shook it. "Uh huh. See you around," I said as I started walking away.

Poor guy. Between the fact that he looked like a drowned gopher and the fact that I had had my fingers crossed behind my back when I had agreed, I almost felt bad for him.

chapter two: *josh*

It's funny how when something's meant to be, all these things happen to just make them . . . well, *be*. Like in *Knocked Up*, when Seth Rogen gets Katherine Heigl pregnant—first it seems like they'd never make it as a couple and then they end up realizing they do love each other even though he's a schlub and she's gorgeous.

And like with the documentary.

Flashback to the night before the purse-in-the-fountain incident. Me and my best friend, Steven Blecher, were hanging out at this coffeehouse called Java the Hut on Vine Street in Hollywood, where Quentin and Judd (that's Tarantino, as in *Pulp Fiction* and Apatow, as in *The 40-Year-Old Virgin* and the above-mentioned *Knocked Up*) have been known to stop in when they're editing movies at one of the various postproduction places in the area. Quentin and I are buds. Okay, well, I met him once when he spoke at our school's Film Society, so maybe we're not best friends, but we *have* exchanged dialogue.

As Steven bickered via IM with some kid at NYU film school that he met in a MySpace group devoted to Steven Spielberg about where *Jaws* had been shot, I worked on my essay for my USC application. "Do you think I should tell them that my dream is to become the Woody Allen of the twenty-first century, or do you think they'll get that when they watch *Andy Hull*?" I asked Steven. Because the competition to get into the film school was insane, the week before I had decided I'd submit a short film with my application. My plan was to make one called *Andy Hull*, which I saw as being similar to *Annie Hall*—Woody's 1977 masterpiece—but instead of being about a nerdy, neurotic middle-aged guy, it would be about a nerdy, neurotic teenage girl. I even had my leading lady picked out—Diane Lowenstein, a girl who my friend Ari had gone to theater camp with the summer before.

"Dude, I told you to bag that *Andy Hull* idea," Steven said as he broke off a huge chunk of my brownie. "It's lame." Steven's a bit on the tubby side. My mom's always on me to lighten up on the sugar, but honestly, as far as I'm concerned, it's preparation for later when I'm doing night shoots and need a quick pick-me-up. "If you're going to blatantly rip off a movie that's already been made, at least find some Japanese horror one no one's seen instead of something so mainstream."

I shook my head. "That's way too 2005." I sighed and tipped my chair back. "I just need to face it—I'm undergoing my first official creative block. I feel like Nicolas Cage in *Adaptation* when he couldn't write the script."

I would have done anything for Quentin to walk in at that moment so I could ask him what *he* did when he was blocked creatively, but I had no such luck. Instead I had to wait a full twenty-four hours, until I ran into Dylan. If you had told me even a week before that Dylan Schoenfield of all people would have ended up being my muse, I would have laughed in your face. Not only is she spoiled and stuck-up, but she's also über-popular. Like Best Dressed/Homecoming Queen/Miss February in "The Girls of Castle Heights Calendar" popular. Like Dylan-Has-2,028-Friends-on-MySpace popular.

Me? I have 612. And most are fellow movie buffs. I suffer from the opposite problem: not many people at Castle Heights know who I am. It's not like I'm some weird loner who wears a Black Flag T-shirt and trench coat and army boots—I mean, I have friends, like the guys in the Film Society and Russian Club—but I'm a film geek. And proud of it, I might say. I already know that I'll be quoted in the articles about me in *Film Threat* ten years from now as saying that I didn't come into my own until my twenties, and I'm fine with that. Everyone knows that every artist who's any good wasn't popular in high school. Take Tim (that's Burton, as in *Edward Scissorhands* and *Beetlejuice*)—I highly doubt *he* was prom king at his high school.

To me, the idea of doing a documentary about cool kids in high school was as original as it got. Sure, it had been done, but everyone knew that even though *Laguna*

Beach was quote-unquote reality television, it was about as real as the idea of me getting crowned homecoming king that fall. My documentary—which, during the drive home from The Dell that day I had decided would be called *The View from the Top of Castle Heights*—would be a no-holds-barred look at the beautiful people. The good, the bad, the ugly—no one and nothing would be spared in my quest for the truth of what really went on behind the velvet ropes that led to Castle Heights' cool crowd. And because we were talking about popularity in glitzy, sunny Los Angeles rather than, say, gray, rainy Portland, Oregon, it would be even *more* intriguing to audiences.

After saving Dylan's bag—and getting zero thanks, which shouldn't have been much of a surprise since she walked around acting as if life was a movie that had been written as a starring vehicle for her while the rest of us were just supporting characters—I went home and put together a killer proposal for the documentary. Block gone, as my fingers flew across the keyboard I felt like how Woody must have felt when he came up with the idea for *Annie Hall*; or Quentin, when he came up with the idea for *Pulp Fiction*; or Martin, when he came up with the idea for *Taxi Driver*. (That's Martin as in Martin Scorsese, another one of my favorite directors.)

After letting it sit for a day, and doing a rewrite on Thursday night, I stopped at the post office after school on Friday afternoon and mailed off my application—I even splurged and spent a little extra to get delivery confirmation—and then I went to work at Good Buys, where I'm a member of the Geek Gang and fix people's computers. I don't like to advertise this because if the people at Good Buys ever found out I'd most likely be fired, but I'm a film geek rather than a computer one. Obviously I know that you can't go wrong with pushing control/alt/delete all at once, which is how I usually try to solve a problem, but if that doesn't fix it that's when I call Microsoft or Mac's help line. To my credit, it's not like I pretended to know a lot during my interview, but Raymond, my boss (a budding filmmaker himself), said that I was the only person he had ever met who knew the little-known fact that Quentin collected board games that were based on old TV shows such as *The Dukes of Hazzard* and *I Dream of Jeannie*. How exactly that came up in conversation I don't remember, but I do know that it got me the job.

"I assume you're aware that Spike Jonze started out in documentaries before he did *Being John Malkovich* and *Adaptation,* Agent Rosen?" Raymond asked that afternoon as he tinkered with a laptop that had an "I Love My Spoiled Rotten Cat" sticker on the front. The store was relatively empty, even though we were running one of our Just-Because-It's-Friday-Get-60-Percent-Off sales. We're the white-trash cousin to Best Buy and Circuit City. We don't carry any of the fancy Japanese name-brand electronics like Sony or Toshiba—most of our stuff comes from Kuala Lumpur or Pakistan, and from the number of customer complaints we receive, it's built to last for approximately six weeks.

"Actually, it was music videos," I said, tapping my foot on the counter in time to the Muzak version of Michael Jackson's "Thriller." "Hey, seeing that it's so dead, can I take off my tie?" I was allowed to wear my Geek Gang T-shirt when I was on the road doing house calls, but per Corporate, I had to wear a white oxford and clip-on tie when I worked in the store.

"No you may not, Agent Rosen," Raymond replied as he yanked my hand away from my neck. "When you're on the clock, that stays on your neck." He pushed my feet off the counter so hard I almost fell off my chair. "Feet on the floor. And it wasn't music videos—it was documentaries."

I sighed as I readjusted the tie. Raymond *always* thought he was right. "Nope—I'm pretty sure it was music videos, Raymond."

He looked around to make sure no one had heard me even though the only people in the department are an elderly couple who, from the way they were yelling at each other, seemed to be wearing hearing aids. "When we're at work, it's *Agent* Strauss, Agent Rosen," he whispered. After having worked with him for a few months, I was starting to understand why Raymond didn't have all that many friends. And people called *me* a geek?

I went to the Geek Gang computer and Googled Spike Jonze, clicking open one of the articles that came up. I pointed to it. "See?" I said.

Raymond looked around to make sure no one was looking, since this was a non-company-related Google. Once he was sure the coast was clear, he began to study it like it was some top-secret government document, stroking his pimply chin. "I stand corrected, Agent Rosen. It seems that you are correct," he said, closing out the Spike Jonze window. "At any rate, I agree that you do in fact have a real chance here to expose the seamy underbelly of the world of popularity. Perhaps when you're done, you could try to get it into Sundance or one of the other festivals. You could pitch it as '*Lord of the Flies:* Beverly Hills-Style.'"

"That's exactly what I was thinking!" I said excitedly. Raymond may have been a nightmare boss, but he was a real visionary when it came to film stuff. In fact, he was a USC film school grad himself. Some people might think that the fact that he's making fifteen dollars an hour as manager of the Geek Gang and not off making millions of dollars a year directing films might not be a good sign, but that's just because he's spent the last four years writing a horror-slash-action film called *Send in the Killer Clowns* that he likes to pitch as "*Die Hard* at a circus" and he doesn't want to try to sell it until he does another rewrite.

"Tell me more about this girl. What's her name—Delilah?"

"Dylan," I corrected.

"So what's she like? Other than popular."

I reached for the Coke I had hidden behind the

computer. "Let's see . . . she's spoiled. And self-centered. And thinks the world revolves around her. And walks down the hall like she owns the school. And won't talk to anyone who's not in the ninety-ninth percentile of popularity."

"In other words, she's prom-queen material," Raymond said.

I nodded. "Remember the Heathers in *Heathers*?"

"Of course," Raymond scoffed. "That was Michael Lehmann's masterpiece. Even though he did get to work with the babedacious Uma Thurman in *The Truth About Cats and Dogs* a few years later."

"Well, think of all three Heathers times a hundred," I said.

He stroked his chin again. "Hmm . . . sounds like you have your work cut out for you. Is she pretty?"

I shrugged. "Yeah, if you like blondes with blue eyes." Which I didn't. I liked brunettes with violet eyes. Specifically brunettes with violet eyes named Amy Loubalu who were seniors at Castle Heights. As far as I was concerned, Amy was the most beautiful—not to mention the nicest—girl at Castle Heights. Back before my parents' divorce, when we still lived in Brentwood, I used to see her at Jamba Juice with the kids she babysat on the weekends. She always went out of her way to say hi to me and ask for a list of movies she should rent from Netflix, but most times I just clammed up and could barely speak, afraid that I'd get Tourette's syndrome and just say "You're so beautiful" over and over again.

"So when do you start?" Raymond asked as he straightened his own tie.

"I'm hoping Monday. I'm going to call Dylan when I get home and try and set up a prepro meeting for sometime this weekend."

He nodded. "Excellent, Agent Rosen." He grabbed me by the shoulders. "Just remember one thing."

I leaned my head back as far as I could without breaking my neck so I could get away from the garlic fumes left over from the baba ghanoush pita sandwich Raymond had had for lunch. "This is *your* movie. *You're* the director. This is *not* a collaboration—it's your singular vision. So don't give in to her. No matter how used she is to getting her way or how pretty she is. Understand?"

I nodded. "I understand."

"You're a filmmaker," he continued, getting more and more riled up. "A *truthteller*. You can't worry about hurting people's feelings. You're on this planet to serve your muse. Look at me, for example—do you think I *enjoy* having to deal with idiots who don't realize that if they keep powering off their computers without logging off first, sooner or later there's going to be a problem?"

I shook my head and took a step back.

"No!" he exclaimed. "I don't enjoy it—I *loathe* it! But I do it because it's mindless and therefore allows me to conserve my creative energy so I can continue to work on *Send in the Killer Clowns*, which is destined to become a cult classic if anyone's smart enough to recognize its brilliance." He grabbed me by the shoulders. "But *you*, Agent Rosen, have the opportunity of a lifetime—a chance to show all your fellow geeks and the geeks-in-training of the next generation that they're not missing out on anything by not being in the cool crowd. That, in fact, maybe their lack of cool is saving them from selling their souls and going over to the dark side!" He leaned in closer. "Don't let them down, Agent Rosen. Leave something behind that you and generations of misunderstood geniuses to come will be proud of." He let go of me. "Understood?"

I nodded.

Talk about a tall order.

When I got home, Mom was at yet another one of her Learning Annex classes (her postdivorce hobby), so I grabbed a bag of Chips Ahoy I had stashed away on top of my closet and went into the family room. Postdivorce we moved to a house in Beachwood Canyon, which is in Hollywood. It's small, but it's right under the Hollywood sign, which is obviously a terrific example of foreshadowing in terms of my future. Ever since Dad left Mom two years before for one of his actress clients (he's an entertainment attorney, which means along with agents and managers, he negotiates deals for actors) and shafted Mom in the divorce, money has been really tight.

Our house is cool—built in 1923, with a lot of built-in

bookcases for my DVDs. I like it better on this side of town because when you're a director, it's very important to keep it real and stay in touch with the regular Joe moviegoing public, and Hollywood, with its mix of ethnic groups and high crime rate, is a lot more real than snooty Brentwood. Plus, there's a great used-record store down the street on Franklin Avenue where Quentin has been known to pop in from time to time.

After I settled myself on the wicker couch that Mom had gotten at the Rose Bowl flea market a few weeks earlier (ever since the divorce she's been on a nothing-should-match-in-order-to-reflect-the-randomness-of-life kick) I called Dylan. Let me rephrase that: I called the number that Dylan had given me. An old woman answered, who, when I asked to speak to Dylan, started screaming in Russian and hung up on me. So I called back, and this time a man answered.

"Hi, is Dylan there?" I asked.

"Who?" he demanded.

"Dylan. Dylan Schoenfield?"

"You have wrong number," the man boomed.

"Um, are you sure?" I asked.

"Who this?" he demanded.

"This is Josh Rosen. I'm a classmate of Dylan's."

"I tell you—no Dylan here! Now you never call here again!" he said, slamming the phone down.

Forget my promise to Raymond that I was going to

make the documentary of my generation. At this point there wasn't going to *be* a documentary.

Amy Loubalu never would've done anything as cruel as give me the wrong number after I risked my life for her (which, by the way, I would have gladly done, no questions asked). In fact, I bet Amy would've let me take her out for a Jamba Juice in return.

"I can't believe you're really going to do this," said my friend Ari on Monday during lunch as he, Steven, and I sat at our usual table in the far right corner of the cafeteria near the garbage bins. Tall and thin with receding brown hair and black-rimmed glasses, Ari's a dead ringer for Steven Soderbergh, the guy who directed *Ocean's Eleven*, not to mention *Ocean's Twelve* and *Ocean's Thirteen*. I took a picture of the two of them together when Steven gave a Film Society talk and they look like they could be father and son.

I stood up and straightened my own glasses. Even though I had stopped at LensCrafters on Saturday, my frames were still crooked from when I risked my life to save Dylan's bag. If I wasn't such a good guy, I would've built the cost of the repairs into the budget. "What do you mean you can't believe I'm going to do this? Of *course* I'm going to do this!" I pointed to the latest issue of *Filmmaker* magazine that he had been flipping through. "You think anyone in there would let a little thing like a wrong number stop them? Would Spielberg ever have considered ending *E.T.* any other way than Henry Thomas putting E.T. in the basket of his bike and riding off?"

"Dude, I think you need a *passport* to go over there," said Steven, who was busy texting some girl named Amber who lived in Kansas whom he had met in a MySpace group for *The Simpsons*. So far he had ignored her requests for a picture (the picture on his page was of Homer), and who knew if she'd still be interested in him once he did send one. His hope was that girls in the Midwest liked tubby guys with blond hair that tended to get greasy within an hour of washing it.

I stood there looking at my two friends and sighed. I had had a feeling I'd run up against this, and had luckily written a script for it over the weekend. "Okay, listen up: just this summer we were talking about how we wanted our senior year to be memorable, right?"

Ari pulled at his ear, which is a thing he does when he gets nervous, while Steven texted.

"Right?" I said again, yanking Steven's Treo out of his hand.

They finally nodded.

"And we also talked about how *Revenge of the Nerds* was such a great wish-fulfillment movie and Judd Apatow should definitely remake it, right?"

"Yeah?" said Ari warily.

"So this is our chance!" I exclaimed. "With this documentary, not only will we have the opportunity to shake it up a bit, but we can do our own *Revenge of the Nerds* remake. Think about it—we'll get to go to parties—"

"And be around girls," Steven said with a faraway look in his eyes.

"Exactly! And be around girls! And there's also the fact that we'll . . . get to go to parties," I said. Obviously I hadn't thought much past the party part.

"And be around girls," Steven said again.

"And be around girls," I agreed. "Guys, this is a once-in-a-lifetime opportunity," I said. "A chance to leave the sidelines and start to *experience* life so we have a wealth of material to tap into for our art down the line."

"But you're always saying that popularity is overrated and that you'd rather stick needles in your eyes than spend a night at a stupid keg party," said Ari.

"Who cares what my personal beliefs are!" I said, grabbing one of the carrot sticks that Steven's mom packed in his lunch every day. "What's important here is that if I ever make a movie that has a keg-party scene, I'll want it to be as authentic as possible and therefore I should make sure I go to at least one."

"Dude—you're right. This is our chance to finally get into the game," Steven said excitedly.

"But I hate sports," said Ari. "I have no eye-hand coordination."

I sighed. "Just insert whatever metaphor works for you, okay?" I replied. "So are you with me or what? Because I can't do this alone. Behind every great director is an even better director of photography and soundman, and for good or for bad, you guys are all I've got."

"I'm in," said Steven. "Especially since there's the possibility of girls being involved."

We looked at Ari.

"Me, too, I guess," he replied. "As long as this social-life thing doesn't get in the way of my homework. Yale's a lot harder to get into than USC."

"Not the film school," I corrected as I took my inhaler out of my pocket for a quick hit before putting it down on the table. "Now, if you'll excuse me, I'm off to change the course of our fate." After taking a few steps, I turned. "But if I'm not back in ten minutes or so, you should probably come look for me."

"Don't you want to take your inhaler?" Ari yelled. "In case you have some sort of allergic reaction to being in such close proximity to all that popularity?"

As a group of tree huggers looked up from their brown rice and veggies, I could feel myself start to flush. "Give me a break," I said, rolling my eyes. "I've been around popular people before."

"When?" asked Steven.

I thought about it. "When I met Stan Lee at Comic-Con two years ago," I finally said. Stan Lee was the co-creator of *Spider-Man* and *X-Men* among other things.

The two of them looked at each other and shrugged.

"I'll be fine," I said. And with that I began the long

walk to The Ramp. The Ramp leads to this raised platform in the corner of the cafeteria where there are ten or so tables, and the popular kids sit there, which makes them not only figuratively but literally above us nonpopular kids. (I had already mapped out the shot I would be using in the documentary to show this poetic tidbit.) As you can imagine, there's been a lot of flak about The Ramp over the years. In fact, rumor has it that this sophomore named Cindy Gold wrote a really intense letter to the editor of the *Castle Heights Courier* about it a few months ago, but the administration ended up putting the kibosh on it. They wouldn't let the paper print it because The Ramp was a gift from the Smallwood family—who have three very popular daughters who had sat up there over the years, including Madison, who's a senior like me—and they had just agreed to pay for a new Olympic-size pool.

By the time I was halfway across the cafeteria, my heart felt like it was going to leap out of my chest or I was going to throw up or—worst-case scenario—both, so I turned around and went back to the guys.

"I'm worried that the high altitude of The Ramp might make my asthma kick in," I said as I picked up my inhaler and put it in my pocket.

Steven snorted and went back to texting, while Ari patted me on the arm.

"It's okay to admit that you're scared," he said. "*I'm* scared for you, and I'm not even going anywhere."

"I'm not scared," I scoffed. "I just can't afford to have an asthma attack and end up in the hospital."

"Dude, you probably don't even *have* asthma," Steven said. "You just use that thing when you're nervous."

"I do, too, have asthma!" I replied. "It's not that uncommon—I just read that six to eighteen percent of young athletes have it."

"But you're not an athlete," Ari said.

"Okay, well, if you want to get type A about it, no, I'm not. But still. Look, I don't have time to debate this—now if you'll excuse me, I have a job to do."

As I made my way across the cafeteria again, I had to admit to myself that maybe I was just the *slightest* bit nervous. Even though I had just given the guys that rousing pep talk about how this could be the very thing that changed our lives, the truth is I'm not big on being the center of attention, which is what tends to happen when kids have the nerve to venture out of their normal cafeteria seating areas. At work or in the Film Society or the Russian Club, I'm fine—in fact, if there were an alternate universe made up entirely of geeks at Castle Heights, there'd be a good chance I'd win Most Popular—but when I'm around normal people I tend to go one of two ways: I either clam up completely or I can't stop talking. Neither is all that attractive.

As I stood in front of The Ramp, I craned my neck to watch as Dylan held court over Hannah Mornell, Lola

Leighton, and a bunch of other popular girls. From the way she was stabbing her fork in the air, I could see she was up in arms about something. Was that girl ever not in diva mode? Probably had to do with one of her credit cards being mistakenly declined or something like that.

Knowing it was important to let the talent know who was in charge ASAP (i.e., me), I cleared my throat. "Dylan?" I squeaked. I had been hoping for something a little more booming and authoritative.

"Take two," I murmured. "Hi, Dylan?" I said a little louder, netting me some astonished looks from the table of not-Ramp-worthy-but-semipopular girls to my right. I felt like Romeo calling up to Juliet, but instead of a ruffled shirt and tights, I was wearing Converse high-tops and an *Apocalypse Now* T-shirt.

Still oblivious, Dylan was now passing her bag—the one that I had saved from drowning—around the table for everyone to examine. "Arturo said that if I had gotten it out of the water two minutes earlier," she was saying, "he could've gotten it so that it looked new again rather than only as good as new, but that guy who got it out for me was just *so* slow!"

I couldn't believe what I was hearing. I risk my life by going into unchlorinated water and *this* was the thanks I get—being given a wrong number and called "slow"?! Who did Dylan Schoenfield think she was? The princess of Castle Heights High or something?

"Okay, just calm down," I murmured to myself as I reached into my pocket for my inhaler. "Calm down and *focus*." After a quick prayer to my spiritual directors (Woody, Quentin, Martin), I began my slow ascent up The Ramp.

You know those dreams where you look down and realize you're buck naked? Yeah, well, that's how I felt. Once everyone on The Ramp realized that someone Uncool had entered a Cool Zone, all conversations ground to a halt. And it didn't help things when I tripped on my untied sneaker lace and my arm landed in Debra Resnicoff's burger and fries.

"Hey, isn't that that geek guy from the fountain?" I heard Lola say.

"Where?" Dylan asked.

"Right there. Wiping ketchup off his arm."

"Omigod. It is," Dylan replied.

As I turned to look at them, I saw Dylan quickly bury her head in a magazine.

I walked over and stood in front of her. "Hi, Dylan," I said.

She looked up from the magazine. "Oh, *hey*, James," she said, trying to sound surprised but doing a horrible job. "How *are* you?!" It was a good thing this was a documentary and not a regular movie because the girl couldn't act her way out of a paper bag.

"It's Josh," I corrected. "And I'm okay," I replied, wiping the last bit of ketchup off my elbow with my finger. Not seeing a napkin anywhere, I stuck it in my mouth.

"Eww," Dylan said. "that's *disgusting.*"

From the looks on the other girls' faces, it seemed they felt the same way. My face was so hot I felt like half of it had melted down my neck, which I'm sure was due to the high altitude of The Ramp rather than nerves or anything like that. "So, uh, it seems that when you wrote your number down the other day, you messed up on a few numbers or something." I had decided that the best way to approach this was by not accusing her of being a jerk.

"I did? Huh. How weird," she said as Lola and Hannah started giggling.

"Yeah," I replied. I could feel myself starting to sweat. Definitely the altitude. "Honest mistake, I'm sure. Anyway, even though I then tried every configuration of the numbers that I could come up with, I couldn't get you."

"Okay, listen," Dylan said. "I talked it over with my friends and my boyfriend this weekend—you *do* know I've been going out with Asher Ellis since sophomore year, right?"

I nodded.

"And I don't think the documentary thing is a good idea, so I'm not going to do it."

"What?! Why not?" I tried not to panic, but my voice came out sounding like I was on helium.

"Well, frankly, *I* don't have a problem with it because, you know, everyone's always saying I'm super photogenic and even if the camera puts fifteen pounds on me I'll still look okay, but other people"—she looked at Lola—"are worried that because you're not in the same crowd as us—"

"Try *no* crowd," interjected Lola.

"—you may be using this as an opportunity to get back at those of us who are cool," Dylan continued. "Know what I mean?"

"Yeah, kind of like that stupid movie from the eighties that's always on cable—" Lola said.

"*Revenge of the Nerds*," Hannah finished.

I couldn't believe this—I knew Dylan was stuck-up, but I hadn't realized anyone could be so cruel. Did she not know what it felt like to have a dream? And did she not realize that at this very moment she was in the midst of squashing mine underneath her shoe?

"Excuse me for one second, please," I said as I marched to the corner of The Ramp and took out my inhaler. "Stay calm," I said to myself as I breathed in. All great films hit road bumps on their way to getting made. There was no reason to get worried.

I marched back. "It's not my intention to make you look bad," I assured her. "Like all the best documentaries, it's going to be really fair and balanced—I swear," I promised. Great. Now I would have to work extra hard to make sure it was fair and balanced.

"Yeah, well, I still don't think it's a good idea. But thanks for asking," she said as she picked up the magazine again and started flipping through it.

Okay, so maybe there *was* a reason to worry. "But . . . you promised," I said. I could feel the back of my neck start to itch, which often happened when things didn't go the way I had written them in the imaginary movie that was continuously playing in my head. According to WebMD, that was one of the main symptoms of seborrheic keratosis, which was a thickening of the skin from age. I really hoped it wasn't that.

"Well, now I'm un-promising." She shrugged without looking up.

"But . . . you can't," I said.

She looked up. "Oh, really? Why?" she asked, her eyes blazing. Dylan was *not* someone who was used to being told what she could and couldn't do.

I thought about it. "Well . . . because." Apparently my A's in English for having such a way with words didn't translate into conversations with popular people.

"I think we should ask Asher about this," she said. "Asher!" she yelled to the table of surfer-looking dudes next to her.

I reminded myself to keep breathing. While Asher and I were probably around the same weight, he's about five inches taller than me. He's got that typical L.A. surfer-dude look—blond hair that's on the longish side and a year-round tan. Either he was hard of hearing, or he was ignoring her.

"Asher!" she yelled again.

"What?" he finally said.

"Come here for a second," she ordered.

"Why?"

"Because I need to ask you something, babe."

My neck was now itching *bad*. I couldn't believe this was happening. "But what about my USC application?" I panicked. "I already sent it off with a proposal for the documentary."

"Maybe you could just do a documentary about the uncool kids," suggested Hannah helpfully.

"Or better yet," said Dylan, "why don't you do a documentary about my archenemy? You could call it *Girls Who Try and Steal Other Girls' Boyfriends*?" She picked up her fork and jabbed it toward the middle of the cafeteria. "I'm sure *some* people would just *love* the attention."

I looked over to see what Dylan was scowling at, and it suddenly became even more difficult for me to breathe. Walking—no, *swaying*—across the cafeteria floor was Amy Loubalu. As she walked toward her table with her hamburger (I loved a girl who wasn't afraid to eat meat), every guy on The Ramp stared. Including Asher. You'd think that the beautiful/nice combination would have earned Amy a prime seat on The Ramp, but the truth was she didn't have a lot of friends. I didn't meet her until high school, but I heard that she had been one of the most popular girls at Curtis, the junior high she went to. At the start of sophomore year a rumor started going around that Amy was dating a twenty-five-year-old talent agent, which I found hard to believe, and by that summer, her reputation had made it so that her only real friend was Whitney Lewin.

By now Asher had finished watching the Amy Loubalu show and was standing over Dylan's shoulder, picking the tomatoes out of her barely touched salad. "What is it?" he asked, annoyed.

"This is the guy who wants to do a movie based on my life," Dylan replied.

Oh, please. That movie had already been done. It was called *Clueless*.

"It's a documentary. About popularity," I explained.

"Sounds cool." He shrugged as he started to walk back to his table.

"He's got a lot on his mind," said Dylan.

If I were him, I'd be trying to figure out how to break up with her.

"Listen," she said. "I just don't feel comfortable doing this."

"But—" I began.

"But what?" she snapped.

Here was my chance to stand up for myself. To give the speech the hero in a movie gives where at the end of it there's applause because he's touched everyone's souls, changed their lives, and made them look at life in a different way.

"Nothing," I said, starting toward the stairs.

"But I'll be back," I whispered. Somehow it didn't have the same impact as when Arnold said it in *The Terminator*.

As I walked back down The Ramp, I tried to hold my head high but it was difficult. It was one thing to wimp out around Amy Loubalu, but it was another to watch my dream of becoming the most acclaimed director of my generation go up in smoke because Dylan Schoenfield had no sense of right or wrong.

chapter three: *dylan*

Random Fact number 210 you should know about me: unless they come in shopping bags that say Fred Segal or Kitson, I'm not big on surprises. In fact, it's more like the opposite: I prefer routine. For instance, if I open the fridge and see a bunch of Weight Watchers strawberry-banana and key-lime nonfat yogurts rolling around instead of a nice, even row of vanillas (my breakfast every morning for the last two years), I start to get a little anxious.

So you can imagine how I felt when I got home on Friday at 5:30—after stopping at Fred Segal for a quick jog-through to start scoping out possible dresses for the Fall Fling formal in November (six weeks away, but it's never too early to start preparing)—and Daddy's car was in the circular driveway of our Spanish-style house. This was so not part of the routine I was used to. Daddy's a workaholic and never leaves the office before 8:30, even on Christmas Eve. What was even more weird was that parked right behind his black Jaguar was a beat-up old blue Volvo that not only looked like it hadn't been through a car wash in years, but had a *Neil Diamond* bumper sticker on it. In case you don't know who Neil Diamond is—not that you could be blamed seeing that he's super old and was popular way back in the *seventies*—he's this dorky singer who, from the pictures of him on Daddy's CDs, is obsessed with sequins and rhinestones.

Parking my red BMW behind the Volvo, I made my way toward the house. *"Hola,* José!" I sang. He's our gardener, who's married to Marta, our housekeeper.

He looked up from where he was pruning some roses. *"Hola,* Miss Dylan," he yelled back. Our house is on an acre of land—huge for L.A. standards—so José's a very busy guy.

I felt very lucky that I was exposed to so many different cultures living in L.A. Between José and Marta, who were from El Salvador, Kathy, my Vietnamese manicurist, and Zora, the Bulgarian woman who waxed my eyebrows, I was one of the most well-rounded people I knew.

"Daddy?" I yelled as I stashed my Fred Segal bags in the front hall closet. I must have this disease that makes it impossible for me to walk out of a store without buying at least a T-shirt.

"We're in the family room," he yelled back.

I figured the other half of "we" had to be whoever the Neil Diamond–loving person was. Maybe one of Daddy's fraternity brothers from Northwestern back in the day who now worked for Greenpeace or one of those other annoying organizations that stalked poor innocent people like myself when all we wanted was to get some frozen yogurt at Pinkberry. Those people *always* drove beat-up Volvos.

As I walked into the room, I stopped short. I *wish* it had been a friend of Daddy's. It wasn't—it was none other than that Geek Boy James or Joe or Josh or whatever his name was. The one who got my purse out of the fountain the week before and thought I owed him my firstborn child because of it. I couldn't believe it—I had already told him I wasn't interested in doing his dumb movie. What part of *no* did he not understand? Talk about not letting something go.

I thought I was going to throw up. Not just because Geek Boy was in my house, but because he and Daddy were sitting on the black suede couch watching a baseball game surrounded by corned-beef and pastrami sandwiches, pickles, knishes, and black-and-white cookies from Nate 'n Al's, my most favorite delicatessen back before I gave up carbs my freshman year.

"Hi, honey!" Daddy said through a mouthful of knish. Other than the fact that Daddy was about twenty-five pounds overweight and a few inches taller, he was a dead ringer for the actor Dustin Hoffman.

"Hi," I said. I tried not to look at the black-and-white cookies, with their thick, creamy icing. Personally, I think that in addition to the PSA announcements on television about the dangers of drugs, they should also do some about black-and-whites because they're way more addictive than any drug could ever be. "Um, would someone like to tell me what's going on here?" I asked as I plopped down on a matching suede club chair and held my breath so I couldn't smell the cookies and risk triggering a snackcident.

"I was just telling Josh about Neil's concert at the Greek back in '78 while we had a little nosh," Daddy replied.

A little? There was enough food on the stone coffee table for a small bar mitzvah.

As I exhaled, the sweet smell of sugar entered my nose. I quickly reached into my purse and shoved three pieces of gum in my mouth. "I can see that," I said. "But what is he *doing* here?"

"Well, from what I understand, apparently you two had come to an agreement about letting him film you for his documentary and now you're trying to renege," Daddy said in his scary I'm-the-Real-Estate-King-of-L.A. voice.

I looked over at Geek Boy, who was innocently biting into a pickle, and gave him my dirtiest look, the one usually reserved for Amy Loubalu.

"I wasn't *trying* to renege," I said. "I *did* renege. I mean, what if he tries to portray me as all spoiled and mean and stuff? We all know that's so not who I am, but let's face it—that's what sells. Just look at reality television."

"I told you," said Geek Boy as he took out that stupid inhaler he always carried around. "That's not my intention at all. Excuse me just a second." He squirted it in his mouth. "Asthma," he explained.

"My brother is asthmatic!" exclaimed Daddy, as if somehow this made them soul mates.

"Really? That's so cool. I mean, not that he suffers from asthma, of course, but just that . . . never mind. Anyway, as I was saying." He reached into his pocket and took out a wrinkled piece of paper and began to read from it. "'I just thought it would be interesting to view popularity from a sociological perspective. An anthropological look at the social hierarchy of modern-day high schools. If you go back through the history of film, you'll see that over the decades—'"

"Okay, seeing that I haven't had my afternoon Red Bull, my head's a little fuzzy, so I'm not even going to pretend to understand what you're saying," I replied, turning toward Daddy, who was now chomping away on his triple-decker-corned-beef/chopped-liver sandwich. "Daddy, you know what it's like to have people write and say mean things about you. Don't you think I'm doing the right thing?"

He took a swig of Dr. Brown's Cream Soda. "No. I don't," he said. "Especially since all this kid's ever wanted was to go to USC film school. Do you know that he works twenty hours a week to help his mother pay the tuition at that school of yours?"

"What, you want me to go get a *job*?" I shot back. What was next? Spending the summer volunteering in Africa?

"That's not what I'm saying. I'm just saying that Josh

49

here knows the value of a dollar. You know, when I was you kids' age—"

"I know, I know," I cut in. "You and Grandma and Grandpa and Uncle Marvin lived in a two-bedroom apartment in Queens—"

"Marvin's the one with asthma," Daddy explained to Geek Boy.

"—and not only did you have a paper route in the morning, but you worked in a shoe store after school," I continued. *"And* you also had to walk a mile in the snow to get there. *And* you paid your own way through City College."

"Exactly. That's the kind of thing that would give you Beverly Hills kids an ulcer."

"Actually, Mr. Schoenfield, I live in Hollywood," said Geek Boy, who had now moved on to one of the black-and-whites, eating it just the way I used to back in the day—first a bite of the chocolate side, then the vanilla, then the chocolate, and so on. As my stomach started to rumble, I took out another piece of gum and shoved it in my mouth.

"You *do?*" I asked. The only time my friends and I went to Hollywood was for the Billion Dollar Babes sample sale. In my book, anything east of La Cienega Boulevard was considered sketchy. Except, of course, for the stretch of Third Street from Orlando to Fairfax with all the cute boutiques.

"Yeah," he said. "In Beachwood Canyon. Right down

the street from the Hollywood sign." He fiddled with the inhaler. "I find it very inspirational for my craft, especially since it's the area where Doug Liman shot the Vince Vaughn and John Favreau movie *Swingers* in 1996, which is such a terrific example of independent filmmaking on so many levels—"

Why he thought I would care less about something like that was beyond my comprehension, even if Vince Vaughn was a total hottie. "How nice for you," I replied. I looked at my watch—it was already six and I was supposed to meet Hannah and Lola at Olympic Spa for body scrubs (run by Koreans—yet *more* well-roundedness!) at seven. "Listen, I hate to break up this party, but it's Friday night and I have plans. It was nice seeing you again . . ."

"Josh."

"Josh," I said, giving him the biggest smile I could muster. "I'm sure I'll see you around at school. I'll even say hi to you from now on." Maybe going the nice route would make him leave me alone. "Have a great weekend," I said as I started to walk out of the room, stopping to smooth out the Navajo rug that Daddy had bought when we went skiing in New Mexico last year. Frankly, I wasn't a fan of Southwestern decor, which was how Daddy had had the family room remodeled after a psychic he met on a ski lift that same trip told him he had been a Native American in a past life. But since, as previously mentioned, I *didn't* work, I had no say in the matter, according to Daddy.

"Dylan," I heard Daddy growl. The growl was never a good sign.

I turned around and gave *him* a smile as well. "Yeah?"

He didn't smile back. "Get back here, please."

I turned around and walked over to the couch, putting my arms around his neck. "Yes, Daddy?" I said as sweetly as I could, trying not to glare at Josh, who was examining a piece of parsley as if he had never seen one before.

"Here's what Josh and I think would be fair: for the next month, Josh will get to film you and your friends one day a week at school during lunch, one afternoon a week after school, and one Friday or Saturday night. And while you won't have final cut, you will retain the right to give notes on the rough cut of the film so that you're not unfairly or unflatteringly portrayed."

I let go of his neck and stood up. "You're *serious*?!" I squeaked.

I could see Josh cringe as he started munching away on the parsley. I couldn't believe it—my father, the man who loved me more than anything, the man who ate small real estate developers for breakfast—had totally sold me down the river just because Geek Boy reminded him of what it was like to grow up poor and listen to some jumpsuit-wearing singer.

"As a heart attack," he replied.

"You know I hate when you joke about that," I said.

"I know, I know. I'm sorry. But, yes, I'm serious," he said as he hoisted himself out of his seat. "So serious that if I find out that you don't cooperate, you're not going to that dance you've been talking about."

"What?! But I *have* to go—I'm the Leaf Queen!"

Josh was halfway through a snort when I whipped my head toward him.

"Is something funny?" I asked in an icy tone.

The snort changed into a coughing fit.

"I guess not," he said when he was done. "It just, you know . . . sounds funny. Like something you'd buy at Home Depot or somewhere like that."

I glared at him.

"Or not," he added.

"The Leaf Queen is a very important tradition at Castle Heights," I explained. "Nine out of the last ten Leaf Queens have gone on to be prom queens. Everyone except for Adriana Castelli and that's because she happened to be in rehab at the time. And just today I saw the greatest dress. It's pale pink with—"

"Well, the only place you're going to be wearing that dress is here in the house if you don't let Josh make his documentary," said Daddy. "So I'll leave you kids to figure out the details." He stopped in front of Josh and put out his hand. "Nice meeting you, Josh. Good luck with your project. I'm very impressed with your drive."

"Thanks, Mr. Schoenfield," Geek Boy said as he shook it. "I really appreciate your offer to sponsor it and, you know, pay for the film and stuff like that."

"Daddy, you're *paying* for this?!"

He shrugged. "Why not? It's a tax write-off. See you kids later."

As soon as he left the room, I flopped down on the other end of the couch, which made Geek Boy move even farther into his corner, as if he were afraid of getting cooties.

I was so mad I wanted to scream. "I can't believe you came over to tell on me," I said. "What are you, seven?"

"I came over here to try and talk things out with you," he said defensively, "but you weren't here, and so we started talking, and before I knew it, the Nate 'n Al's guy was here."

I shook my head. "I can't *stand* parent kids."

"Huh?"

"Parent kids—kids who suck up to parents."

He shrugged. "I don't suck up to them—they just always seem to really like me. In fact, back in third grade, when I was best friends with Toby Wasserman—"

I put up my hand to stop him. "Okay, halt. Listen, while I'd really like to play *This Is Your Life* with you, I don't have the time right now. So three days a week for one month—" I started counting on my fingers. "That's—"

"Twelve days," he said. "No, wait—actually, because October is a long month, it'll actually be fourteen days, because it's a month with five weeks rather than—"

I put up my hand once more. "Okay, halt again. If we're going to be working together, which it looks like we *are*, you're going to have to stop with the Wikipedia stuff."

54

"Fine," he mumbled, reaching for a piece of white of a black-and-white.

"Although I'm impressed," I said.

"You are?" he asked, surprised, as he chewed away.

I got up and went to my purse for another piece of gum. "I mean, pretending to love Neil Diamond just to bond with my dad? That's pretty genius. How'd you find out about that anyway?"

"Huh?"

"How'd you know he's a Neil lover?" I asked as I shoved another two pieces in my mouth.

"I didn't. When I rang the doorbell your dad answered and he saw my bumper sticker."

"Yeah, but how'd you know to put the bumper sticker on?" Holding my nose, I picked up the rest of the black-and-white with a napkin and threw it in the bag of garbage. It was bad enough I was going to have to do this stupid thing—I certainly wasn't going to risk gaining weight as well. I sat back down on the couch.

"What are you talking about?"

"I mean you don't actually *like* Neil Diamond."

He was quiet.

"Omigod—you *do* like Neil Diamond. By any chance, are you aware of the fact that you're the only one under fifty who would ever admit that?"

He shrugged. "If you take the time to listen, his lyrics are pretty amazing. Almost on par with Bob Dylan or Neil Young. 'I Am . . . I Said'? That's as deep as it gets."

"Excuse me," I said, "but *'I am, I said/To no one there/ And no one heard at all/Not even the chair'*? How is a chair supposed to hear? It's a chair!"

"Oh. So you're familiar with Neil's lyrics?" he asked, surprised.

"Of course I'm familiar with them," I replied. "It's all my parents played in the car when we used to go on road trips when I was little." After Mom died, Daddy stopped listening to Neil because he said it reminded him too much of her, but unfortunately the damage had been done—all the lyrics to songs like "Cracklin' Rosie," "Song Sung Blue," and "Sweet Caroline" were permanently etched in my brain. I'm sure when I go into therapy in my twenties I'd be spending a few sessions on how it had traumatized me.

"Cool. I haven't thought too much about the score yet, and obviously with our limited budget, we wouldn't be able to license one of his songs," he said, "but my friend Steven's older brother Jason knows the cousin of one the guys in Super Diamond, and maybe we'd be able to get them to give us one of their songs cheap."

I gave him a look.

"Or not," he added. "Look, Dylan, I know you don't want to do this, but I think I've come up with a way to make it worth your while."

I gave him a doubtful look. "How?"

"Well, I've been thinking about it, and if you want to submit the documentary with *your* college applications, I wouldn't have a problem with that. As long as I get proper credit."

At this news, my ears perked up. "Huh. Do you think they'd let me submit that instead of writing an essay?"

"They might."

The one thing that had been keeping me up nights—other than what I was going to wear to Fall Fling and why Asher preferred to spend his Saturday nights watching grown men beat up on each other at Ultimate Fighting championships rather than with me—were my college essays. I may have been a lot of things—not least of all super popular, charming, and the fashion icon of Castle Heights—but "good student" wasn't in the top ten answers to "Who Is Dylan Schoenfield?" While Hannah was on the any-college-as-long-as-it's-Ivy track and Lola was set on going to one of those artsy colleges back east where you couldn't tell the difference between the boys and the girls, I had accepted that I would go somewhere local like UC Santa Cruz or Santa Barbara, where Asher would spend most of his time surfing and I'd major in art history because then I'd have something to talk about at cocktail parties when I got older. But even though they weren't that difficult (all you needed was to maintain a GPA of 2.5 and a tan), you *did* need to write an essay, which wasn't on my list of fun things to do.

"Well, seeing that not going to Fall Fling isn't an option, I guess I don't have a choice." I sighed. "Meet me on The

Ramp at lunch on Monday and you can start then. But I'm telling you, I don't care what my father says—if I see that you're trying to make me look bad, the deal's off. Got it?"

"Got it," he replied, nibbling away on the black side of another cookie.

"And don't think that this means that all of a sudden we're like *friends*, or anything," I said. "It's strictly business. Oh, and in case you didn't know, Asher and I are super serious, so if you were thinking of using this documentary thing as a way to, you know, *hit on me* or anything, it's not going to work."

"Don't worry," Geek Boy said. "Like you said, it's strictly business. But who knows—maybe this'll be the start of a long and rewarding working relationship and we'll be Woody and Jean Doumanian."

"Huh?"

"Woody Allen and his producing partner," he explained.

Woody Allen . . . the name sounded vaguely familiar. "Does he go to our school?"

Geek Boy looked like he was going to throw up all the deli food he had just eaten. "Woody Allen was only the greatest director of the twentieth century."

"So he's dead now?" I asked.

"No. He's still alive. It's just that his movies aren't as good as they used to be. They're decent, because he's Woody, but nothing like his classics."

"Oh."

"*Annie Hall*? *Manhattan*?"

I shrugged.

"*Hannah and Her Sisters*?" he asked with disbelief.

"Hannah doesn't have any sisters. She's got an older brother, Warren. He goes to Stanford."

"It's the name of one of Woody's movies," he explained.

"Oh." I shrugged. "Never saw it."

He continued looking queasy and sighed.

Sheesh—*someone* was taking this movie stuff *way* too seriously. "What?" I asked.

"Nothing," he said as he stood up and put out his hand. "So we have a deal?"

I put mine out as well. "I guess so."

As I walked him to what he called the Neilmobile (Hello? Can you *get* cheesier than that?) I tried to look at the bright side of things: helping Geek Boy fulfill his dream of getting into USC film school had to balance out whatever bad karma I may have had.

Not that I had any, of course.

chapter four: *josh*

I don't know who was more excited about the documentary—Steven or my mom.

"Dude, you're *so* right—the more I think about it, the more I realize this thing is totally going to change our lives," said Steven that Saturday afternoon as the two of us sat on the kitchen floor unraveling the cables for the microphones we'd be using on Monday.

"Yeah," I said glumly. "If we survive it." Already I had received a three-page single-spaced e-mail from Dylan about the documentary. There needed to be a makeup and wardrobe budget (yeah, right); I couldn't shoot her if she was PMSing and therefore retaining water (whatever *that* meant); she had approval over which of her friends were on camera—the list went on and on. We hadn't even started and she was making the biggest stars in Hollywood look easygoing. "Forget about getting it done," I said. "I'll be happy if I can just stop her from texting me every five minutes with yet another demand. Maybe this wasn't such a good idea—"

"Dude! What are you talking about?! This is what we've been waiting for," Steven said as he wiped the sweat off his face with the vintage Sundance Film Festival '02 T-shirt he had scored on eBay. "The chance to let all those popular girls see what they've been missing by dating jocks."

"He's right, honey," said Mom as she fixed him a plate of brown rice and veggies even though we had stopped at In-N-Out Burger less than an hour before on our way back from the rental place. "Your father was a jock and look how that turned out." Dad had been on the tennis team at UCLA, which is where they met.

"Everyone knows that it's always the unpopular guys who end up with the best chicks," announced Steven.

"Yeah, in, like, a John Hughes movie," I replied.

"Or a Woody Allen one," Mom added.

She *did* have a point.

Steven stood up and walked over to the baby-blue linoleum table that Mom had gotten at the Santa Monica flea market right after we moved. If Mom wasn't at the Learning Annex, she was at a flea market. "Look at Spielberg, dude—are you going to sit there and tell me that even though she's pushing fifty, Kate Capshaw isn't still a total fox? No offense about the age thing, Sandy." Mom liked my friends to call her by her first name—something about putting everyone on an even playing field. At forty-five, Mom was still looking pretty good herself. In fact, ever since she had stopped straightening her brown hair and let it grow so that it was now long and curly, she looked more like a poet (yet another Learning Annex course) and less like a lady who spent her days lunching, which is what she used to do before the divorce.

"No offense taken, Steven," said Mom. "In fact, just last night I was reading that perimenopause is when women really begin to step into their sexual power."

"Mom." I blushed. "Please. We have company."

That was another by-product of the divorce: really *open* communication. That part I could've done without sometimes.

"Once you go nerd, you don't go back," Steven said.

"It's true," said my mom, who had recently started dating an accountant named Larry from the Intro to Persian Mystic Poetry class she had taken a few months earlier. "I can't begin to explain the difference when you're with someone who's taken the time to read *The Female Body: An Owner's Manual*—"

"Okay, moving on," I said, in hopes of stopping her before she embarrassed me a lot rather than her usual little. It was great to see Mom happy again after those last few years with Dad, but in my opinion, she was taking this rediscover-your-inner-self thing a little too seriously. "All I care about is getting the footage so I can get into USC and hopefully get a scholarship. I'm not in this for dates." At least not with Dylan or any of her equally stuck-up friends. Now, Amy Loubalu—that was another story. Amy was as perfect as the cinematography in *The Godfather*. The way her brown hair swung just so when she walked. And her eyes, which were on the violet side of blue, a color so unique that even the Crayola people wouldn't have been able to come up with a name for it. And her incredible organizational skills—the way she made sure to use the same color pen for whatever notebook she was writing in, so that everything about English was red, and physics was green, and—

"Josh? What do you think?" I heard my mom say.

"Huh?" Whenever Amy popped into my head—which was more and more often since she had changed lockers and was now four down from me—I tended to lose track of time.

"I asked if you wanted me to take you to Loehmann's and get you a few new pairs of slacks, now that your social circle is going to be widening so much," she said.

"Thanks, Mom, but I think I'll be fine in jeans." The only person I knew who wore "slacks" was my eighty-five-year-old grandfather in Scottsdale, Arizona.

Just then my phone buzzed. When I picked it up, there was yet another text from Dylan. *Trying to get in to see my colorist to get my roots done today but if not will have to hold off on shooting till I do.*

And by the time I was done dealing with Dylan, I was going to *feel* like I was eighty-five.

I like to think of myself as a pretty calm, cool, and collected guy—think George Clooney circa *Out of Sight*, without the movie-star looks—but by the time third period rolled around that Monday, I had already gone through an entire roll of Tums.

"Here," Steven whispered from the desk next to me in calculus, holding out a box of Mike and Ikes. "Have some of these. They'll settle your stomach."

"No, thanks," I whispered back. "I think they'll just make me throw up," I said. Maybe it was better to just *dream* of one day becoming a director instead of actually becoming a director.

By lunch, my upset stomach had been joined by a buzzing in my head. "Maybe we should hold off on starting until I go to the doctor and get an MRI," I announced to the guys as we stood at the entrance of the cafeteria with all our gear, which included two video cameras, two booms, and a handful of lights. "I might have a brain tumor."

"Maybe you're just wimping out," replied Steven as he hoisted the boom from one arm to another, almost decapitating Sloane Simons in the process.

"Or maybe it's MS," I added. "It says on WebMD that ringing in the head is also a symptom of MS."

"Or maybe you're just wimping out," said Steven.

"You know, studies have shown that high levels of stress can indeed manifest into all sorts of diseases," argued Ari as he laid the cables on the ground. I could always depend on Ari to back me up on medical issues.

Steven pointed to my inhaler, which I had been holding in my hand like a good-luck charm all day. "Just take another hit off that thing and let's get on with it already."

I did as I was told and immediately felt better. "So are we ready?"

"I was *born* ready," said Steven.

"You were *born* to get your butt kicked," replied Ari. "Josh, maybe Hannah Mornell was right—maybe a look at *un*popularity would be more interesting."

I shook my head and stood up tall, which was a rare occurrence seeing that slumping was my default mode. "No. This is our opportunity to make a difference, like Robert Redford and Dustin Hoffman as Bob Woodward and Carl Bernstein in *All the President's Men* when they exposed Watergate. Or Sally Field as Norma Rae in *Norma Rae* when she got better working conditions for the factory workers." I stood up even taller. "We've come too far—we can't turn back now."

"We haven't even started," corrected Ari.

"We're starting right now," I said. "Come on."

With that, the three of us walked across the cafeteria with the same amount of purpose as if it were downtown Baghdad and we were part of the *ABC World News Tonight* team.

I just prayed we didn't step on any land mines on the way.

From the second we got up on The Ramp, it became clear that Dylan Schoenfield made Mrs. Tashlock, my trig teacher junior year who took points off if your paper had any creases in it, seem like the most easygoing person on the planet.

"Here's a few more do's and don'ts," she said as we sat at a table with her, Hannah and Lola, and their three very bland-looking salads. Not one of them had bacon bits or croutons on them. "Josh. *Josh.* Are you listening to me?"

I wasn't. I was too busy gazing down at the cafeteria floor from this new vantage point. I hadn't really had a chance to take it in when I was up here before. I think I had expected it to look like the view from an airplane, but it wasn't all that different. The people on the main floor looked exactly like they always did. It was a bit disappointing, to be honest.

"Sorry. What?" I asked, turning my attention back to her.

She thrust a few typed pages in my hand.

"'Rule number 22: Do NOT shoot me from the right'," I read. "How come?"

"Because I don't want anyone to see the hideous chicken-pox scar on my eyelid," she replied, undoing her blonde ponytail and smoothing it out so it fell in front of her face.

"What scar?" I asked.

She yanked her hair off her face and leaned forward.

"Watch it!" I yelped, yanking her open Diet Coke can out of the way before it could spill on the expensive post-divorce-guilt camera my dad had bought me.

"*This* scar," said Dylan as she pointed to her eyelid.

Steven leaned in for a better look. "I don't see anything."

"Welcome to my world," grumbled Lola, who was chewing each small forkful of salad at least fifty times before she swallowed. What was up with girls and the food stuff? I bet Amy Loubalu didn't have weird food stuff going on. As beautiful and graceful as she was, I had a hunch that not only wasn't she afraid of meat, but that she could jam three fries in her mouth and still look great.

"Look—there's Asher," Dylan said.

He was walking up The Ramp carrying a tray with two pieces of pizza, three cartons of milk, onion rings, and a cupcake.

"Asher!" she yelled, waving. Who knew such a tiny body could contain such a loud voice?

Like the other day, he tried to ignore her and keep walking.

"Babe! Over here!" she yelled louder.

He looked at his table of surfer buds and with a sigh trudged toward us. "Hey," he said with the amount of enthusiasm usually reserved for a dentist visit.

"Sit next to me," she said, pushing Ari off his seat so Asher could have it.

He looked like he'd rather do anything but. "Nah, I'm

going to sit with my hombres," he replied, gesturing with his chin at the next table.

"Oh," she said, looking disappointed. "Text me later, then?"

He shrugged. "I guess," he replied as he walked away.

"We're really good at making sure we don't spend every minute together," Dylan explained. "'Cause that's *so* not healthy."

"Yeah, codependence is a killer," said Steven.

As Dylan settled back in her chair, she looked at Steven as if just noticing his existence for the first time. "Um, I don't mean to be rude, but who exactly are you?"

"I'm Steven Blecher, the sound guy."

She gave him a blank look.

"You paid me twenty bucks freshman year to dissect your fetal pig for you in biology, remember?"

"Vaguely." She turned to Ari. "And you are?"

"Ari Tenser, the lighting guy," he mumbled. "We were in home ec together sophomore year. You paid me fifteen dollars to make your Irish soda bread for you for the final."

"Huh. Are there more of you guys?" she asked.

"More of us what?" I replied.

"Geeks."

I wondered if she really was that rude, or if she had some sort of medical condition where the filter between her brain and her mouth had been broken since birth.

"Actually, we're *film* geeks," I replied. "There's a big difference between us and the *regular* geeks."

"How so?" asked Hannah as she daintily ate some raisins.

"Well, film geeks are just . . . cooler. More creative," I replied. "Less pocket protector and more visionary."

"But you're still a geek," Dylan said.

"Technically, yes," I agreed, "but ever since Quentin came on the scene, *film geek* doesn't have the same negative connotation."

"Who's Quentin?" she said. "Does he go to our school, too?"

Did this girl know *anything* that didn't have to do with shopping and makeup? "Quentin Tarantino?" I replied. "Director of *Pulp Fiction*? *Kill Bill: Volume 1*? *Kill Bill: Volume 2*?"

"Look, I'm going to tell you right now," she huffed, "unless it's a romantic comedy, I've probably never seen it, okay? But whatever—the fact remains you're still a geek." She smoothed her hair. "Now back to the movie—if I'm able to see the scar when I watch it, then you'll have to cut it out," she warned.

I closed my eyes and, taking Mom up on her suggestion to creatively visualize whenever I got anxious, envisioned myself giving the valedictorian speech at USC while Steven Spielberg sat next to me. "Listen, I promise that all of your demands will be met," I said as I looked at my watch. Lunch was nearly half over. "We should get started."

"But what about lunch?" Steven asked.

I gave him a look.

"What? You know I don't work well when I'm hungry."

"It seems to me you'll be okay if you miss a meal or two," said Lola, who still hadn't made a dent in her salad.

He patted his stomach, making it sound like a tin drum. "More of me to love, ladies. More of me to love."

The girls looked like they were about to throw up. This was officially off to a bad start.

Dylan took out her lip gloss and shrugged. "Okay, but I sure hope you took the time to look over the memo I sent you this weekend. Because I'd hate for you to spend a month shooting this and then find out you can't use it because you didn't meet my terms."

I sighed. This was going to be the longest five weeks of my life.

"Okay, so, there's three levels of popularity . . . " Lola was in the middle of explaining as a group of kids stood behind me while I aimed the camera at her and Hannah.

"There's low-level popularity," Hannah said, pointing to a table at the end of The Ramp. "Like Ashley and Britney Turner and those girls." I turned and zoomed in to get a shot. It was like *Attack of the Killer Clones*. All the girls were wearing jeans and the exact same style long-sleeved T-shirt, just in different colors.

"Wow. From this angle they look like a roll of Life Savers," I said from behind the camera.

Lola and Hannah laughed. "Score one for the geek," I announced. "I can't believe I made you guys laugh." Which made them laugh again. There was something about being behind a camera that made me a lot more relaxed. Maybe I should approach Amy Loubalu with a camera and ask her out that way. Then, of course, I'd have to bring it on our date as well, which would be awkward if I took her to a movie or something.

Lola turned toward Dylan. "He's funny," she said. "Who knew?"

From the bored look on her face as she filed her nails, Dylan didn't agree. "Any idea when we might get back to *me*?" she asked without looking up.

Lola and Hannah looked at each other and rolled their eyes.

"In a minute," I replied. "I promise."

"Anyway, after that comes midlevel popularity," Lola said, pointing to a table a little closer to where we were sitting. "That would be Lisa Eaton and Shannon Hall and those girls." I turned the camera to get a shot of Lisa and Shannon huddled together, flipping through the pages of a fashion magazine. Unlike Ashley and Britney, who wore guilty looks, as if they were just waiting to be found out and kicked off

The Ramp, Lisa and Shannon were laid-back to the point where I wondered if they were about to start snoring.

"And then there's us." Hannah smiled. "High-level popularity. Obvious by the fact that we have the prime table smack in the middle of The Ramp." She smoothed her red bob, looking even more like Molly Ringwald in *The Breakfast Club* than she usually did. "It's okay if you want to come in for a close-up, you know."

"Um, hi, everyone? Excuse me," said Dylan. "This isn't in the memo, but I'd like to add, 'The only close-ups will be of me.' "

"But every time I've asked you a question so far, you've put your hand in front of your face and said, 'No comment,'" I said.

"That's just because unlike *some* people," she said with a glance at Lola and Hannah, "it takes me a little longer to trust people. However, now that I see that you know what you're doing, I'm ready to talk. Wait—hold on one second." She flipped her hair upside down and scrubbed at the sides of her head before flipping it back up. "Okay— *now* I'm ready."

I turned the camera toward her. I had to admit, the camera did love her, especially her blue eyes. And it made the little bump in her nose less pronounced. "So Dylan Schoenfield," I said in my best documentarian voice, which Ari said made me sound like the CNN announcer, "as last year's junior prom queen, as well as past Spring

Fling princess, and homecoming queen, you're obviously one of, if not *the* most, popular girl at Castle Heights."

She sat up a little straighter and smiled into the camera like a TV anchorwoman.

"And yet, as we all know from *People* magazine and *Entertainment Tonight*," I continued, "even the beautiful and popular people are still human. So can you tell us a little bit about the pitfalls of popularity? You know, the downside of it?"

Dylan twisted a piece of hair around her finger as she thought about it. "Well, for good or for bad, when you're popular, you just can't escape the limelight," she said. "Take Angelina Jolie, for instance. Her mom dies and she loses a few pounds because she's overcome with grief and people say she's anorexic. And then she goes on one of her trips to Asia to get another kid and eats too much rice and people say she's getting fat. I mean, the poor woman just cannot win, you know?"

"So you're saying that when you're popular there's this pressure to be thin?" I asked.

"Well, yeah, but that's a whole other issue. What I mean is that when you're popular, you have to be super nice to *everyone* all the time. Even when you have PMS. Because if you're not, then before you know it, it's all over school." Suddenly her face scrunched up like she had eaten tuna fish that had been left out in the sun. "Omigod—*what* is Susan Adelson *wearing*?" As we all turned to look, I saw Susan walking across the cafeteria in jeans and a red sweater.

"Jeans and a red sweater?" I said.

"Uh, yeah, and *open-toe* Birkenstocks," she replied. "Rule number 731: unless you were brought up in, I don't know, *Iowa* or somewhere like that, everyone knows you don't wear open-toed shoes after October first. Granted this is California, but still."

So much for the nice-to-everyone part.

She snapped her fingers for me to move the camera back on her. "But getting back to what I was saying—see, it's like there's this magnifying glass on you *all the time.* So that's why if you're popular, you're better off being friends with and dating other popular people. Sort of how actors date other actors. There's just a shorthand there that makes it easier."

As she got up and walked over to Asher's table, I picked up the camera and started to follow her, stopping when I realized the guys weren't with me. "What are you guys doing? C'mon."

Ari looked terrified. "Do we have to?

I sighed and kept going.

Dylan put her arms around Asher's neck from behind as he studied a magazine. "That's why Asher and I are such a perfect match. We're kind of like the celebrity couple of Castle Heights, right, babe?"

As he unwrapped her arms from his neck, Asher

continued to study the magazine, which, when I zoomed in, I could see it was the *Sports Illustrated* swimsuit issue.

"*Asher,*" Dylan said, punching him on the shoulder.

He looked up. "Hey, you know I don't like you touching me in public."

After he turned back to the magazine, I could see the hurt that flashed across Dylan's face, but by the time she had turned back to the camera, she was smiling. "You can cut that last part out," she said. "We can do an episode on him later," she said as she walked back to our table.

"But if you're only hanging out with people who are just like you," I asked when she had sat back down, "then how are you supposed to broaden your perspective on life?"

While she took a sip of her Evian and pondered what I thought was a very deep and thought-provoking question, I zoomed in for a close-up. "Well, that's what vacations are for," she finally replied. "Like when my dad takes me to Hawaii for Christmas break, or Aspen for winter break, I meet lots of different people from all over the world. Those trips are very enlightening."

Yeah, if you want to enlighten yourself about how *other* rich people live. I couldn't believe how out of touch with common man she was. I bet she had never even *been* to my side of town. "Okay, let me ask you this, then: Was there ever a time when you *weren't* popular? When you were just, you know, normal?"

"Uh-oh," I could hear Hannah whisper off to the side.

Dylan hesitated. "Okay, I need you to cut for a second," she said, putting her hand in front of the camera and knocking me in the nose in the process.

"Ouch," I said.

"I think before we continue, you really need to look over those rules I gave you. Specifically Rules 41 to 45, which are all about creating something that's fair and balanced."

"But why is that an unfair question?" I asked.

"Because if you read the list, you'll see that you're to stay focused on the *present*. I mean, what, I'm supposed to hang out with *un*popular people, like you and your friends? I didn't make the rules, Josh—I just follow them." She started gathering up her books. "It's from following the rules that I've gotten where I am and I'm certainly not going to let you guys paint me as some total bitch because you're jealous of that."

"If the shoe fits . . . " said Steven under his breath.

"Excuse me?" Dylan demanded.

"Nothing," I said. "Just ignore him. Sometimes he gets minor Tourette's syndrome."

"Well, I think you've gotten enough for today," she announced as she started walking down The Ramp.

I sighed as I patted my pocket to make sure my inhaler was still there. If she kept throwing fits like this, I'd end up having a seven-minute documentary to show. Now I understood why Dylan was so far up the Castle Heights food chain—no one else in their right mind would want to be near her.

* * * * * * *

One of the classic story lines in movies is this: boy meets girl. Boy and girl can't stand each other. Boy and girl realize that, actually, they love each other. Boy and girl live happily ever after. I knew right away that Dylan and I were going to stay stuck in the can't-stand-each-other phase of the movie rather than pass go and live happily ever after.

On Wednesday afternoon at 1:45, Dylan sent me a text telling me that she had decided that she was willing to let me accompany her and the girls to Robertson Boulevard, which was a street with lots of expensive boutiques.

But I have an allergist appointment, I texted back. My doctor was concerned about how often I used my inhaler and was always telling me it wasn't an antianxiety aid, which bothered me to no end because I *didn't* use it for anxiety—I had allergies. Could I help it if I had been born three weeks premature and my lungs never developed properly?

OBVIOUSLY as much as u call yrself a FILMMAKER u don't take it all that SERIOUSLY!!!! was the text I got back.

Luckily I was able to reschedule the appointment, but I was starting to understand why so many directors were in such bad physical shape—when you were invested in a movie, it was all-consuming. Everything suffered: your health, your relationship. Luckily I didn't have one of those, but if I *did* have a girlfriend—like, say, someone like Amy Loubalu—I bet she'd be very understanding and supportive about dating an artist.

* ★ ＊ ★ ＊ ★ ＊

"Tell me again what this has to do with school and popularity," I asked later as I trudged behind the girls on Robertson Boulevard trying to juggle their packages and my camera. I was on my own, as Steven's mom wouldn't let him skip his weekly weigh-in at Weight Watchers (he kept gaining instead of losing, which may have had something to do with the fact that he'd eat entire boxes of 100-calorie Chips Ahoy cookies instead of just one package). Ari had tryouts for the musical version of *Macbeth* (he was shy in a group, but when you put him onstage, he rocked).

"As ambassadors of popularity, we owe it to everyone to look our best," Dylan explained. "Omigod—this is my absolute *favorite* store!" she squealed for the third time in fifteen minutes, pointing to a place called Magique that had mannequins wearing ripped clothes that made them resemble the homeless ladies on Hollywood Boulevard.

As the three of them ran inside, I followed, but not before the door smacked me in the face.

"I bet no one treats Quentin like this," I grumbled as I juggled the bags and the camera and I opened the door. Once inside I plopped down on an overstuffed chair and tried not to cringe from the techno music that was blaring through the speakers as the girls rifled through the clothing racks. I took out the camera and panned around the store. So *this* is where popular girls spend their afternoons. I felt like I had found the secret passage to the inner sanctum.

"Are you with the paparazzi?" sniffed the salesgirl whose pale skin and dark lips made her look like Morticia from the classic TV show *The Addams Family*.

"No. I'm a director," I said proudly.

Her snooty look was replaced by a smile. "Oh yeah? I just happen to have a copy of my headshot and acting reel in my bag." She gave me what I guessed was supposed to be a sexy look, although it was more like she needed to go to the bathroom. "I'd love you to take a look when you have a moment."

"Oh. I'm not—I mean I'm still in high school. This is a documentary I'm doing to get into film school—"

She walked away before I could even finish my sentence.

Dylan came out of the dressing room wearing a dress that looked like a Hefty garbage bag with armholes. "Okay—you can start filming now."

With the camera in one hand, I used the other to reach into my pocket and pull out the list I had made during physics class entitled "Questions to Ask Popular People." It was a little trashed, due to the fact that I had spilled salsa on it that afternoon, but it was still readable. "What would a typical night out for a popular couple be?" I read from the list, before looking up at her. "What do you and Asher usually do?"

"You mean when he's not off at those stupid Ultimate Fighting things?" asked Lola as she came out of her dressing room dressed in something that looked half spacesuit/half army uniform.

"He doesn't do that *every* weekend," replied Dylan.

Hannah came out wearing something that looked like a nun's habit. "When was the last time you guys even hung out?" she asked.

"We hang out all the time," said Dylan defensively. "We hung out . . . three weekends ago!"

"You mean that night that he was supposed to meet you at Heidi Lehmann's party and didn't show up until ten and then only stayed for fifteen minutes?" Lola retorted.

I just kept moving the camera back and forth like I was at a tennis match, trying not to look too excited. Catfights always helped heighten the drama of a film.

"Excuse me for not being one of those girls who's so insecure she needs to be with her boyfriend twenty-four/ seven," Dylan huffed as she marched over and put her hand on the camera lens. "Okay, you need to cut."

"Ow," I said as the camera bopped me in the nose again.

She put her hands on her hips. "Rule number 876: no talking about my relationship on camera. Some things need to remain private and personal."

"Especially when they're, like, *ending*," said Lola quietly.

"What?" Dylan snapped.

"Nothing," Lola said as she disappeared back into her dressing room.

"Okay, I think we've had enough for today," Dylan said as she marched back to her own.

Hannah walked up to the camera. "You're not going to put that part in, are you?"

I shrugged. "I don't know. Why?"

"Because it just makes us as popular girls look . . . I don't know . . . *bitchy*. And we're so not." She leaned in closer. "You probably won't get this because you're a guy, but seeing that the three of us are best friends, we're on the same cycle and it's, you know, *that time of the month*, so we're all a little oversensitive. I mean, as you know, usually we're super sweet. Well, maybe Lola isn't, but Dylan and I are."

So much for loyalty among friends.

"So will you keep this part out?" she whispered. "Because even though I don't come across as bad, I don't want to be thought of as a bitch because I'm friends with them, you know?"

"How about I think about it?" I whispered back.

"That would be great," she said with a smile before she ran off to her dressing room.

Even with our Just-Because-It's-Thursday-Again-Get-70-Percent-Off sale, work was still dead the next day. I spent most of my shift trying to convince an elderly couple that it wasn't that their ungrateful daughter-in-law had given them a defective laptop, but, rather, they needed to turn it *on* first in order for it to work. At 6:30, as I was getting my stuff out of my locker at work and about to head over to the New Beverly for a double feature of the Chinese director Wong Kar-wai's work, which I had been looking forward to for months (especially since Quentin was a huge fan of his as well and was sometimes known to show up at the New Beverly on occasion), my phone rang.

When DYLAN flashed across the screen, I sighed. This was the fifth call in three hours. Apparently in addition to being her director, I was also a human weather vane, a human calculator, and a human MapQuest.

"Hi, Dylan," I said as I answered the phone.

"Josh?"

"Yeah?"

"It's Dylan."

"I know. I just said that," I said, reaching for my inhaler. It had gotten to the point where just the sound of her *voice* made my lungs start to constrict. I made a mental note to go on WebMD when I got home to find out if you could be physically allergic to a person.

"So listen," she said. "My car won't start *again*—I can't even *tell* you how many problems I've had with this thing, it's beyond annoying—and if it's not too much of a hassle, I really need you to come pick me up and drive me to Pilates in Santa Monica because my trainer said that if I cancel one more time she's going to drop me as a client, and with Fall Fling coming up, I can't afford to have even a trace of a poochy belly and I would've asked Marta, our housekeeper, to do it but she's already left because she had to go to church because it's some saint's day and Hannah and Lola can't do it because Hannah's getting her hair cut and Lola's at her Adopted Ethnic Children of White Families therapy group, so there's really no one else for me to ask, and seeing that you're my director and want this documentary to be as good as it can be, I know you want me to be in the best possible shape I can be, which is why I thought that if you're not doing anything right now, maybe *you* could take me."

"But we weren't supposed to get together until Saturday—"

"Okay, well, obviously this film isn't all that important to you. And, you know, if it's not important to *you*, then I'm not sure why it should be important to *me*, so maybe I should just explain to my dad that you couldn't be bothered."

I wondered if Dylan had ever considered a career as a politician. Her blackmailing skills were beyond impressive.

"The problem is I'm just finishing up at work," I said, "so I'm all the way across town—"

"That's okay. I don't need to be there until seven, so we have some time."

"Yeah, but traffic this time of day is pretty awful, so—"

Her sigh almost broke my eardrum. "Look, Josh— I'll just cut to the chase: for someone like myself who's already got major trust issues, I'm not sure that I'm going to be able to work with someone who's so unsupportive of me."

Here was a perfect opportunity for me to practice what my mom liked to call "showing up for myself." Not letting someone take advantage of me, or not putting my needs to the side just so they'd like me or approve of me. To stop being a wimp and rolling over.

I took a deep breath. "What's your address again?"

Yes, I needed to show up for myself. But even more important was getting this documentary done. After my parents' divorce my grades had gone down, and I've never been a good test taker (I went through an entire inhaler during the SATs), so if I wanted to get into the most competitive film school in the world, I needed this documentary to be as kick-ass as possible. Even if it meant having to suck it up and become Dylan's personal assistant for the next few weeks.

"Seven-two-one-seven Luna Drive," she replied.

"Give me a half hour," I said, glancing at the picture I kept taped to the inside of my locker of Quentin holding up his Independent Spirit Award for *Pulp Fiction.* All the stars in that cast put together couldn't be as high maintenance as Dylan.

"Okay, so before Pilates we just have to make one quick stop at Alice, this little boutique on Montana Avenue,"

Dylan said as she got into the Neilmobile. She looked around the car. "How *old* is this thing anyway?"

"It's an '87."

She wrinkled her nose. "Is it *safe*?"

I nodded. "Volvos are known for being the most reliable car there is. In fact, in 2005 they did this study where—"

"Okay, FYI? I'm *so* not interested in facts and figures," she said as she fastened her seat belt. "I already have enough stuff to think about, thankyouverymuch."

Like what color nail polish to wear? I thought to myself as I put the car into drive.

As we crawled down Sunset Boulevard in the bumper-to-bumper traffic, she reached for the stereo. "We need some tunes." As she clicked it on, Neil Diamond's "Holly Holy" boomed out of the speakers and she turned to me. "You're *kidding* me, right?"

"It *is* called the Neilmobile." I shrugged.

"Okay, well, I'm afraid this is going to make me throw up, so can we please listen to something else? Especially since I'm starting to freak out with all this traffic."

I shrugged. "If you want. Personally, I find Neil very relaxing. Like vocal yoga or something." I definitely needed all the help I could get at that moment to relax. Being alone with Dylan in such close proximity made me anxious.

She gave me a look. "Personally, I find Neil really annoying." After nixing all my preset classic-rock stations, she landed on a Top 40 station. "Omigod, I *love* this song!" she shrieked as some overproduced, bass-thumping, alien-voice-sounding garbage filled the speakers. As if having to listen to the song wasn't bad enough, Dylan started to *sing*. At the top of her lungs.

I had never heard anything more frightening in my life.

I took my eyes off the road to see if she was being serious or if she had a knack for comedy that I hadn't been aware of up until this point, but apparently she *was* serious. And things got even more frightening when she started "dancing" in her seat, which resembled an epileptic seizure.

She opened her eyes. "Don't you love this song?" she demanded.

"Uh—" I wanted to say that since I wasn't a tween girl, the answer was no, but I didn't think that would help on the bonding front.

"Last week my teacher played it in Yoga Booty Ballet and I went *insane*. Everyone was saying I should *so* try and get on *American Idol*."

Before I could come up with a reply that would neither offend nor encourage her, the Neilmobile began to make a sound that was somewhere between a donkey braying and a mouse squeaking.

"*What* is that noise?!" Dylan yelled, clutching my arm so tight I almost swerved right into a limo. She may have been tiny, but she was *strong*.

I reached into my pocket for my inhaler. "I'm not sure,"

I panicked. "The only other time I heard something like this was when—"

As the Neilmobile started to slow down, I managed to make it over to the far-right lane of Sunset.

"—I ran out of gas a few months ago," I finished.

Which, from the way the car drifted to a full stop, was apparently happening again.

"Are you saying we're out of gas?" Dylan asked.

I looked at the gas gauge. "Well, since the needle is on the far, far, far left of the *E*, yeah, I'd say that's probably the case."

The Neilmobile coughed up one last sputter and then got quiet.

"I cannot *believe* this!" Dylan yelled. "I mean, who runs out of gas on Sunset Boulevard? During rush hour?!"

"Look, it's not like I planned it or anything," I said defensively between inhaler squirts. "I thought I had enough to get you to your Pilales thing—"

"Pi*la*tes," she corrected. "Like *latte*, the drink." She started fanning herself. "Look at this—you've gotten me so freaked out I'm *sweating*." She took out a towel from her workout bag and started dabbing at her forehead. "I *hate* sweating."

"I *would've* stopped to get more gas on my way here, but you were in such a hurry," I snapped.

"Safety should always come first," she said, sounding like a PSA as she dabbed away.

"You've never run out of gas before?" I asked, inhaling with the inhaler again.

"Well, yes, I have, but at least it was on the *freeway*," she shot back.

"And that would be better because . . . ?" I asked.

She thought about it. "I don't know. It just is. Listen, if I'm still going to make it to Pilates I really don't have time to fight with you about this right now. Do you have a Triple-A card with you?" she asked as she took out her phone.

"Yeah, but my mom never paid the renewal fee, so it's expired."

If looks could kill, I would've been a victim from *Saw 4*. "So *now* what do we do?" she asked.

"Well, do you have a Triple-A card?" I asked.

"No. I switched wallets this morning because I was using my Rachel Romanoff bag instead of the Serge Sanchez and the black of the wallet clashed with the black of the bag. I mean, they're close but that kind of thing really bothers me even though Hannah swears it's not a big deal."

Why she thought this stuff was of interest to another human being was beyond me. "I guess I could call Steven or Ari and ask them to come by. Or maybe you could call Asher." I picked up my phone.

The look she gave me would have melted the Wicked Witch of the West. "Or not," I added.

"Why don't you just call a tow truck?" she asked as she went back to fanning herself.

"Good idea," I said as I started to dial the phone. In the entire time I had spent with her, that was the smartest thing that she had ever said. "Uh oh," I said a moment later.

"What?"

I looked at my phone, where none of the bars were lit up. "No reception." There was a stretch of Sunset that was known for being a dead zone. Apparently we were in it.

Dylan started banging her head against the back of the seat. "I. Can. Not. Believe. This."

"I know there's a gas station a little ways up the street," I offered.

"How far?"

"I don't know . . . a mile?"

"You want me to walk a *mile*?!"

Frankly, I didn't care if she walked at all—by this point, I just wanted her out of my car. I liked to think of myself as a pretty patient guy, but as my mom's friend Jo'Say liked to say, she was working my last nerve. Between the personal-assistant stuff, and the chauffeur stuff, and the insults, I had had it. "If you want, you can stay in the car," I said.

"By myself?! I could get raped or killed."

I looked at the Range Rovers, Mercedes, and BMWs whizzing by. "I'm thinking there's not a lot of serial killers in this part of town," I replied.

She grabbed her bag. "No way. I'm coming with you."

"Whatever you say." I sighed as we got out of the car, taking my video camera with me in case someone did try

89

and break in. *Maybe the documentary wasn't such a great idea after all,* I thought.

Within ten minutes *maybe* had changed to *definitely*. After having to listen to Dylan's complaints that it was too cold, too loud, and her feet hurt, I decided that not only did I no longer care if I got into USC, but I would've given up my entire Martin Scorsese library of movies just to not have to deal with her anymore. How Asher put up with her was beyond my comprehension. Maybe he wore invisible earbuds.

"How much longer?" she called out from behind me for the second time in two minutes as we trekked up Sunset toward Brentwood as cars whizzed by. Because we were in the residential area, there weren't even sidewalks—just narrow shoulders. Every time a car rounded the bend I was sure we were going to be toast.

"I don't know . . . five more minutes?" I called back. The truth was, my feet were hurting as well. Not that I'd need them if I were roadkill.

"You said that five minutes ago!" she retorted.

That was the thing about L.A.—as a rule of thumb, everything was twenty minutes away from wherever you were. Since we had been walking for about fifteen, I thought it was a safe answer. However, what I didn't realize until that moment was that everything was twenty minutes away by *car*—not foot.

As we turned a corner, I saw the bright shining lights of a Mobil station. I had never been so happy to see a gas station in my life, even when Mom and I were driving to Scottsdale, Arizona, to visit my grandparents and I had drunk so much water I thought my bladder was going to explode and we were on a stretch of the 10 freeway where there's nothing for miles.

"Omigodomigodomigod!" I heard her yelp. Thinking that she was as excited as I was to see that we were almost at our destination, I just kept walking until a few moments later she screamed "JOSSSSSSHHHH!"

I turned back to see her flat on her butt holding her ankle. "Ouchouchouchouch," she moaned, looking like a bad actress in a fifth-rate horror movie.

"What happened?" I sighed as I walked toward her.

"What do you *think* happened? I tripped on some stupid rock and broke my ankle."

I looked at her foot, which looked fine to me. "Can you wiggle your foot?"

She moved it a little, wincing with pain. "Yeah, but it kills."

"If you can move it, it's not broken. It's probably just a slight sprain."

"Sprained?! How long is it going to be sprained?" she asked, nearly in hysterics. "Will it be better for Fall Fling? It's got to be better for Fall Fling. I'm not showing up in, like, *flip-flops* or something ridiculous like that!" She started to cry. "What if I can't wear my silver Christian Louboutins?"

I had no idea who or what a Christian Louboutin was, but it certainly wasn't the time to find out. "Okay, let me think of the best way to handle this . . . why don't you wait here and I'll run to the gas station and get someone to drive back here and pick you up."

"Don't you think we should call an ambulance so I can get to a hospital?"

I wondered if Urbandictionary.com had a picture of Dylan under *drama queen*. "As long as we get some ice on it soon, I think you'll be okay. Plus this is a dead zone with no cell reception."

"You can't just leave me here by the side of the road!" she said.

"Well, what are my options? Carry you?"

The way that she looked at me made me realize that as far as she was concerned, that was a perfectly viable option.

"But I have a weak lower back. My doctor says I'm prone to herniated disks," I said.

"And I'm a young girl wearing a tank top who can't walk, lying on the side of a road," she shot back. "I mean, hello? How would I defend myself if a serial killer stopped?"

After two minutes of hanging out with her, any serial killer with half a brain would realize that having to listen to Dylan was more trouble than it was worth and would go in search of a different victim.

"And, you know, if my *dad* found out about this, I don't think he'd be too thrilled . . . " she added.

I thought about it. His daughter was a pain in the butt, but Mr. Schoenfield *was* paying for the documentary. Taking a deep breath, I hoisted her up into my arms like a groom about to carry a bride over a threshold and began to trudge toward the gas station.

"I don't want to be a pain and ask you to stop so I can get my sunglasses out of my bag, so do you think you could move a little so that the sun isn't directly in my eyes?"

I did what she asked, but I didn't even try and hide my sigh.

"Thank you," she said.

I walked a few more yards.

"And do you think you could move your left hand up about two inches? It's jamming into my spine and it feels like I'm about to be paralyzed."

Again, I did what she asked, not really caring if I dropped her in the process.

"Thanks."

We—or rather, *I*—walked a little farther. "I feel like I'm in *The African Queen* or something like that," I said.

She looked around. "Um, sorry, but from what I've seen on TV, L.A. looks nothing like Africa."

"It's a movie," I explained.

"Who's in it?"

"Humphrey Bogart and Katharine Hepburn."

"Never heard of them."

Of course she hadn't. I bet Amy Loubalu had seen *The African Queen*. Okay, maybe she hadn't because it was from 1951, but I bet she had at least heard of it. Or, if we were dating and I suggested we watch it on a Friday night with a big bowl of popcorn with Tabasco sauce, she would've gotten into it.

"So I'm curious—what were you thinking driving around with so little gas?" she asked. "I mean, it's one thing if, you know, it's just *you* in the car, but don't you think it's a little selfish to put another person's life in jeopardy like that?"

I stopped walking. "Wait a second—*you're* calling *me* selfish?"

"Yeah, I guess I am. Which, frankly, is a little disappointing. I mean, just yesterday Lola and Hannah were saying how they thought you were actually a pretty decent guy, and they basically had me convinced, but now? Not so much."

Luckily we had gotten to a part of Sunset that had sidewalks, so I didn't feel so bad when I set her down. It wasn't like I dumped her next to a guardrail or something, but from the look on her face, you would've thought I dumped her in a pig's trough or something. But I had had it. Forget about the documentary—there was no way I could put up with her for the next four weeks. "And if you ask *me*, demanding that someone put aside whatever plans they may have had and drive across town just so someone else can go to a stupid exercise class because they want to look good for a stupid dance isn't a little selfish—it's a *lot* selfish."

"I can't believe you just called me selfish!" she said. I wondered if she was considering becoming an actress, because the wounded look on her face was beyond believable. "I'm really sorry to have to say this, but I don't think this is going to work out, Josh."

"Yeah, I agree," I agreed.

"I mean, up until today I thought you were harmless, but to now see this other side of you that's so . . . *cruel* . . . Wait—what did you say?"

"I said that I agree," I snapped. "I'll e-mail the USC people and tell them that an emergency came up and I won't be able to do the documentary." Out of habit I went to reach for my inhaler, but I realized I didn't need it. Instead of being freaked out about this turn of events, I actually felt empowered. Who knew standing up for yourself could feel so good?

"Oh. Okay. Yeah, that's probably best," she replied. Were my glasses smudged, or did she look a little disappointed? Not that I gave a rat's butt. From now on, I didn't care *what* Dylan Schoenfield looked or felt like. I was finally free.

I started walking toward the gas station.

"Wait—what about my foot?!" she yelled after me. "Aren't you going to carry me the rest of the way?"

Even with the roar of the traffic that was whizzing by, I bet they could hear my laugh all the way across town at USC.

"You're amazing, you know that? From the moment I

got your dumb bag out of the fountain, you've acted like *I* owed *you* something," I said. "I have no idea how you got to be so popular, but I'll tell you this much—it's definitely not because of your winning personality. You've insulted me, you've insulted my friends, and guess what? I'm not going to take it anymore! I'd rather be a geek than a selfish, self-centered, materialistic . . . mean girl."

For once in her life, Dylan Schoenfield had nothing to say. She just stood there with her mouth open so wide you could've fit a bus in there.

I wish I could say I just kept walking and never talked to Dylan again, but because I'm Jewish, the guilt of leaving her there—especially if her foot *was* screwed up—would've been too much to handle. That being said, I wasn't a complete doormat: I refused to carry her. Instead I let her lean her hand on my shoulder like a crutch while she hopped on one foot, so it took us twice as long to go those last few yards to the gas station.

But that was as far as I went. It's not like I talked to her or anything. While I waited for the gas-station guy to fill up a container with gas for me to take back to my car, she dialed her phone.

"Asher? Hey, babe, it's me." She turned her back to me. "Listen, I have a huge favor to ask . . . Asher? Asher, are you there? . . . Well, do you think you can turn the TV down for a second?"

Before starting the documentary, I had always thought

Asher was an idiot. But after spending time with Dylan, I knew he was an even *bigger* idiot for dating her.

"That's much better," she went on. "So I was wondering whether you could come pick me up at the Mobil station at the corner of Sunset and Barrington . . . it's a long story, but"—she whipped around and gave me a dirty look—"basically Geek Boy almost had us *killed* . . . so can you come get me?" Her face fell. "Oh . . . yeah, I understand . . . no, I know how tired you get after eating Mexican food . . . I'll just call you when I get home, then . . . bye." She turned to me. "Not that it's any of your business, but he's in the middle of something very important," she explained.

I could think of lots of important things to do rather than help her out. Like, say, clipping my toenails.

After the gas-station attendant handed me the container of gas, I turned to her. "Well, I'm going now."

"Fine. Have a nice life," she snapped.

"You, too," I replied.

I was feeling pretty good about myself by the time I got back to the car. "Raymond's right," I said out loud after I filled the tank and got into the Neilmobile. "If I'm going to be an A-list director, I need to stay true to my artistic vision." I was a creative guy—I'd have no problem coming up with an equally good idea for another documentary. Maybe I'd take Hannah's advice and do one on the unpopular crowd. That could work. It would be like Judd Apatow's classic television series *Freaks and Geeks*, but just the "geeks" part. In fact, the more I thought about it, the more it seemed like a much better idea than focusing on the popular crowd. The whole popular thing had been done to death anyway.

When I got home, there was an e-mail waiting for me.

Dear Josh:

Thank you for your recent application to the USC School of Cinematic Arts. I'm not in the habit of e-mailing prospective students, but I felt compelled to let you know that I applaud your innovation in being so proactive in today's competitive admission process by going above and beyond the usual application process. This year we've had more early-admissions candidates like yourself than ever before, setting the bar for admissions even higher. To that end, we on the admissions committee find the notion of popularity a subject of worthy exploration. It's not like anyone would be interested in watching a documentary about *un*popular people, now, would they?

We very much look forward to seeing your finished documentary. Without making any promises, it's my feeling that someone as proactive as yourself might also deserve a scholarship. USC is proud to have cultivated many forward-thinking, aspiring filmmakers over the years, and I have a feeling someone of your caliber would be a fine addition to the family.

Best regards,

Murray Sheingold

Admissions Director

I couldn't believe it—I had received an e-mail from the *admissions director* of USC even though he was not—and I quote—*in the habit* of doing things like that. As far as I was concerned, I was basically in! But there was a slight problem: I had just told Dylan Schoenfield, the most popular girl at Castle Heights, off. And called off the very documentary about popularity that USC was *very much looking forward to seeing.*

Other than rigging the voting and assuring her I'd make it so that she won that stupid Leaf Queen crown she wanted, how on earth was I going to convince her to let me keep doing the documentary?

With a sigh, I sat back in my chair and did the only thing I could think of to stop myself from jumping out of my second-floor bedroom window.

I reached for my inhaler.

chapter five: *dylan*

This is the thing about geeks: they may *look* all innocent and goofy—like raccoons or squirrels—but once you get close to them you realize they're super dangerous, to the point where they can give you rabies or something equally disgusting.

"I cannot *believe* I was dumb enough to let my dad force me into this thing in the first place." I was sitting with Lola at Pinkberry after she came to get me at the gas station. I inhaled my green-tea yogurt with mango and coconut. It was bad enough that I had been insulted the way I had, but the fact that Josh had upset me to the point that I was stress eating like this was even worse.

"Did he really call you selfish to your face?" Lola asked as I dug my spoon into her yogurt as well.

"Um, *yeah.* Can you believe that anyone would say something so viciously untrue like that?" I replied. "I'm tell-ing you, I knew something was wrong that very first day when he brought up that question about whether there was a time when I wasn't popular."

I'm one of those people who tries really hard to stay in the moment rather than live in the past. So because I try to live in the now, I don't find it necessary to bring up the fact that when I started at Curtis Middle School in fifth grade I was a dead ringer for a Jewish Ugly Betty and spent every lunch period for the first month hiding out in the girls' bathroom.

Lola shrugged. "I don't know—I think the from-unpopular-to-popular angle is good. It makes it like one of those from-rags-to-riches stories that my mom used to read me when I was little about Chinese people so I wouldn't feel ashamed of where I came from."

"Okay, so maybe I know what it's like to spend recess inside reading a Judy Blume book instead of playing kick-ball with the other kids," I admitted as I dug in my wallet for some money so I could get another yogurt. This is why I didn't like talking about the past—more stress eating. "But all that was so long ago, why bring it up? It would be like if he had asked you on camera about those few months in eighth grade when your mother made you wear those satin embroidered shirts every day so you'd feel more con-nected to your heritage."

Lola cringed. "I guess you're right."

"And I'm certainly not giving Amy Loubalu credit for my popularity on camera," I announced.

Lola shrugged. "I know you hate her, but she did help you out a lot."

"Are you kidding? How so?"

"Let's see—inviting you to sit with us at lunch," she replied. "Taking you to the Beverly Center and telling you what to buy so you stopped looking like the poster child for What Not to Wear If You'd Like to Have a Social Life."

"Okay, fine, maybe that *was* kind of nice of her," I said, "but it was *me* who spent all those hours reading books like *101 Ways to Become Popular!* and *Up the Social Ladder in Ten Easy Steps!* And I think anyone with half a brain would agree that the way she then stabbed me in the back with an ice pick by stealing Michael Rosenberg away from me in eighth grade cancels out all of that. *Especially* since, as my best best friend, she knew full well how madly in love with him I was."

Lola looked hurt. "I thought *I've* always been your best best friend."

"You are," I quickly said. "I mean, you *were*. You were and are." With everything I had just gone through, I didn't need to risk having someone *else* turn on me. I stood up, hopping on my good foot. "I'll be right back. I need more yogurt."

As I waited for the girl with the pierced eyebrow and lip behind the counter (did Pinkberry not care about the image they were giving off to potential customers? Talk about an appetite suppressant) to add the real chocolate chips to my large cup of yogurt, instead of the yogurt ones, I thought about how tough it was to be me. No matter how nice I was to people, there was always going to be someone looking to take me down just because I was good-looking and had great fashion sense and a really hot boyfriend, even if he wasn't as available during crises as I'd like him to be.

I was glad that Josh had agreed with me that we should call the documentary off. That way Daddy couldn't accuse me of reneging on the deal. And even if Josh *hadn't* agreed with me, I'm sure Daddy would've understood once I explained to him what happened. I mean, to put someone's life in jeopardy by driving around with no gas and then almost leave them by the side of the road with a semisprained ankle, which meant that it would have been next to impossible for them to get away from a psycho-pathic killer? That, as far as I was concerned, was beyond unacceptable.

Not to mention then saying I was selfish and self-centered.

Like I could ever trust someone like that.

"Hey, Josh," Hannah said with a smile the next day during lunch as I was in the middle of trying to convince her and Lola that, yes, I did need the cane I had been using all day because, yes, my foot was swollen even if they couldn't see it. I don't know *what* she was putting in her Red Bulls, but somehow she had gotten it into her head that Josh was a nice guy and that I was being too hard on him about the running-out-of-gas thing.

I turned around to see Mr. Irresponsible Driver himself standing behind me looking as nervous as ever. "Hey, guys," he said. He pointed to my foot. "How is it?"

"Like *you* care," I sniffed.

"I do care. I left you a few voice mails and texts last night to check on you."

A *few*? Try like ten. First he had insulted me—now he was stalking me. Asher should've been the one checking in on me, but when I texted him to tell him about how mean Josh had been to me, he didn't even respond. I know some people would think that was rude, but I'm sure it's just because he was really worried about the geometry midterm he had coming up the following week, seeing that he had already failed the class twice. Being the only senior in a class of sophomores couldn't have been easy, especially when you're as sensitive as Asher is.

"It's fine," said Lola. "It's not even swollen."

I shot her a dirty look. It was exactly this kind of traitorlike behavior that explained why Amy had had best-best-friend status over her back in the day. "It is, too," I insisted.

"Well, like I said in my messages," Josh said, "I'm really sorry, and if there's anything I can do—"

"I think you've done enough," I snapped.

He took a deep breath. "Um, do you think I could talk to you alone for a second?"

Hannah stood up. "Come on, Lola—let's go look at that 'Twenty Years of Fall Fling Fashion' photo exhibit they just put up outside of the auditorium." Even though Hannah was definitely the sweeter one, and I could usually count on her to be a lot more understanding than Lola, when I told her what had happened with Josh and how he had called me selfish and self-centered, all she had said was "Wow. He really had the nerve to say that to your face?"

After they walked away, Josh sat down and took out his inhaler. Honestly, he was going to end up in Inhalers Anonymous if he didn't watch out. "I know that yesterday I got a little upset, but the truth is—" He stopped for a second and looked down at the crowd. "I still can't get over how undramatic the view is from up here."

I rolled my eyes. "Just because we're popular doesn't mean we live on another *planet*, Josh."

"I guess," he agreed. "Anyway, so as I was saying, the truth is that I've been thinking a lot about the documentary and I know I said that I agreed with you that we should just forget about it, but the more I think about it, the more I feel it can really . . . *help* people."

"Me? Help people? But I'm so self-centered," I said sarcastically.

"Like I said in my e-mail, I don't know what came over me yesterday," Josh said. He held up his inhaler. "I think maybe the inhaler I was using yesterday was past its expiration date or something and I had some sort of psychotic reaction that made me start spouting lies."

I folded my arms across my chest. "I may not get as good grades as you, but I'm not a total idiot, Josh. Don't think you can talk yourself out of the damage you've done."

He held up his hand. "Just hear me out," he said. "You know how sometimes girls who are really popular get a bad rap for being snotty or stuck-up?"

I glared at him. "Of course. That's the story of my life."

"Okay, so through this, you'll be able to help the reputation of *all* popular girls by showing the world that that's not true."

I sighed. "Look, Josh, I'm all about being of service to my fellow humankind, but I'm sorry—in this case I just don't feel I can trust you."

"Okay, I get it." He sighed. "I just thought that with what's going on with Dakota Greene and all, it might have come in handy . . ."

As I stopped examining my invisible swollen ankle, my head snapped up so fast I'm surprised I didn't sprain my neck as well. "What are you talking about?" Next to Amy Loubalu, there was no one I disliked more in school than Dakota Greene. Talk about willing to go to any lengths to take away my queen/princess status at every school function. Last year she had tried to set up a raffle where everyone who voted for her for junior prom queen was entered to win a $250 gift certificate to Bloomingdale's until the principal found out and threatened to expel her.

He shrugged. "I heard she's starting to campaign for prom queen."

"But prom's still eight months, one week, and three days away," I said.

"Yeah, but she hired some sort of political consultant that her dad knows and he came up with a plan of action. Supposedly she's started handing out questionnaires about what people look for in a prom queen."

"I cannot *believe* her," I said as I paced around the table. Miraculously, my ankle seemed to be fine. "I mean, it's pathetic how seriously some girls take these things, don't you think?"

A small smile started to creep over his face as he nodded. "And I was thinking if we did the documentary, then I could cut together a short trailer for you to post online and hand out to people so you can start campaigning, too."

As I thought about it, I realized that Josh was onto something. Not only had I been looking for an opportunity to be of service to my fellow humankind that didn't involve picking up garbage, but this one didn't even involve having to change my schedule around in any way. I just had to keep being me. Forget using the documentary in place of my college application essay—more importantly, I'd have a ninety-minute prom campaign ad.

I held out my hand. "It's a deal," I said.

That Tuesday night, while hunting around in the freezer for something low-calorie yet delicious, I came up with a brilliant idea; a way to show voters a whole other side to myself that would be sure to melt their hearts.

I picked up the phone to call Josh.

"Hello?" said the woman who answered the phone as some folk music played in the background.

"Hi, is Josh there please?" I asked, settling myself on the stool in front of the island in the kitchen with a pint of Mint Carob Chip Rice Dream. It wasn't *that* low-calorie, but it *was* nondairy, so it wasn't as bad as regular ice cream.

"Why yes, he is," the woman said, sounding like she had just won the lottery or something. "May I ask who's calling?"

It was so weird to talk to a nanny or housekeeper who was American. "This is Dylan Schoenfield."

"Just one second. Josh!" I heard her scream, even though she had covered the receiver. "It's for you. It's *Dylan.*"

"Hey, Dylan," he said when he picked up.

"Hi."

"Did he pick up?" the woman said. "Josh? Are you there? Did you pick up?"

"Mom, I have it. You can hang up now," he said.

"Okay, honey. Well, Dylan, I hope we get the chance

to meet at some point. Josh has told me *so* much about you."

"*Mom*, please. Hang up now, okay?"

"Okay, sweetie. Bye, Dylan."

"Bye, Mrs. Rosen," I said, speed-walking around the perimeter of the kitchen to burn off the Rice Dream. Our kitchen is pretty big, so I figured it was decent exercise.

"Actually, it's Goodstein. When I married Josh's father, I kept my name, which turned out to be a good thing on so many levels, especially since we're now divorced—"

"*Good-bye*, Mom," Josh said.

"But I always tell Josh's friends to call me Sandy anyway. How can I expect to really get to know you kids if we're starting our relationship with such a wall between us?"

"Okay, you really need to hang up now, Mom."

"I am. Bye, kids,"

"Bye . . . Sandy," I said.

We waited to hear the click of the phone being hung up, but it didn't come.

"Mom, I can hear you breathing," Josh said.

Finally the click came.

"Omigod—she's hysterical," I said, plopping myself back down on the stool and eating what was left of the pint.

"Yeah, well, I'll trade you. I'm sure your mother is a million times closer to normal than mine is."

"Actually, mine's dead," I said.

"Oh. That's right. I'm sorry—"

"It's okay. So listen—the reason I'm calling is because I thought that maybe after school tomorrow you'd like to come with me to the Amanda Foundation."

"Isn't that an animal rescue organization?" he asked.

"Uh-huh."

"Oh. Are you getting a dog?"

"Nope."

"A cat?"

"Uh-uh."

"A rabbit?"

"A *rabbit*? Who would get a rabbit for a pet? No. I'm not big on things that shed—I just thought it would be good for the documentary. Especially since Lola heard from Beth Lapkin who heard from Shelley McCrory that Dakota just placed an order for a hundred bedazzled 'Dakota Greene for Prom Queen' T-shirts. I'm thinking maybe some footage of me playing with a bundle of fluffy kittens is the way to go."

He didn't say anything.

"Josh? Are you there?"

"Yeah. It's just . . . nothing," he mumbled. "It'll be fine. I'll just make sure to have an extra inhaler with me."

I rolled my eyes. "Let me guess: you're allergic to animals, too."

"I can't remember if I was tested by the allergist for

animal dander, but I'm sure I am. I was three weeks premature, so—"

"—you don't have a strong immune system. Yeah, I know," I replied.

He was quiet again. "Plus . . . forget it."

"What?"

"It's just that . . . well, there was an incident," he finally said.

"What kind of incident?" I asked warily.

"An incident with a guinea pig I brought home over Christmas vacation in fourth grade. Pepper was his name."

"What happened to Pepper?"

"He kept giving me these pleading looks like he was really hungry, so I threw in a head of lettuce before I went to bed one night and then . . . "

"Then what?"

"Well, apparently guinea pigs don't know when to stop eating, so he didn't. And he . . . exploded."

"Ewwww!" I shrieked. "That's *disgusting!*"

"Yeah, it kind of was," he agreed. "So ever since then, I tend to avoid being around animals whenever I can. It's a post-traumatic-stress thing."

"Oh."

"But maybe this is a good opportunity for me to try and get over it. I should probably start getting some experience working under less-than-perfect circumstances, for when I'm a real director."

"Are you sure?" I asked. I had to give him credit—having once had a teddy bear that exploded in the washing machine when I was four, I knew how traumatic seeing an animal's intestines could be.

"Yeah. It'll be okay. I'm sure I'll have to work with animals at some point. I might as well start now."

I had always been under the impression that geeks were frightened of their own shadows, but I had to admit that Josh was being pretty brave.

That was the thing about people—sometimes they actually surprised you.

As soon as I walked into Good Buys the next afternoon with the three shopping bags I had accumulated in the last hour, I totally understood why Josh's shirt had said GEEK GANG that first day I met him—*everyone* in there was kind of geeky, from the people who worked there to the customers. Unlike the Apple Store or Circuit City, which were super loud and made you feel like you had had seven energy drinks, the vibe in Good Buys was more like a funeral.

I walked over to the neon Geek Gang sign where a guy with glasses and a wart on the right side of his nose was reading a magazine called *Fangoria* that had a picture of a guy dripping blood on the cover.

"Hi," I said, trying not to look at the wart. Facial disfigurations tend to make me nauseous.

He looked up. "Hello," he replied. "I'm Agent Raymond Strauss, director of intelligence for The Dell branch of the Geek Gang. How can I help you today?"

"I'm looking for Josh Rosen," I said.

He scratched his nose, right near the wart. "And you *a-r-e*?"

"Dylan Schoenfield."

"Ah. So *you're* Dylan." He nodded as he brought his walkie-talkie up to his mouth. "Agent Rosen, Agent Rosen. Please report to the command station. You have a visitor. Over."

"How cool!" I said excitedly. "I totally feel like I'm in an episode of *24*!"

Now, I thought that was pretty funny, but by the stone-faced stare I got in return, apparently Agent Raymond or whatever his name was didn't think so. Josh must've known how weird this guy was, too, because within thirty seconds he was trotting up to us with his video camera, all out of breath in his white shirt and creased black pants.

"Omigod—is that a *clip-on* tie?" I asked, grabbing for it.

"Hey! Don't—"

"I guess it is," I said as it popped off.

"Give me that," he said, taking it back and clipping it back on. When he was done he turned to the wart guy. "Okay, Raymond, I'm leaving."

"So I'll see you at fifteen-hundred hours tomorrow, Agent Rosen?" he asked.

He rolled his eyes. "Yes, Raymond—I'll see you at *three* o'clock." He turned to me. "You ready?"

I nodded.

He reached for two of my shopping bags. "Here, let me take these."

"Oh. You don't have to—"

"It's okay," he said, leading the way to the door. Asher *never* carried my bags for me. In fact, one time when he dragged me to a sporting-goods store, he actually made *me* carry *his* stuff so he could flip through the latest issue of *Surf's Up!* on the way back to the car.

"Is that guy really like that or is he an actor?" I asked when we got outside the store. Even though it was five o'clock on a weekday, the mall was packed. Sure, New York City might beat L.A. when it comes to museums and the symphony and all that cultural stuff, but no one can touch us when it comes to shopping.

"Unfortunately he's really like that," Josh said as he unpacked his video camera. "Uh-oh," he said as he examined it.

"What's the matter?" I asked, panicked. The last time he had said "Uh-oh" I had ended up stranded on the side of Sunset Boulevard.

"The battery's dead."

I relaxed. "Oh. So now what?"

"Well, I guess I could buy one at work, but even with my discount it's pretty expensive, so if it's okay with you,

I'd rather recharge it at home and do this some other time," he said.

"Oh. Okay," I said, trying not to sound too disappointed.

"Look, I feel bad about having made you wait around for me," he said. "Can I, uh, buy you something to eat to make up for it?"

Fighting my way through the crowds at Nordstrom's yearly half-off sale earlier *had* sapped a lot of my strength. But still—he was . . . *him* and I was . . . *me*. "You mean sit down at a table in a restaurant alone together?"

He shrugged. "Well, yeah. Unless you want a Hot Dog on a Stick from a cart. Other than the fact that they smell like formaldehyde, they're pretty good."

My stomach started to rumble. "I guess having a meal together would be okay." My eyes narrowed. "But you're not thinking of it as a *date*, are you?"

He snorted. "No. Of course not."

I was glad we were on the same page, but he didn't need to *snort* about it.

"Our relationship is strictly professional. I'm just trying to be a nice guy, seeing that you came all the way over here for nothing."

"Okay, then. So where should we go?"

"I usually go over to Du-par's at the Farmers Market," he replied.

The Farmers Market was within walking distance of

The Dell. It had been built in the 1930s and had a bunch of different mom-and-pop food stands and restaurants from Mexican to Korean. Daddy had tried to buy that land as well when he started developing The Dell, but backed down after he received a petition with over a thousand signatures from people who were against it. As there wasn't one health-conscious restaurant in the bunch, I thought that getting rid of it and putting up a gym was a good idea, but for some reason people tend to like greasy food and old-fashioned soft-serve ice-cream cones. Go figure.

"Isn't that like a pancake place?" I asked.

"Well, yeah, they have pancakes, but it's more like a diner."

I highly doubted that there'd be anything on the menu that was less than fifteen Weight Watchers points, but anything sounded better than a hot dog on a stick.

"Sure. That sounds fine," I said.

Plus, it was a very nondatelike place.

If you ever want to find the over-sixty-five crowd in L.A., just go to Du-par's at 5:15 P.M., because they're all there, eating their Salisbury-steak-and-baked-potato dinners. It was sweet to see so many old couples in love. Who knew—maybe Asher and I would eat here when we got old, too. That is, if I could get him to spend some time with me. Or just even *talk* to me. While Asher may be super hot, he's next to hopeless when it comes to communicating. When we were first going out, he'd at least *try* to keep the conversation going. Granted, it was usually him going on and on about Ultimate Fighting or surfing or some other subject that I had zero interest in while I said things like "uh-huh," "mm-hm," and "oh, really?" every few minutes to make him think that I was listening, but he didn't even do *that* anymore. Now our conversations went more like this:

Me: Hey, Asher.

Him: What up?

Me: Nothing. Just wanted to say hi.

Him: Hey, can I call/text you later? I'm kind of busy at the moment.

Me: Sure. Well, bye . . . love ya!

Him: Later.

We had been together for two years, so I realized it wasn't going to be like it was in the beginning when all we did was make out and tell each other how hot the other looked that day. However, in the book *How to Put the Sizzle Back in Your Marriage* that Lola stole from her mom's nightstand drawer a few months ago and gave to me, it said that communication was the keystone to a successful relationship and that if one of the partners was always giving one-word answers or saying things like "Can we talk later? I'm kind of busy," then chances were the marriage was in trouble.

And I also knew from having read the copy of *Men Are*

from Mars, Women Are from Venus that Hannah took from *her* mom's nightstand drawer that men just aren't into talking as much as we women are because they'd rather be off *fixing* something. But I also knew from the book that there were some guys out there who not only *like* to talk, but who know how to have a dialogue instead of a monologue.

Asher just didn't happen to be one of them.

At least not at the moment. But that was okay—I could train him. Like a puppy. I mean, he *was* super hot.

"This is so trippy," I said as I squinted against the fluorescent light and took a bite of my iceberg-lettuce salad with Russian dressing. Usually I avoid dressing like the plague, but when I asked for balsamic vinaigrette, Doris, our yellow-haired waitress who seemed to never have heard the word *sunblock* before, looked at me like I was speaking Swahili so I decided to just go with the flow. "I don't know if I've ever seen polyester-and-elastic-waist pants up close before."

Josh took a bite of his club sandwich. "I know it's not written up in a gossip blog or anything like that," he said, "but I have seen a few celebrities in here from time to time."

"Like who?"

"Like . . . Janusz Kaminski."

"Who?"

"Janusz Kaminski!" he said with his mouth full.

"Okay. A) Rule number 732: the talking-with-your-mouth-full? Totally gross, so please refrain."

He finished chewing and wiped his mouth with a

napkin. "Sorry. I guess I've been spending too much time with Steven."

"And B) Who on earth is Shamu Kazinsky?"

Josh looked at me like I had just stood up on the table and started barking. "Janusz Kaminski. Only one of the best cinematographers of all time. He shot a lot of Steven's movies."

"Steven your friend?"

As he took a sip of his milk, I cringed. First of all, who over the age of five drank milk with a meal? And second, did he not know how much fat was in that glass?

"No. Steven *Spielberg,*" he replied.

"You know Steven Spielberg?" I asked, impressed.

"Not exactly," he admitted. "But I'm sure I'll meet him one day. Anyway, I'm not quite sure it was Janusz because I only saw him from the back and it was right before I got my new prescription for my glasses—"

"Okay, sorry, but that's *not* a celebrity," I replied.

He shrugged. "In the film world, he is." I guess my fry envy was showing because he pushed his plate toward me. "Want one?"

I shook my head. "No thanks. I try and only have carbs one night every other weekend."

He shook his head. "I'll never understand girls and food. I bet you could eat at In-N-Out Burger every day for the next five years and still be skinny."

"That's so not true, but it's still really sweet of you to say that," I replied. His fries *did* look good. "Okay, maybe

I'll have *one*," I said as I reached for one and dipped it in the ketchup/mayonnaise concoction he had made. "Omigod— these are amazing," I said with my mouth full.

"You're talking with your mouth full," he said.

I finished chewing and dabbed at the corners of my mouth. "I am not." I reached for another fry. "I'm just going to have one more, if that's okay." It couldn't hurt. I had already fallen off the wagon with the Russian dressing.

"Have as many as you want," he said.

Wow. How nice to be around a guy who encouraged a girl to eat—even if he was a geek. The few times I had tried to snag a fry from Asher's plate, he always gave me a look like he had just caught me shooting drugs or something. But now one turned into two turned into him ordering me my own side of fries. I felt a little self-conscious pigging out like that in front of him, but soon I relaxed. I didn't even get upset and say, "Excuse me, but are you *kidding*?" when an old man and woman shuffling past our booth stopped to say what a cute couple we made.

"You really love movies, don't you?" I asked as I scarfed down some of the onion rings he had ordered for us. (Well, he *said* they were for us, but I don't particularly like them, which is why I only had seven or so.)

He nodded as he dipped one of them in the salsa/mustard combination he had whipped up. Although it sounded disgusting, it was pretty yummy.

"How come?"

He shrugged. "'Cause I guess I find real life over-rated."

"Yeah, but if you're spending your time watching movies all day and night, then you're not exactly giving real life a chance," I replied.

He thought about it. "I guess you have a bit of a point."

Um, *duh.*

"I don't know," he continued. "They've just always been a way for me to escape. Especially when my parents started fighting a lot, before my dad moved out."

"What happened?"

"He started having an affair with one of his clients. An actress-slash-yoga teacher. She's twenty-three."

"What *is* it with these old guys and younger girls? And all their names end in *i*—Brandi, Staci, Lesli."

"Or it's Amber. That's my dad's new wife's name, and Steven's dad's girlfriend's name—"

"Omigod—that's *my* dad's girlfriend's name, too! She works at Neiman Marcus. She came over for dinner once and kept looking at me like I was an ugly piece of furniture that she couldn't wait to donate to Goodwill."

"Yeah, well, my dad basically *did* get rid of me. I talk to his assistant more than I talk to him. The last time we did talk, it was so that he could tell me that Amber was pregnant and that she was going to have the baby at home in the bathtub and they wanted me to videotape it."

"Eww," I said, suddenly no longer hungry. I pushed the onion rings away.

"I know. That's partly why I want to do the doc—so I can get a scholarship and not have to depend on him anymore."

As Josh mixed together mustard and A.1 steak sauce as another potential dip for the fries and rings, I thought about how weird it must have been to have to worry about scholarships and not getting sick because you didn't have health insurance. It was as if he was one of those characters in a fairy tale who was kicked to the curb and forced to wander in a dark forest for years. Before he started eating again, he took out his inhaler from his back pocket and sat it down on the table.

"Are you worried you're going to have an asthma attack while you eat?" I asked, pointing at it.

"No. It was in my back pocket, so it's hard to sit up straight, which is what I need to do in order to digest my food properly."

This guy was *weird.* "What's up with that thing anyway?" I asked.

He looked up from his plate. "What do you mean?"

"You're like my dad and his black Amex card," I said. "You never leave home without it."

"I told you—I have asthma. Probably because I was born—"

"Premature. I know," I replied.

"It's *medical*," he insisted. "I can even show you the note from my allergist that he wrote me for gym class."

"That's okay," I said.

"Do you want dessert?" he asked, changing the subject.

"No thanks. I'm not all that hungry," I replied as I looked at my watch. "And I should probably get going anyway."

He looked at the check and threw down some bills.

"I'll get it," I said quickly.

"Nope. I got it." Josh smiled.

I opened my wallet and took out a twenty. "No, really—you can put the money toward health insurance or something." I hoped that wasn't rude.

"Don't worry about it," he said.

Huh. Now if I had said that to Asher, not only would he have taken it, but he also would have asked me for gas money.

"Sorry again about the dead battery," he said as we stood in front of the parking structure. He was parked in employee parking, which was down five levels, while my BMW was in my special VIP spot right near the entrance.

"Don't worry about it. It wasn't half as bad as I thought it would be," I replied. "I mean, it was actually kind of . . . fun." Who knew? It was nice to be around someone who was just normal, rather than perfectly put together and glancing around the room all the time to see what everyone else was doing and if anyone else was looking at them.

"Yeah. It was," he replied, sounding somewhat amazed as well. "Well, see you at school tomorrow."

"Okay. And I'm not sure what I'm doing this weekend, but as soon as I do, I'll let you know so you can have your one weekend night of filming."

"That would be great," he said.

I reached over and pushed his hair out of his eyes. "You know, you should really think about getting a haircut because your eyes aren't half bad. That shade of green is *very* in this season."

He turned bright red and pushed it back into his face. "Thanks," he mumbled.

"See you *mañana*," I said as I started walking toward my car. Obviously Josh was a geek, but maybe he wasn't a *total* geek. Sure, he had no fashion sense whatsoever, and the inhaler thing was *so* not sexy, and there was the talking-while-chewing thing. But as my grandmother says, there's a lid for every pot, so I'm sure he'll end up with someone.

chapter six: *josh*

Other than one time last year when Mom made me take out her college roommate's niece who was visiting from Des Moines, Iowa, the following Saturday night was the only time in my seventeen years on the planet that I ever spent a weekend night with a girl. Granted, it was business-related, but, still, when you spend most weekend nights hanging out in your room IMing with guys from Amsterdam debating whether *The Godfather* or *Godfather Part II* was Coppola's masterpiece, spending it at the movies with girls who smell good definitely warrants the bringing of the inhaler. Not because I was nervous. Just in case I was allergic to any perfume they may be wearing.

"Wait! Just one more picture!" Mom said, chasing me outside with her camera.

"Mom, please go back inside," I pleaded as a hipster couple walking past our house gave me a strange look. "Now, please, if possible."

"Honey, it's very important to honor the special moments in life. I was just reading an article in the *New York Times* about how ours is one of the only cultures that has forsaken ritual—"

"That's great, Mom, but can we talk about it tomorrow?" I asked, practically running to the Neilmobile. The problem was it wouldn't start, which, sadly, was becoming a common occurrence ever since I had run out of gas the week before. Unlike the car's namesake, who continued to get better with age, as shown by his CD *12 Songs*, the Neilmobile was losing its mojo.

"Just great," I said, after the occasional sputtering of the engine turned to complete silence.

The other problem was that Mom's beat-up old Volvo—which we called the Mitchellmobile, because of its Joni Mitchell bumper sticker—had gone into the shop that morning because its brakes were failing, and wouldn't be ready until Monday.

I looked over at the Geekmobile, which was the car I used when I needed to make Geek Gang house calls. I was in luck because I hadn't had time to return it at the end of work that day. Mrs. Spivakowsky, the old Russian woman at my last stop, had made me sit there for twenty minutes digesting the baklava and milk she had force-fed me even though I very nicely told her that I was pretty sure the twenty-minute rule was for swimming and not driving. Other than the fact that it says GEEK GANG in huge letters on both doors and it's a blue-and-yellow Mini Cooper—which makes it resemble a clown car—it's not so bad. But I could only imagine what Dylan would have to say about it. Since Du-par's, she'd called me a few times about documentary stuff, but we had ended up staying on the phone talking. I had never met someone who had so many opinions.

"So usually we spend our Saturday nights at a party," yelled Dylan into the camera as we waited in line at the Arclight movie theater with every other high-school girl in the city to see the latest teen romantic comedy where a spoiled rich girl and a boy from the wrong side of the tracks fell in love after lots of misunderstandings. Because we were in such a public place, I had decided to nix the sound boom and lights. I liked the idea of shaking it up and giving it a Marty Scorsese/au naturel look, but that meant that Steven and Ari had nothing to do. Steven didn't care, as it gave him the opportunity (and freed both hands) to shovel popcorn in his mouth, but without having a giant light or a camera to hide behind, Ari looked pretty miserable. When you were six feet (and still growing) like he was and had ears that stuck out, you didn't exactly blend into the crowd.

"Can you step closer to the camera?" I yelled.

"Sure," she said. "Like this?" she yelled as she stepped up so close she almost smacked me in the nose again.

I stepped back a foot, knocking into a very large bald man.

"Whoops," I said. "Sorry about that."

He didn't look amused, so I quickly moved to the side, this time almost knocking into a woman in a wheelchair. I hadn't counted on filmmaking being so dangerous.

Once I was no longer in danger of hurting anyone or getting my butt kicked, I put the camera back up to my face. "So you were saying . . ."

"I was saying that because the only party going on tonight was Ashley and Britney Turner's—"

"Which is *so* B-minus/C list—" said Lola as she moved in front of Hannah, almost edging her out of the frame.

"—we decided to save our energy for next weekend, which is when Lisa Eaton is having her Halloween party," finished Dylan.

"Sorry. Hold on a second," I said as I put the camera down. I turned to Steven, who was standing next to me shoveling popcorn into his mouth, and gave him a look.

"What?" he said with his mouth full.

"Their voices are going to be drowned out by the sound of you crunching," I said. "Plus, it's rude to talk with your mouth full."

He shoveled more of the box into his mouth. "Since when did you become the Polite Police?" he asked between crunches.

"Forget it. Just . . . do you think you could not eat until we're done?"

"Dude, I haven't eaten all day," he replied.

"You had a Double-Double and fries from In-N-Out

an hour ago," said Ari, who had put his hoodie up and was slouching in an attempt to make himself blend in more.

"You know what? Maybe I should just go—" Steven said with a scowl.

"Fine. You can eat—just go do it away from the mike," I said.

"Um, hello?" said Dylan. "Can we get back to work?"

I put the camera back up to my face. "Okay. So you were saying . . . "

Hannah moved back into the frame and used her hip to push Lola back. For girls who were supposed to be, as Hannah was always saying, best best friends, they sure were competitive. "We were saying that we were saving our energy for next weekend. Especially since Lisa Eaton's brother is going to be home from Stanford that weekend. I'm going to hit him up and see if he can talk to the admissions people for me."

Lola rolled her eyes. "Talk about using this thing as an opportunity to make it all about you," she said under her breath. Man, these popular girls might look all delicate, but they most definitely played for keeps.

Dylan, on the other hand, stood there in the middle like she belonged on a float in a parade. "I mean, I guess if we wanted to be nice, we could show up and raise the cool factor," she said, "but frankly, I get really sick of always being the one giving and never getting in return. You know what I mean?"

"Yeah, it's sort of like how my mom likes to farm me

out to all her divorced friends to hook up all their electronic equipment because there's no husband around to do it," said Steven as he tossed his empty popcorn box in the trash.

Dylan pondered this. "Sort of," she replied. "But not really."

"Plus she gets sick of having to answer the question 'Are you and Asher even still dating anymore?'" added Lola.

From the way Dylan looked at her like she was Drew Barrymore in *Firestarter*, this wasn't the right thing to say.

"Just because we're dating doesn't mean we have to spend twenty-four hours a day together," she said defensively.

"Do you guys spend *any* time together?" asked Steven.

"Of course we do," she replied. "I just happen to not be completely codependent."

"My mom was so codependent that she had to go to this *rehab* for codependence," said Hannah.

"Every once in a while we like to give each other room to breathe," Dylan continued. "Which is why, *yet again*, he's at some Ultimate Fighting thing in Long Beach with his stupid friends," Dylan said. "Wait—can you edit out the 'stupid' part? Never mind—I'll just say it again." She fluffed her hair and clapped her hands together. "Take two: 'Which is why he's at some Ultimate Fighting thing in Long Beach with his friends.'"

There's something about viewing people from behind a camera that makes it so that you start seeing them differently. This thing kicks in where because you're so focused on their faces, you realize that sometimes what their faces say versus what's coming out of their mouths are miles apart. So when Dylan said, "Whatever. It's fine. I'd much rather be one of those girls who gives their boyfriends space rather than smothers them," I could tell from the look on her face that, in fact, it *wasn't* fine. That it was so not fine to the point where she looked like she was about to cry.

"I think I'm going to turn the camera off for now so I can save the battery," I said.

"That's probably a good idea," Dylan agreed. While I much preferred Amy Loubalu's dark and exotic beauty over Dylan's blonde hair and blue eyes, when she smiled like she did then—kind of sweet and sad at the same time—she looked . . . real.

Just then the "Sold Out" sign started blinking and a chorus of *awwww*s could be heard.

Lola turned to Hannah. "I *told* you we should have bought tickets online."

"Some of us were studying because we'd actually like to get into a decent college," she shot back.

"We could see the new Robert Rodriguez movie," Steven said. "It's supposed to be awesome—total blood and gore."

"Um, *eww*," said Lola.

"That new dance movie looks cute," suggested Hannah.

The guys and I looked at one another—and *we* were supposed to be the geeks in this group?

"We could get something to eat," I suggested.

Dylan looked up from her Sidekick. "Nope. We're going to a party."

"But I thought you said Ashley and Britney's was going to be lame?" Hannah said.

"It is—which is why we're going to a *UCLA frat party!*" she squealed. "Shannon Hall's there now and says it's totally happening. Omigod—this will be *so* cool for the documentary!"

"All right!" said Steven, holding out his hand to Lola for a high five, which, not surprisingly, wasn't returned.

The contents of my stomach shifted and I made a mental note to look up the symptom on WebMD when I got home. "I don't think that's such a great idea," I said.

"Dude, what are you talking about? It's a *great* idea," said Steven. "College girls, dude. They're mature. They'll appreciate us," he said pointedly with a glance toward Lola. She didn't notice him because along with the other two, she was entrenched in fixing her makeup. They didn't even need mirrors to do it.

I turned to Ari. "You don't want to go, do you?"

He shrugged. "It could be fun. Especially if some of

the theater group is there. They just did a mime version of *Rent* and I have some questions about the technical aspect that—"

"Josh, it's going to be awesome," promised Steven.

Dylan flipped her head up and shook out her hair. "For once he's right," she said. "Why don't you want to go?" she asked, reaching into her bag for a different pair of shoes.

"It's not that I don't want to go. Of course I *want* to go," I replied. "It's just that I don't think we should."

"Why?" asked Steven. So much for my best friend supporting me unconditionally, no questions asked.

"Because tonight's supposed to be about the documentary . . . capturing the girls in their regular Saturday-night stuff. And so to go to a college frat party, where there are big frat guys who probably don't want us breathing their air, it's just not the authentic inside look at Castle Heights popularity I envision. It's a different movie. It's *Old School.*"

"But it's a college frat party—nothing's cooler than that," said Lola.

I made sure to keep my arms glued to my sides because I knew without looking that I was sweating. Big-time.

"It just doesn't jibe with my artistic vision," I said.

"It'll be *fine,*" said Dylan. "Trust me."

There was that "fine" word again. And for the second time that night, I didn't believe her.

* ★ * ★ * ★ *

You know that old movie *National Lampoon's Animal House*? The one where John Belushi crushes beer cans on his head without flinching? Well, before we even got inside, I could tell from the amount of noise coming from the house that the ZBTs of UCLA made *Animal House* seem like an ABC Family Channel movie. Not to mention all the beer cans and tequila bottles littering the front lawn. And the rope hanging down from one of the third-floor windows that was made of girls' bras.

"Maybe we should just wait out here," I said, sidestepping a banged-up stuffed UCLA Bruin bear, the school's mascot, as we made our way up the driveway. "We could take exit polls or something. Like they do during the election." A tingling started above my right eye, which I knew from WebMD to be a sign of nystagmus, a syndrome where your eye moved from side to side.

Dylan put her hands on her hips. "I don't understand why you're so scared."

I took out my inhaler. "I'm not scared," I scoffed. "Why would I be scared of a bunch of dumb frat guys? It's just not my scene."

"Okay, Josh? Don't take this the wrong way, but from everything you've told me, it sounds like other than dark movie theaters, you don't exactly *have* a scene," she replied.

"That's not true," I corrected. "There's the going to Du-par's and discussing-the-movie-afterward part."

"Right. With other guys who don't have a scene other than hanging out in dark movie theaters." She grabbed my arm and yanked me toward the door. "You wanted popular, right? Well, only the most popular of the popular have the guts to crash a frat party. Now come on."

I took a deep breath and let myself be led inside.

Total pandemonium. Kids being sprayed with beer, Hacky Sack games, a Bruin bear-costumed being cheered on while doing flaming shots of some sort of alcohol.

So *this* is what I had been missing all these years. Although I had seen countless movies about this kind of thing, from *National Lampoon's Animal House* to *Old School*, I had never come anywhere near to witnessing it up close. Here I was, finally in the inner sanctum of guyhood, surrounded by testosterone and college girls in tank tops and miniskirts, and yet I could only think of one thing.

"Wow. It really smells like dirty feet in here," I said to Steven.

"Dude, this is total awesomeness to the nth degree," whispered Steven as we stood at the edge of the living room taking in the group of tank-topped, miniskirted girls dancing together to Jay-Z.

"Look at that sound system," said Ari.

I started sneezing from the cloud of cigar smoke that was permanently lodged in the middle of the room. Great. Now I probably *would* have an asthma attack.

"You guys want a beer?" asked Dylan, pointing toward

one of the twenty kegs that were scattered around the room.

"No thanks. I don't like to drink when I'm working," I replied. The truth was that I didn't like to drink, period. After spending five hours last spring break with my head in the toilet puking up crème de menthe and peppermint schnapps when Steven and I raided his grandmother's liquor shelf at her condo in Boca Raton, Florida, the thought of alcohol made me woozy.

"Okay, well, I'm going to have one," Dylan said, heading over to a keg where three ZBT–T-shirt–wearing guys were standing.

Within two minutes Steven had inserted himself into a Ping-Pong game while Ari had found the *Rent* crew. At least that's who I figured they were with their white-painted faces. When had my friends become so outgoing? Lola and Hannah had drifted off toward the sliding-glass door to the backyard, where two thick-necked football players were entertaining them with riddles. Not even jokes, but riddles, like the ones on the bottom of Bazooka bubble gum wrappers. And they were *laughing*. I could just imagine trying to win Amy Loubalu over with riddles. She was so nice she'd probably laugh anyway, but still.

So with everyone off doing their thing, that left me alone. In the middle of a fraternity keg party with huge sweat stains under my arms, holding a video camera. I wondered how long it would be before I was thrown in the pool or something equally humiliating. As I stood there praying that the cops didn't show up and bust me for underage drinking even though I wasn't even drinking, two guys wearing ZBT shirts started walking toward me.

"Great. I never even got a chance to finish my first film and now I'm going to die," I murmured.

"Hey, pledge, go get me a beer," said the taller, better-looking one.

"And when you're done with that, get me that chick's phone number," said the shorter one, pointing to a cute redhead.

I gulped and willed myself not to reach for my inhaler. "Uh, I would, but I'm not one of the pledges," I said.

"You're not?" said the good-looking one.

I shook my head. "No. I don't even go to school here. I'm a senior in high school, so I wouldn't want to take any jobs away from any of the pledges, you know?"

"Dude, you're in high school?" the short one asked.

I nodded, holding my breath. Maybe that was the wrong thing to say.

"And you had the guts to crash one of *our* parties?" said the other one.

"Well, see, I'm doing a documentary for my USC application—"

The good-looking one narrowed his eyes. "Dude, why would you want to go to USC?"

I had forgotten how much of a rivalry there was

between the two colleges. Probably not the smartest thing to say.

"Yeah, but only because of their film school. Because UCLA has a great film school, too, but—"

"Ohhhh, a *film geek*," said the short one. The way he said it made me think that wasn't necessarily a good thing.

"Watch it—my little sister's a film geek," said the good-looking one.

Maybe there was a god.

"Anyway, one of the girls I'm focusing on heard about this party and thought it would be good to include in the documentary," I continued. "See, it's all about popularity—"

"We're the most popular frat on campus," said the short one proudly.

"Exactly," I said. "So that's why I was hoping to get some footage. I'm thinking I'll use a flash-forward-after-high-school dissolve effect." It amazed me how easy it was to think on your feet when you were scared for your life.

They nodded, impressed. "So you wanna film us?" asked the good-looking one.

"That would be great," I replied.

Who knew frat parties could be so fun?

I sat on the couch and zoomed in for a close-up on Lice, the short one (his real name was Arthur, but there had been an incident back in freshman year). "Dude, you have no idea how important ZBT is to me, man," he said, almost in tears. "It saved my life." He swiped at his face. "Before I got here, I was just a dweeb from Nebraska. And now, little dude? Look at me—I'm golden."

"Yeah, but sometimes being a ZBT is tough," admitted Whit, the tall one. "People think all you do is party and never read a book, but that's just a misconception. I'm an eighteenth-century French-literature major—do you have any idea how hard it is to keep up with the reading load?"

I nodded sympathetically. "That sounds tough."

I felt a hand on my shoulder. "There you are," slurred Dylan, plopping down on the couch. She looked at the guys and thrust her hand out. "I'm Dylan. Howyadoing."

They looked at each other nervously and stood up. "Nice talking with you, little dude," said Lice. "But we're gonna bolt now."

"Yeah," agreed Whit. "I try not to be within a fifty-foot radius of drunk high-school girls. Good luck."

I turned to Dylan, who let out a huge burp.

That didn't sound like a bad rule of thumb to live by.

"You wanna know the best thing about being popular?" she slurred a few minutes later as I tried to get her to drink from the bottle of water I had gotten her.

"Sure," I answered, ducking to avoid the football game that was being played over my head and knocking over my can of Coke, which, from the amount of dust on it, was probably the only nonalcoholic beverage in the entire house.

"Once you're in the club, it never ends. First it's proms, then frat parties, then, after you get married, there's the country club." She leaned over to the camera. "Are you getting all this?"

"Uh-huh," I replied. I didn't mention that I had neglected to actually turn the camera *on*. I know that when I came up with the idea for the documentary I had said it was be a no-holds-barred, down-and-dirty look at popularity, but as I sat there with Dylan right then, the idea of shooting her when she was drunk felt uncool. Even though she thought I was a geek and probably wouldn't have thought twice about filming me if the tables were turned, I found myself feeling oddly protective of her.

"You know, I just have to say that for a geek, you're not all that geeky," she slurred. As she leaned forward, she toppled over. "*Oooof.*"

"Uh, thanks. Maybe we should go," I said as I tried to help her up.

Which was hard to do when she was in the process of throwing up on my sneakers.

"Okay—now I think we should *definitely* go," I said. Lice and Whit were cool, but I didn't think they'd appreciate vomit all over their ugly plaid couch.

"I think I'm going to be sick," Dylan moaned.

I looked at my brand new Chuck Taylor Converses,

which were slowly turning from red to pink. "I think you already were," I replied, lifting her up and dragging her toward the bathroom, averting my eyes from the lacy bra strap that had popped out of her shirt. "Why don't you get cleaned up while I round everyone up so we can get out of here?"

"I'm never drinking again," she moaned.

I shoved her inside. "I'll be back in a minute," I promised as I shut the door.

I turned around to find that in the short time since we had left the couch the crowd seemed to have doubled in size. It was next to impossible to find Steven and everyone else, especially since the average height of the guys in the room was about six foot four. Apparently ZBT was made up of equal-opportunity partiers, because in addition to the frat boys and sorority girls who filled the house, I could see that there were also some Goth girls and Mohawked guys lounging around.

"Hey, Josh," I heard a girl's voice say above the thumping rap music that flooded the place, making it seem like an earthquake that had no intention of stopping.

I turned around to find Amy Loubalu, dressed in jeans and a light purple T-shirt that made her eyes even *more* beautiful, as if that were possible.

"Amy. Wow—how weird to find you at a college frat party. You know, since both of us are still in high school and underage," I babbled.

Could I have said anything *more* stupid?

"Which means, you know, we'd probably be arrested or something if the police showed up," I added.

Apparently I could.

She smiled the same smile that, for more nights than I could remember, had been the last image in my brain before I fell asleep. Not wide, but rather just enough of a hint of her straight white teeth to make you want to really make her laugh so you could hopefully see more. "I guess you're right." She chuckled. "So who are you here with?"

"Ah, I'm here with Steven and Ari and . . . some other people. You?"

"I came with Whitney," she said, pointing to Whitney Lewin, who was in the process of making out with a very short guy wearing a dress. "She's dating one of the pledges." Whitney also went to Castle Heights but I didn't really know her very well. Not because she was popular, but because she refused to speak to any guy who wasn't at least a year older than we were, which meant that now that we were seniors, she didn't talk to anyone but Amy. "Do you smell something weird?" She sniffed.

I moved back a few inches. "That would be my shoes. One of my, uh, friends had a little accident."

Again with that smile. "Got it. Oh, hey, I heard about your film. I'd love to see it when it's done—I love documentaries."

Not only was Amy Loubalu the most beautiful girl in the world—she was also *smart*. What more could a guy want?

"Sure," I said. "That would be great." Out of the corner of my eye I saw Dylan wobbling toward us. "But, uh, I should go find my friends because it's kind of late and we were just leaving—"

"There you are!" said Dylan, who, in trying to clean herself up, looked like she had taken a shower with her clothes on. Her cardigan sweater was buttoned wrong and her skirt was all wrinkled. She was still tipsy, but not so tipsy that she didn't realize who was standing in front of her. "Oh. Look who's here," she sniffed.

"Hi, Dylan," Amy said.

A group of pledges in a conga line came in between us and Amy. Dylan turned to me. "So now you're talking to my archenemy?"

Archenemy? *Amy Loubalou* was Dylan's archenemy? But she was so . . . perfect.

Amy smiled at both of us. Not many girls would be able to manage a smile that looked that genuine to their archenemy. Amy wasn't just beautiful and smart—she was *classy* to boot.

"I was right," Dylan said, "you totally *are Single White Female*-ing me!"

"What are you talking about?" Amy asked.

"First Michael Rosenberg and now him," she said, pointing at me.

I was just as confused as Amy.

"Not that I'm dating him or anything—our relationship

143

is strictly business, seeing that I'm the star of his movie. But don't think I haven't seen you throwing yourself at Asher."

Throwing up in the middle of the room at a frat party may not have been any big deal, but judging from the way a few of the partygoers were now staring at us, a potential catfight between two girls *was*.

Dylan grabbed Amy's sleeve and yanked her off to the side. I couldn't hear what was being said, but from the way Dylan was swaying back and forth and jabbing her finger in the air, she was obviously going off on Amy. Amy, to her credit, just stood there, patiently listening without interrupting. In fact, she even reached out and steadied Dylan a few times so she wouldn't fall over. It was in heightened moments of drama like this where one's true character really came out, and it was comforting to see that Amy was as classy as I had always imagined.

"Dude, this is *awesome*," Steven said. "Are you getting this?" he asked, pointing at the camera.

I held the camera protectively. "This isn't TMZ, Steven," I snapped.

He looked at me, amazed. "When did you and Dylan become all BFF?"

"We're not. It's just . . . " It was just what? I had no idea. Over the last few days instead of finding everything about Dylan annoying, now I only found sixty-five percent of it annoying. I turned to our little group, who had now gathered next to me. "Are you guys ready to go? I think Dylan should probably call it a night." By this time Whitney had rescued Amy, and Dylan was sitting on the stairs with her head between her legs.

The three of them, along with Lola, looked at each other. "There's no reason we *all* have to leave, is there?" asked Lola.

"Yeah," agreed Hannah. "There's two football players who seem to be really into us. They tell the funniest riddles."

So much for Dylan's best friends being there for her through thick and thin.

"Ari and I will make sure the girls get home okay," added Steven, who had his car with him.

"Ari, you don't really want to stay, do you?"

He thought about it. "Actually, I do," he admitted, as amazed about the fact as I was.

"So I'm assuming I'm driving Dylan home?" I asked.

They all nodded.

"So we're going to get back to the party. See ya," Hannah said, walking back toward the kitchen.

"What about her car?"

"I'll bring her back tomorrow to get it," Lola replied, running toward Hannah.

Even if I had wanted to protest, it wouldn't have mattered because they had all disappeared before my mouth was even fully open. I looked at Dylan, who was about to go tumbling down the steps headfirst, and sighed. "Let's get out of here," I said, hoisting her to a semistanding position before she broke her neck.

Apparently my job responsibilities as director extended far beyond what would end up on-screen.

"Where we going?" Dylan mumbled as I carried her down the street.

"To my car."

"Shotgun!" she yelled in my ear.

"Ouch. My ear. Since it's just you and me, I think you win," I said. That being said, because she was now wearing the pizza that we had grabbed before the party, I had been hoping to put her in the backseat.

When we reached the Geekmobile, I sat her down on the curb while I found my keys. However, unlike a Weeble, she didn't just wobble—she fell down.

"Talk about being committed to my art," I said as I hoisted her back up to a semisitting-but-more-about-to-fall-over-any-minute position. "I bet Woody never had to deal with anything like this."

Just then she opened her eyes.

"What. Is. That?" she said.

"It's the Geekmobile," I replied.

"The *what*?"

"My Geekmobile. Well, technically, it's not *my* Geekmobile—I mean, the registration is under Good Buys' name."

"And you want me to *ride* in there?" she asked.

"It's a very smooth ride," I said defensively. "Plus it gets great mileage, even if it isn't hybrid." I had written the Good Buys headquarters a few e-mails about how, in the spirit of helping the environment, they should switch from Mini Coopers to Priuses, but so far I hadn't heard back.

Holding my nose so I didn't have to breathe in Eau de Vomit, I settled Dylan in the passenger seat. Once I got into the driver's seat, I looked at my watch. "Shoot. It's already eleven-thirty."

"It is? It's still so early! We should go do something!" she slurred, bouncing up and down in the seat.

"Don't you have a curfew?" I asked

"I'm not sure. I never asked."

I took out my phone. "Well, I do, and it's midnight, so I need to call my mom and tell her I'll be a few minutes late."

"You have a currrrfewwww? Awww . . . that's so cuuuute!" she brayed.

Wow. I hadn't realized real live drunk people were as annoying as they were in movies. When I got Mom on the phone she was still so thrilled about the fact that I was socializing with non–Film Society–related people that she told me to stay out as late as I wanted.

The first few minutes of the ride were uneventful. Relaxing even, because there was no traffic on Sunset Boulevard, which happens as often as snow in L.A. But as soon as Dylan started fooling around with my iPod, I knew there was going to be trouble.

"Um, Dylan, maybe you should just hang your head out the window and enjoy the fresh air," I said as I tried to grab it away from her.

"Excuse me, but I'm not a *dog*. Plus it's Saturday night—we need some tunes."

Before I could stop her, "Cherry, Cherry" by Neil Diamond was booming out of the speakers. *"Baby loves me, yes, yes she does,"* Dylan screeched.

Once again, the shock of how bad her voice was almost made me swerve. She hadn't been lying about her knowledge of Neil's work. I had to admit it was impressive, because other than myself, I had never met anyone under the age of sixty who knew all the words to a Neil Diamond song.

"She got the way to groove me, Cherry baby," she howled.

I couldn't believe what I was witnessing—any and all coolness that Dylan Schoenfield had was nowhere to be found. Right before my very eyes she had turned into a complete and utter geek.

"Come on, Josh—sing with me," she demanded, grabbing my arm and almost making me swerve into oncoming traffic.

"No, it's okay—you seem to be doing a pretty good job soloing it."

"But it's no fun to sing alone. Please?"

"She got the way to move me," I halfheartedly sang along with her.

"No—you have to *really* sing," she ordered. "Otherwise it doesn't count."

"*She got the way to groove me,*" I sang louder.

"*Cherry baby!*" she screamed as she bounced up and down in her seat.

"*Cherry baby!*" I screamed louder.

We looked at each other and started cracking up. If anyone had told me a few weeks ago that I'd be singing a Neil Diamond duet with the most popular girl in school while zooming down Sunset Boulevard at midnight on a Saturday in the Geekmobile, I would've said they were nuts. It was like something out of a John Hughes movie.

We had made our way through a pig-latin version of "Song Song Blue" and were just finishing up "Cracklin' Rosie" as I pulled into her driveway.

"Omigod I haven't laughed that hard in *forever*," she said as I turned off the ignition. It seemed the combination of fresh air and singing had sobered her up, because she was no longer slurring. And there wasn't a trace of her usual I'm-Dylan-Schoenfield-*That's*-Why whininess.

"Me, either," I agreed, fiddling with the camera case. "That was almost as funny as *Annie Hall*."

She started twirling a lock of hair around her finger. "Annie Hall . . . her name sounds familiar . . . didn't she graduate last year?"

This time, instead of getting annoyed at her lack of Woody knowledge, I laughed. "No. *Annie Hall* isn't a person. It's the name of a Woody Allen movie."

"Oh. Isn't that from like a *hundred* years ago?"

I shrugged. "1977."

"Never seen it. What's it about?"

"About these two people who are complete opposites who fall in love," I replied as I continued pulling at a loose thread on my case.

"Ooh—kind of like *Knocked Up!*" she said. "I *loved Knocked Up!*" She had twirled her hair so much that it had ended up in a knot. I almost pointed it out to her, but decided against it. There was something about seeing her look less than perfect that was refreshing.

"Um, sort of. It's a classic. Voted number thirty-five on AFI's list of Top One Hundred American Films of all time." I pulled the camera out. "Is it cool if I film you for a bit?"

"*Ew*, I look hideous!" she said.

"No you don't. Plus the way the moonlight is coming in the window is really cool. Spooky, like a John Carpenter movie or something."

"Who?"

"He's another director. So can I?"

She shrugged. "I guess so." She sighed. She flipped down the mirror on the visor and started smoothing her hair and then stopped. "Oh, whatever—if I see it and think I look like a troll, I'll just have you cut it out."

As I focused in on her, she settled back in her seat and looked at me. "You really *are* a walking Wikipedia when it comes to movies, aren't you?"

"I guess," I said. This camera picked up everything, and as I zoomed in, I could see a big pimple on her chin that wasn't noticeable before. Who would have thought Dylan Schoenfield had oil glands?

As I zoomed back out (I know I had said I wanted this to be as real as possible, but I also didn't want to nauseate people), she sighed and a wistful look came over her face. It was weird how sometimes when people looked sad, they became even better looking. "I bet that's a really cool feeling—to have something you're so psyched about," she said quietly. "You know, like a real passion. Something to write about on your college essays."

I cleared my throat. "Don't you have a hobby or something like that?" Seeing this other, more real side of Dylan was a little disconcerting. If someone who had it all figured out got bummed out, why were the rest of us even trying?

She shrugged. "No. Not really." She fiddled with the fringe on her purse. "I mean, obviously I'm great at accessorizing and I definitely know what makeup color palettes work with different skin tones, but that's not a hobby—that's a . . . *gift*." She looked up from her purse and shrugged. "I don't know," she said quietly. "Sometimes it's like . . . when people see you a certain way, they don't *want* you to change. They just want you to keep being *that* girl— the popular girl."

I zoomed in closer. This was good stuff.

"The one who's five minutes ahead of everyone with the clothes and the bags and the shoes and whatever," she continued. "Believe me, if I were to chuck it all and go all boho hippy and stop shaving my legs, people would freak out. Not just because it would be disgusting, but because they expect me to be . . . well, *me*." She looked down at her lap for a second and then looked up again. "I've been this for so long I wouldn't even know how to go be someone else," she said quietly.

Dylan was right: seeing her act so different—so real—was a little awkward. And with the camera, it made me feel like I was spying on her. But I couldn't seem to put it down.

Then, as if a spell had been broken, she fluffed her hair and sat up straight. "Okay, enough of that. You want to come in and have an Everything-but-the-Kitchen-Sink Special with me?"

"What's that?"

"My dad and I came up with it. Basically you take everything that could be considered part of the dessert family and you mix it together. Ice cream, cookies, chocolate chips, strawberries, caramel sauce, Swiss Miss Diet Hot Cocoa—stuff like that." She turned more to her left. "You're getting my good side, right?" She was back to being the Dylan everyone loved-to-hate-hated-to-love.

I put the camera down. "Yeah. But my arm's getting tired. I think I'll stop for now."

She took out her lip gloss and put some on. "So you want to come in?"

"I would, but I'm already pretty beat and I have to be at work at eleven tomorrow morning," I replied.

"Oh. Okay." She sighed.

"What's wrong?"

"Nothing." She shrugged, looking at the dark house as she sank back against the car seat. "It's just that my dad's been at Amber's like every night this past week and being alone in there skeeves me out." She turned to me. "I know it's babyish, but I get freaked out being alone sometimes."

It was almost easier when Dylan was just obnoxious 24/7. At least then I knew what to expect. But now, with all these news flashes that she could be just as uncomfortable as the rest of us mere mortals—that was throwing a real wrench in things. I sighed. "I guess I should at least *taste* an Everything-but-the-Kitchen-Sink Special," I replied. "So, you know, I can get to sleep. Otherwise I'll be up all night wondering about it."

She smiled. "Really?"

I smiled back and nodded.

She clapped her hands. "Oh, good!" As she reached for the door handle, she turned to me. "But I have to warn you—no one's ever been able to have just a 'taste.'"

Dylan was right—you *can't* have just a taste of an Everything-but-the-Kitchen-Sink Special. You have to scarf it down like you've been stranded on a desert island for three months, and not only is it the first thing other than berries and grass that you've eaten since then, but when it washes up on shore, it comes with a memo that says you'd better scrape up every bite because you won't be getting anything else for *another* three months.

"Who knew that Magic Shell mixed so well with peanut butter?" I asked, sprawled out on one of the couches in her family room in a sugar coma while she took over the other one. "What time is it?"

She lifted her wrist up to her face as if it weighed three hundred pounds. "One o'clock. Do you have to call your mom again?"

"No—she's probably sleeping by now. Plus, the idea of getting up to find my phone feels about as doable as running the L.A. Marathon," I replied. "God, that was good."

As Dylan sat up, a tiny burp came out of her mouth. "Omigod—*excuse me*. That was so gross."

Ha. She should spend an afternoon with Steven if she wanted to see gross.

"I'm glad you liked it," she said as she reached for a few stray M&M's that had managed to escape her spoon and fallen onto the couch. "Asher thinks it's disgusting."

I heaved myself up and reached for the camera. "How come?" I asked, moving the lens from the empty ice-cream containers, candy bags, and hot fudge jar that were sitting on the coffee table to her face.

"He says it'll make me fat."

What a jerk. If he wasn't five inches taller than me, I would've kicked his butt.

"I know that a lot of people gossip about the fact that he doesn't treat me all that well," she replied, trying to wipe the chocolate off her face but failing miserably, "but that's just because they're jealous. We're totally fine."

I nodded behind the camera.

"Really. We are," she said defensively.

I wondered who she was trying to convince—me or herself.

"Anyway, your idea to put the caramel sauce on the dried cranberries? Totally brilliant," she said. "We should write a cookbook or something." Another burp escaped her. "Whoops. And then we'll get a show on the Food Network and I'll star in it and you'll direct it."

I put the camera down and pointed at the seventy-two-inch plasma flat-screen TV. "Speaking of networks, do you think I could turn that on for a sec just to see the picture quality?"

She rolled her eyes. "You sound like my dad." She tossed me the remote. "Here."

As I flipped the channels, I shuddered with excitement. The depth and sharpness of the picture, the vivid color—the minute I made my first chunk of money off one of my films I was buying one of these puppies.

And then—there it was.

I couldn't believe it. There, in seventy-two inches of glorious color and surround sound, were Alvy and Annie meeting for the very first time after tennis.

"I can't believe it," I whispered.

"What? What? What is this? Who's that weird-looking

short guy? And why on earth is that woman wearing a man's tie?" demanded Dylan.

It was like seeing it up on the Arclight screen, except I was on a comfy couch with my sneakers off. I was all for artistic integrity, but if I had to sell out to be able to afford a home-theater system like this, well, then, I would.

"Josh, what *is* this?"

"It's *Annie Hall*," I whispered, still dazed by its Technicolor beauty.

"That movie you were talking about earlier?"

I nodded. The reds were so red; the greens were so green; the sound was so clear. It was like an Everything-but-the–Kitchen-Sink Special, but on the screen.

"Cool. Did it just start?"

I nodded again.

"Let's watch it, then," she said.

Which we did. Well, if you could call Dylan interrupting every two minutes with questions like "Do you think they knew they looked like fashion roadkill back then?" and "Are people really that neurotic, or is it just New Yorkers?" *watching* a movie. As the movie went on, she quieted down, and by the end, when Alvy and Annie ran into each other in front of the Beekman movie theater after they'd broken up, I could tell she had become a Church of Woody convert.

I heard a sniffle and looked over. "Are you crying?" I asked.

"*No*," she said, trying to nonchalantly wipe away the

tears I could see even though she turned her face to the side. She picked up the camera from the coffee table and hid behind it.

"It's okay if you are," I said to the camera. "It's a very moving story." Thinking back to the moment in the car earlier that evening, I thought it was only fair that I open up as well. "You know, I cried the first twenty times I saw it." Wow. Admitting that out loud was hard enough, but when there was a camera in your face? Ouch.

"You did?" she said.

I nodded. "Now I guess I'm just used to it."

She put the camera down. "But Annie was totally right to move to L.A. to be with a successful record producer like Paul Simon rather than a geek like Alvy who's a neurotic hypochondriac."

"Maybe he was born premature and his immune system wasn't that strong," I said defensively. "He never comes out and says that, but that's the subtext I got, which would then explain his fear of getting sick." I bet Amy Loubalu would have compassion for someone who had an underdeveloped immune system.

Dylan reached for the almost-empty caramel jar and scraped her finger along the inside. I couldn't believe there was any room left in her tiny body for even a milligram more food. "Okay, when you use words like *subtext* and stuff like that? Way too film geek."

"Maybe he wasn't as successful as Paul Simon, but what about the fact that he was able to make her laugh?

That's got to count for something, right?" It had to, or else I'd never get a date with Amy or anyone else. "Hey, did you know that the working title of *Annie Hall* was actually *Anhedonia,* which means 'the inability to experience pleasure'?" I asked.

She gave me a weird look. "Why would you think I'd have any reason to know that?"

I shrugged. "I don't know. In case you were in the bookstore and picked up the new biography of Woody that just came out that talks about that."

"Yeah, well, moving on. Josh, I hate to tell you this, but while being able to make someone laugh is great, there are a lot more important things in a relationship."

"Like what?" I asked. I could tell by the way she started shoveling popcorn in her mouth that I had hit a nerve.

"Lots of things," she said, grabbing another handful. "Like . . . you know . . . *chemistry.* Like seeing the person and wanting to kiss them for hours until your lips fall off."

"Okay, yes, I see your point, but what about when you've been together for a while and that part has passed? That's what my mom says happened with my dad. Can't you be attracted to someone because they're smart and funny, too?"

She rolled her eyes. "God, you're such a *romantic.*"

"Is that a bad thing?" I asked.

She shrugged. "It's just so *fairy tale*-like. She stood up and stretched. "I can't stand fairy tales. The princesses in them are so . . . princessy. Ick."

158

Talk about the pot calling the kettle black. I stood up as well and looked at the clock. It was nearly three. "I should go."

"Wait—don't you want a tour of the house or something? Please?" she asked, panicked. "You can film it—you know, give people an inside peek into my world."

Sheesh—she *really* didn't like to be alone. "Sure, I guess," I replied.

The house was big even by Beverly Hills standards, so the tour killed another thirty minutes. Every room looked like it came directly out of a designer showroom—Mom would've had a heart attack from how everything matched so perfectly. While the house was beautiful, there was something off about it—it was like it didn't seem lived in, but was more like a museum. I felt like I should have some sort of admission sticker on my shirt and not talk above a whisper.

"And this is my bedroom," she said, leading me into a room that was bigger than my living room. I panned around with the camera.

"So this is where it all began," I announced. "Where the acorn of popularity turned into a towering oak tree."

She cringed and flopped down on the bed. "You said you're just going to focus on directing and not writing in college, right?"

"Yeah," I replied as I walked over to the closet.

"That's probably a good idea," she agreed.

I motioned to the closet door. "Can I?"

She shrugged.

I flung it open, surprised to find it filled with . . . clothes.

"What's the matter?" she asked.

"I don't know," I replied. I guess I just thought your room would be . . . I don't know . . . different from normal people's."

"Why?"

I shrugged. "Because you're so popular."

She snorted. "Josh, I hate to tell you, but it's not like there's a book floating around with all this secret information about getting and staying popular." She got off her bed and walked over to her bureau and opened a drawer. "Here, look—I even have a junk drawer, just like everyone else."

"Huh," I said, zooming in on the mess of rubber bands, pennies, old movie stubs. Exactly like the junk drawer in my room.

"Come on—let's go downstairs," she said.

"And this is Daddy's office," she said, leading me into a room that was almost the size of our school library.

"Wow," I whispered as I swept the camera across the room, getting footage of the crème de la crème of electronics—computers, stereo, another large-screen TV. I was in heaven. "I feel like I'm at work. Except all this stuff is top-of-the-line rather than the crap we sell." I walked over and zoomed in on one of the framed pictures on the mahogany credenza. "This isn't *you,* is it?" I asked. The girl in the picture was about nine and had hair so curly she looked like she had stuck her finger in a light socket. Plus, the lenses on her glasses weren't Coke-bottle thick—they were more like gallon-size-Martinelli's-apple-juice-bottle thick.

"Don't film that!" she yelped, pushing the camera out of the way so hard I almost dropped it. I felt like one of those paparazzi you hear about that get beat up by actors. She grabbed the picture—and the two others next to it that were just as bad, if not worse— and opened a drawer and threw them in there. "They're from a *very, very* long time ago. For some reason Daddy insists on keeping them up there."

Jeez—talk about an awkward phase. I put the camera back up to my face. "Wow. You sure were . . ."

She folded her hands in front of her chest and turned away. "Hideous? Disgusting? Beyond ugly?" she offered.

"Actually, I was going to say you were kind of . . . I don't know . . . cute. In, you know, a nerdy way," I replied.

"No I wasn't," she said firmly.

"Okay. You weren't," I agreed. Like I said, I didn't have a lot—scratch that—I didn't have *any* experience with girls, but I had seen enough movies to know that sometimes the only thing to do was agree with them no matter what they said.

She opened up the drawer and grabbed one of the

other school pictures, where she had a mouthful of metal and a haircut that made her resemble a hobbit, and examined it before looking up at the camera. "Really? You think I was cute?" she asked.

"Um—" What to say and not get my nose broken?

"If you thought I was cute then, that would be the sweetest thing anyone has ever said to me. I mean, Daddy says he thinks I was cute back then, but he has to say that because he's, you know, my *dad*."

I looked at the picture again. The phrase *a face only a father could love* should have been stamped on the bottom.

"So do you?" she asked.

"Do I what?" I asked back as I started examining the computer monitor as if I had never seen one before.

"Do you think I was cute back then?"

I turned to her and put the camera in front of my face.

"Nuh-uh," she said, taking it out of my hands. "I want to see your face when you answer."

Great. "Well, obviously you, you know, went from being a duckling—not an *ugly* duckling, mind you, more like an . . . awkward duckling—to a swan since then," I explained, "and, uh, I'd be lying if I didn't say that you look a lot better now, but, you weren't, you know . . . *hideous* or anything like that back then."

"I thought you said I was cute."

"I did."

"But just a second ago you said I 'wasn't hideous,' which is a lot different than 'cute.'"

Asher may have been a jerk, but I was overcome with a rush of sympathy for the guy. Did he have to go through this stuff on a regular basis? No wonder he liked to spend his weekends at Ultimate Fighting championships and other places where there weren't a lot of girls. "Hey, did you ever think about joining the Debate Team?" I asked.

"Huh?"

"Never mind. Okay, I'd like to amend my original statement: how about, you were cute in an awkward way?"

She thought about it and then nodded. "I guess that's better than nothing," she said. "You look kind of tired."

That was the understatement of the year. Trying to avoid the minefield of talking about a girl's looks with her was harder than calculus. "Tired? Or kind of tired?" I teased.

"Ha. Ha. Come on, I'll walk you out," she said.

Before she turned off the light I took one more glance at Dylan: The Early Years. It was nice to know that like Quentin when he worked at a video store, everyone had to start somewhere.

chapter seven: *dylan*

The week after the ZBT frat party, something weird started to happen: whenever I was sitting at my desk at home trying to avoid doing my French homework, or stuck in traffic on Wilshire Boulevard on my way to Pilates, instead of texting or calling Lola or Hannah, like I usually did, I found myself texting or calling . . . *Josh*.

In fact, that's what I was doing the following Thursday afternoon when I was *with* Lola and Hannah, at Kathy's Nail Salon, getting our weekly mani/pedis and he was at work.

Josh: OK, best on-screen couples who also are/ were offscreen couples. Go.

We had recently started playing this game where one of us threw out a subject, and the one to come up with an answer that couldn't be topped won.

Me: Angelina Jolie & Brad Pitt

Josh: Woody Allen & Diane Keaton

Me: Ernie & Bert

Josh: ????

Me: From Sesame Street!

Josh: I know that—but I thought it was a given that they had to be HUMAN and not made out of felt!

This made me crack up to the point where I smeared my right pointer finger, which caused Kathy, my manicurist, to not only give me a dirty look, but start chattering in Vietnamese to the rest of the manicurists, who then *all* gave me dirty looks.

"Are you texting with Josh *again*?" asked Lola as Ashley, her manicurist, painted her nails with the same dark color she always wore.

I nodded, careful to sit still as Rachel applied topcoat to my toes. Even though all of the manicurists were Vietnamese, they all had super-American-sounding names.

"So are you guys like totally BFF now?" said Hannah anxiously as Miriam applied a pale pink to her nails. Hannah could be *so* neurotic sometimes. Frankly, that's why I found it so refreshing to talk to Josh. He listened to me, but he also didn't let me get away with things. See, when you're the most popular girl in school, a lot of what you hear is

"Omigod, Dylan—you are *so* right." Especially from people who shall remain nameless, like Hannah. Now, I *am* right a lot of the time, but I'm also human. Sometimes I say things without really thinking about them and they're not right—in fact, sometimes they're downright stupid. Josh had no problem challenging me—like with the Ernie and Bert thing.

"Of course not," I said. "It's just business."

The two of them looked at each other.

"What?" I said.

Lola shrugged. "Nothing. It's just that . . . " She sighed. "Oh, never mind," she said as she picked up a magazine (almost smearing her freshly painted nails) before Miriam yelled at her in Vietnamese and snatched it away from her.

I hated when Lola did that sigh/"Oh, never mind" combination. Talk about passive-aggressive. At least that's what Hannah had said it was when we were talking about it one night on the phone.

"Uh, yes, *mind*. Spill it," I demanded.

She looked at me. "Well, people are . . . *talking*."

"Who's talking about what?"

"People on The Ramp. About how geek-friendly you've become recently."

I turned to Hannah. "Is this true?"

She nodded.

"Look, I'm saying this because I'm your best best friend—" Lola started to say.

"Best friend," Hannah corrected. "We decided we're all equally best friends."

"Well, we *were,* until Josh came into the picture. Anyway, all I want to say is that with Fall Fling coming up, and with Dakota amping up Operation Prom Queen by blogging about the marine she dated last summer—"

"Did you read that last entry, by the way?" Hannah asked. "It's like totally R-rated."

"—I'd just be careful," Lola went on.

"Obviously, being nice to people from every clique is important because you want to get as many votes as possible," explained Hannah, whose father was on the Beverly Hills City Council, "but you don't want to identify *too* much with Josh and those guys."

"Why?" I asked.

"Because of your past," said Lola. "You know, how you yourself used to be a geek." She made sure to say the last part just a *little* bit louder than necessary.

At this, all the manicurists looked up from the various hands and feet they were polishing and looked at me in amazement. My hands started to get clammy. I hadn't even thought about that.

"You don't want anyone to think you've had some sort of psychotic break and are regressing," said Hannah, whose mother was a shrink.

"As if," I said defensively. My phone buzzed and I looked down. *So see u at 7?* said the text from Josh. Last night he had told me that his mom was going to be cooking a bunch of dishes she had learned in her Introduction to Indian Cooking class at the Learning Annex, and when I told him how much I loved Indian food—despite the fact that many of the dishes used cream and were therefore high in fat—he had invited me over. All day I had been looking forward to a home-cooked meal. If you were popular, people automatically assumed that you had plans 24/7, but the truth was that most nights I ended up nuking a Lean Cuisine and eating it by myself while I watched TV.

Yeah, see u then, I typed back. Maybe I *was* spending too much time with Josh—especially since I had a boyfriend and all—but I couldn't *not* go to dinner at his house. That would just be rude.

Plus, I was starved.

As I was standing in front of my walk-in closet trying to put together the perfect home-cooked Indian meal outfit—which, when your closet is as big as mine isn't all that easy—Asher called.

"Hey, babe," I said as I flopped down on my bed and almost slid off onto the floor. After reading about some model's trip to Morocco in *Teen Vogue,* I had recently redecorated my bedroom in a very colorful Moroccan fashion with a silk tapestry as a bedspread. It was gorgeous, but it was super slippery. I couldn't even remember the last time Asher had called me on his own rather than returning one of my calls. Maybe all the thinking I had been doing about how Josh was such a better conversationalist had worked in a reverse-psychology way.

"Hey," Asher replied. "What up?"

Why couldn't he say *"what's up?"* like normal people? More and more, I found myself annoyed by lots of little things about him. For example, the way he didn't even bother to pop a breath mint after eating Mexican food if he knew we were going to make out. Or how he moved his lips when he was reading. Or how he'd pick at his toenails when we were watching TV at my house and then not wash his hands before we ate sushi. Josh was a geek, but Asher was just gross. That being said, I was still totally in love with him. How could I not be, seeing that he was cute, and popular, and . . . cute, and . . . popular. Obviously, he had a lot of other great qualities as well, but I couldn't talk to him, look for an outfit, *and* think of them all at the same time. I sat up and started making an "absolutely not" and a "maybe" pile of outfits. "Nothing. Just, uh, doing my French homework." Not that he would've even cared, but it didn't seem necessary to let him know I was going to Josh's for dinner.

"Oh. Then I should probably let you get back to it," Asher said, sounding relieved.

I walked over to one of my two full-length mirrors and held up a black caftan embroidered with pink stitching before deciding it wouldn't work for dinner, as Morocco and India were very different countries. (I think.) "It's okay. I can talk for a few minutes. How are you?"

"Fine. There was something I wanted to talk to you about, but it can wait, since you're busy and all."

"What is it?" I asked, sitting/sliding back down on my bed and examining my pedicure. I was *so* lucky I could pull off lilac—on a lot of girls, it made them look like they had been dead for a half hour, but on me it looked just great.

"Nothing. We'll talk about it some other time. You should get back to French."

Okay, things were now officially weird. First, calling me on his own rather than returning one of mine, and now turning into the homework police? It was like he had been body-snatched.

"Are you sure?" I asked.

"Yeah. No worries, mon." That was another thing that drove me nuts—the "mon" thing. I mean, with blond hair and blue eyes he wasn't exactly Jamaican. Plus I was his girlfriend, not a smelly *guy*. "I'll see you tomorrow. Later." *Click.*

"Bye," I said to the air.

As I put on a pink-and-blue embroidered silk tunic, I thought about calling Hannah or Lola and telling them about what just happened with Asher, but what had happened earlier at the nail place had me feeling weird. Like Asher said, I was sure it was nothing and everything was fine, but still—when you're a famous and powerful couple, people just *love* to start all kinds of rumors about how you're breaking up. Just look at all the tabloids. There was no way that Asher and I could break up. Seeing that we were like royalty at Castle Heights, that would've devastated the other students.

Beachwood Canyon—the part of town where Josh lived—was actually kind of cute. Well, "cute" in a funky, boho, let's-slum-it-because-we're-so-cool Hollywood way rather than in an everything-matches-just-perfectly Beverly Hills way, which is more my style, but still. All the houses were little, like something out of a fairy tale.

"Oh my—Dylan, honey, you really didn't have to do this," Josh's mom you-must-call-me-Sandy said as the three of us stood in the kitchen checking out the dessert spread I had brought.

"I wasn't sure if, you know, you were a pie person, or a cupcake person, or a frozen-yogurt person, so I decided it would be best to get a variety of stuff," I replied. While it had seemed like a good idea at the time, I could see now that I may have gone a bit overboard.

"Well, I'm just going to have to try a little of everything," Sandy said. "Not like I need it," she added, patting her stomach, which was just the *teensiest* bit poochy. That's what seems to happen to women in their forties no matter how many times a week they do Pilates. I was *so* not looking forward to that. "Shoot—I forgot to get Rolaids!" She turned to me. "Ever since Josh was born, I've had stomach problems. My gastroenterologist says I'm crazy, but I think it might have something to do with the fact that he was premature." She turned to Josh. "Honey, can you do me a favor and run to the drugstore and get some for me?"

Josh paled. "You mean, leave you guys alone?"

She put her arm around me. "Sure—it'll give Dylan and me some time to get to know each other. You know, some girl time."

I started to get nervous, too. Sandy seemed nice enough, but what if she started asking me parentlike questions, like whether I had ever smoked marijuana (I hadn't) or used birth control (not an issue because I was still a virgin). "Come on," she said, picking up a tray of samosas, which were like Indian knishes, and leading me toward the living room. "The dal's not going to be done for another twenty minutes, so let's go sit and chat."

Josh grabbed my arm and leaned in. "If she starts getting really embarrassing, just tell her you have to go to the bathroom and stay in there until I get back," he whispered.

I nodded as Sandy continued to lead me out of the kitchen. Once in the living room, I took the red-and-black paisley couch while she settled into an electric-blue rocking chair with a pink cushion. At first I wondered whether maybe she was color-blind because there was an awful lot of color going on in the room, but strangely enough, it worked.

I pointed at the rocking chair. "What an interesting color combination," I said.

"Thanks," she replied. "I got the chair at the Fairfax flea market and the fabric at the Rose Bowl swap meet." Josh had mentioned Sandy's obsession with flea markets.

"You mean you *made* this?" I asked, impressed, as I nibbled at my samosa.

She nodded proudly. "Yes, I did. That Introduction to Upholstering class I took at the Learning Annex was worth every penny." She pointed at the couch. "I got that at the Santa Monica flea market. Don't worry—I made sure to have it de-flea'd."

Was it my imagination or were the backs of my legs starting to itch?

Although I had worried that, as a mother of a geek, Sandy might wear mom jeans and have a bad perm and no sense of humor, it turned out that she was *so* cool. Most of my friends' moms were so busy with shopping and charity events that I knew them about as well as I knew Juan, the barista at the Starbucks I stopped at every morning on my way to school. Within five minutes of sitting with her, Sandy had told me her entire life story—how, like me, she had grown up in Beverly Hills before she went to UCLA and married Josh's father, who was a law-school student, and became a Brentwood housewife until Josh's dad came home one night and told her he was leaving her for Amber. And how she then had found herself with almost no money and had to move here, but soon discovered she was a lot happier than when she had been rich even if she couldn't afford to shop at Saks anymore. It was a very inspirational story, like something you'd see on a Lifetime Television Original Movie.

"So what about you, Dylan?" Sandy asked as she rocked in the chair. "What kind of life do you envision for yourself in the years to come?"

Wow. This family was really into the deeper questions of life.

"Um, you know, I guess I sort of see myself having the life *you* had—not this part, but the Brentwood part," I replied. "You know, the part with the credit cards."

She laughed. "Well, if that's what you want, then I hope you get it. However, I just want you to know that sometimes when you get close to them, you find that things are a lot different than they look from the outside."

Like Josh, I thought as I reached for another samosa. So what if people were gossiping about my friendship with Josh? Geekiness wasn't a communicable disease like mono. Maybe geeks didn't have a lot of fashion sense, or social skills, but they were people, too, and they had as much of a right to be at Castle Heights as I did. In fact, maybe I would make that my platform for my prom campaign: trying to bridge the gap between the geeks and the popular kids. I'd be an ambassador, like those actresses who travel to third-world countries and adopt babies. Plus, I myself was a living, breathing example that geekiness was something that could be outgrown and overcome. I mean, if anyone was qualified to help the geeks of the world mainstream into a regular social life, it was me.

Omigod—I had found my hobby!

"I'm back," Josh called out as he ran into the room, looking like he had just run the six-hundred-yard dash. His face was all sweaty, his *Close Encounters of the Third Kind* T-shirt was sticking to his body, and his glasses were crooked.

Not only did I have a hobby, but my first rocking chair, so to speak, was standing right in front of me.

Dinner was incredible. I know I tried to only have carbs one night every other weekend, but that night I just couldn't help myself. Everything was just so good—especially the naan, this Indian bread that looks like pizza dough. Plus, since Sandy had cooked everything herself, it would've been rude not to have seconds. And, in the case of something called chana masala—chickpeas cooked in this yummy tomato cream sauce—thirds.

"And then there was the time that we took Josh and his friends to the movies for his fifth-birthday party—" Sandy was saying as we ate dessert. I couldn't believe there was room in my stomach for more food, but seeing that I had eaten one cupcake and three-quarters of a piece of pie, it seemed that there was.

"—and there was this short guy in the audience with glasses," Josh cut in.

Sandy smiled at him. "So Josh got up and walked up to him and tugged on his sleeve and said—"

"'Are you Woody Allen?'" he finished.

The two of them cracked up. Watching them, it was obvious they really did enjoy being with each other. I know Daddy loved me, but on the rare occasions *we* ate dinner together, he always had one eye on the newspaper or the television.

"So was it Woody Allen?" I asked.

Josh shook his head. "No. It was an accountant from the Valley."

"But he was very sweet," said Sandy. "He gave me his card and told me to call if I needed help with my taxes." As she stood up and started walking toward the kitchen, she stopped in front of Josh and ruffled his hair. "Even back then, I could see that Josh would stop at nothing to achieve his dream." She reached down and started covering his head with kisses. "My little filmmaker."

"Mom," he said, pushing her off. He was trying to look embarrassed, but I could see from the small smile on his face that he liked it. They seemed so happy.

Even when it was time to do the dishes and there was no dishwasher.

"I want to thank you for letting Josh do this film," Sandy said as she handed me a plate to dry while Josh was in the other room trying to fix her laptop that she had spilled green tea on earlier that afternoon. "He's been having so much fun. And I think it will really help his chances of getting a scholarship."

"Well, a promise is a promise, so it's not like I could

have ever not followed through," I replied. "And it's been fun."

She stuck her head out of the kitchen to make sure Josh wasn't nearby. "I know I'm biased because I'm his mother, but even if I weren't, it's just that I think he's a terrific kid and it breaks my heart that he spends most of his time at the movies or on the computer. Sure, years from now when he's won his third Academy Award, it probably won't bother me as much"—she smiled—"but I just wish he were in situations more often where he might meet some . . ."

"Girls?" I asked.

She smiled. "Exactly." She washed a mug before handing it to me to dry. Drying dishes was actually very relaxing. Maybe I'd suggest to Marta that she stop using the dishwasher so that we could have some nice bonding time together. "And in addition to Josh being a bona fide genius—we had his IQ tested when he was in kindergarten and he scored a hundred and fifty-five—he also has such a delightful sense of humor. I really do think he's going to be the next Woody Allen. Less neurotic, obviously, because of the therapy I insisted he have after the divorce, but just as clever."

"Mom. What are you *doing*?!" Josh yelped. We turned around from the sink to see him standing there. From the fact that his face was so red, it was obvious he had heard more than enough to know Sandy was trying to do the hard sell of him being good boyfriend material. Little did they know that when I was done with him, thanks to my new hobby, he'd be a *great* boyfriend. Not for me, obviously. But for someone else.

"Oh, hi, honey. We're just having a little girl talk," Sandy replied with a smile. "You didn't tell me what a wonderful conversationalist Dylan is."

I had barely been able to get in two words, but it was nice to know that she was able to tell that about me. Maybe she had taken an Intro to Psychicdom class at some point.

"Come on, Dylan," he said. "There's a DVD I want to lend you that I think you'd like."

I followed him to his bedroom, which, like the other rooms in the house, wasn't all that big, but the way he had decorated the red walls—with lots of movie posters and framed record-album covers—gave it a funky feel. On the wall across from his bed was a bookshelf filled from top to bottom with DVDs. "Wow. Have you actually watched all of these?" I asked.

He nodded.

I walked over and started checking the movies out. "It's like being at Blockbuster," I said. Not only were they in alphabetical order, but they were divided into genres: comedy, action, drama, horror. It was funny—Josh may have been kind of messy with his appearance, but when it came to anything having to do with movies, he was annoyingly neat.

He pulled out a DVD case and handed it to me. "Here."

"What is it?"

"*Manhattan*. Woody's other true masterpiece."

"What's it about?"

"About two opposites who fall in love," he replied.

"But that's what *Annie Hall*'s about. He's not very creative when it comes to thinking up plots, is he?"

He looked at me like I had just killed his dog. That is, if he hadn't been deathly afraid of animals because of the incident with the guinea pig and *had* a dog. "It's a classic story line," he snapped. I was beginning to get that you could never, ever, dis Woody Allen in front of him.

"Okay." I shrugged, walking over to examine his other bookshelf, which was filled with mostly books about movies and biographies about directors.

He took out his camera. "Can I film you? It might be interesting to include some footage of you out of your environment. You know, Dylan-in-a-Film-Geek-World stuff."

"You're not *that* geeky," I said to the camera.

He peeked his head around and looked at me, amazed. "I'm sorry. You're going to have to say that last line again because what I *thought* I heard you say was that I wasn't that geeky."

I shrugged and turned so that he wasn't shooting my right side. "You're not. I mean, yes, you have some serious geek tendencies, but they're not, like, fatal or anything."

I could tell by the way that he quickly burrowed his head back behind the camera that he was all embarrassed.

"You know, Josh, I don't know if you realize this, but you have this annoying habit of hiding behind that thing when you're trying to avoid something."

"I do not," he replied, lifting it up even higher so even more of his face was covered.

"You so do," I said. "Between the camera and your inhaler—"

He put the camera down. "I told you—"

"—your lungs didn't develop properly because you were premature and that's probably why you have asthma. I know, I know." I held out my hand. "Just let me hold on to it for a while," I challenged.

His eyes widened like I had just told him I was canceling his Netflix subscription. "What?"

"I'm not going to take it home or anything. Just while I'm here. I mean, if you're not dependent on it, it shouldn't be a big deal, right?"

He started straightening the stuff on his desk. "I don't know where it is," he lied.

"It's where it always is—in the pocket of your jeans," I said.

Busted, he reached in and took it out. "Okay, but you better remember to give it back to me before you leave," he warned. "The Santa Ana winds are going to be really strong tonight, and because of my lungs, I tend to cough a lot." He started fake-coughing. "As you can see, it's starting to get bad already."

I rolled my eyes as I took the inhaler and shoved it into my own pocket. It was a good thing he was going to be a director and not an actor. "Okay, now you can go back to hiding behind your camera," I said.

He picked it up and started filming me again as I started fiddling with his Luke Skywalker figure on the shelf. "So have *you* ever been in love?" I asked.

"With someone I've actually met in person?"

I nodded.

I could see him slump. "No," came his muffled reply.

"But you've been in love with people you *haven't* met in person?" I asked, almost breaking off Luke's arm as I tried to get it to move the light-wand thingie.

He shrugged as he walked over and took Luke out of my hands, placing him back in his original position on the shelf. "Yeah. You know, girls I've had e-relationships with and stuff. Girls I've met on MySpace and Facebook." I saw him move his hand toward his pocket. "Hey, you still have my inhaler, right?"

I patted my own pocket. "Yup. Right here. Interesting that you get nervous when we start to talk about *girls*," I remarked.

"I'm not nervous," he said.

"Whatever. Anyway, I think it's kind of hard to fall in love with someone if you've never met them in person," I said, flipping through the cases. I'm sorry—I know he knew more about movies than most *Jeopardy!* contestants, but there wasn't *one* silly romantic comedy on any of the three shelves. Mostly they were super old, like from the 1970s, so all the actors on the covers were dressed in hideous clothes with even more hideous hairstyles.

"Not if you have a good imagination." He shrugged.

"So are you in an e-relationship now?" I asked.

He took the DVDs that I had taken out of the bookcase and realphabetized them. "Nope. There was this girl from Boston named Heidi but last week she wrote me that she thinks she might be gay, so that's probably not going to work." After he was done, he picked the camera back up and started hiding again. "And there's a girl here that I'm kind of interested in anyway," he mumbled from behind the lens. The last part was said so softly a normal person would have missed it, but because I have bionic ears when it comes to anything that's considered romantic gossip, I heard it loud and clear.

I stood up and yanked the camera away from him. "Omigod—who?!" I demanded. "Does she go to Castle Heights?"

He nodded, one hand going to his pocket while the other grasped at the air toward the camera.

"OmiGOD," I squealed louder, bouncing on his bed before leaping up again. "You have to tell me who it is! Is she a senior?"

He nodded again and started to cough. "Can I have my inhaler back now?"

"Josh, you're okay. You're going to be fine," I said in an authoritative voice, like you hear ambulance drivers use with car crash victims on TV. "So, do I know her?"

He nodded a third time. "Please can I have it back?"

I sighed and fished it out of my pocket and handed it over.

He took a squirt and closed his eyes. "Much better," he said as he grabbed the camera from the bed.

"But you don't understand—I'm *dying*! You *have* to tell me who it is!" I moved the camera away from his face. "And stop hiding behind that thing."

"I'm not hiding," he replied, his head shrunk down into his shoulders like a turtle. He put the camera down and flopped down face-first on his bed. "I shouldn't have said anything," he moaned into his pillow.

"What? I'm not going to tell anyone. I'm fantastic at keeping secrets. For instance, I never told *anyone* about the fact that Lola made out with Ted Fenton at Cynthia Greenburg's Sweet Sixteen last year even though she was technically still going out with Richie Marino at the time."

He lifted his head off the pillow and looked at me. "Okay, well, you just told *me*," he replied.

"Whatever. I know I can trust you. So who is it?" I couldn't believe that all the time Josh and I had been hanging out, he hadn't mentioned he had a crush. Frankly, I felt a little betrayed. Friends don't let friends not know about their crushes.

"I'm not ready to talk about it yet," he said as he grabbed a little rubber E.T. figurine off his night table.

"But I can *help* you," I said. "You know, give you advice and stuff." I pointed to E.T. "And the first piece of advice is that you might want to put all that stuff away if you ever have a girl over. Not so sexy, you know?" I definitely had my work cut out for me when it came to mainstreaming him into regular society.

"It'd just be a waste of time." He sighed, placing it in a drawer. "Someone like her would never like someone like me."

"You don't know that. Like your mom said, you're kind of a catch—you know, in a mathlete kind of way. And I'm going to help you become an even *bigger* catch," I said. "Okay, even if you're not willing to tell me who she is yet, you've got to at least give me some clues. You said I know her . . . is she one of my good friends? Omigod—is it *Lola*? Do you have a crush on *Lola*?!"

He looked at me like I was crazy. "No. It's not Lola."

I marched over to his closet and flung open the door so I could see exactly what I was dealing with when it came to wardrobe. From the few pairs of jeans, three white oxford shirts, and a suit jacket, it turned out not much. "Good because she's completely obsessed with this guy John Guzman who goes to Buckley, which I *so* don't understand. I mean, who wants to go out with someone who calls himself the Guz? I can't even imagine what he's going to end up wearing to Fall Fling." I turned to look at him. "Wait—is it Hannah?!"

He rolled his eyes. "No. It's not Hannah."

"I'm glad because even though she doesn't want anyone to know yet, Joe Yudin just broke up with Deb Eiseman and asked her to Fall Fling."

He shook his head. "And now I know."

I walked back to the bed and sat down next to him.

He turned his face to the side. "I don't think you're friends with her," he said into the pillow. "In fact, I *know* you're not friends with her."

"Okay, this is so making me crazy. At least tell me if she's blonde or brunette."

He flipped over on his back and stared at the ceiling, a faraway look in his eyes. "A really deep, rich chestnut color, like Faye Dunaway in *Network*."

"Who?" I said.

"Never mind." He sighed.

"How tall is she?" I demanded.

"I don't want to play this game anymore," he said, walking over to the fish tank in the corner of the room.

"I thought you didn't like animals," I said.

"I never said I didn't like them. I said I had issues with them because of the incident," he explained as he sprinkled some food into the tank. "Besides, it's just mammals I have problems with. These are fish."

I shook my head. This was going to be more work than

I thought. "Okay, um, Josh? Rule number 422: whatever you do, don't spend your first date with your crush giving her a biology lesson. Or whatever class it is where we learn about mammals. What's their names?

He looked up. "Orson Welles and François Truffaut."

"Who are Orson Welles and François Truffaut?"

He sighed. "Only two of the most important directors of the twentieth century," he replied.

"Okay, whatever, back to your crush." I picked up my Sidekick. "So she's brunette and I'm *not* friends with her," I said as I scrolled through the address book. The good news was that because we lived in L.A., there were double the amount of blondes than brunettes, so it wouldn't be so difficult to figure this out. "Oh! I know—Karina Morgan."

He turned to me. "Karina Morgan has been to rehab twice in the last year—why would you think I'd have a crush on *her*?"

"Before she became a pillhead she was a *very* nice girl." I continued scrolling through the list. "I know—Stacy Eisenhauser."

He gave me the same look I gave my dad when he had asked me whether I wanted to go to the Neil Diamond concert at the Staples Center with him last year. "Not only does Stacy Eisenhauser look like Rosie O'Donnell, but she came out last year and is dating Jordanna Olson," he said.

"Well, you *did* mention you had a habit of falling for lesbians, so it's not totally out of the realm of possibility," I shot back.

"I can't believe you have her number programmed in your phone."

"That's because she helps me with my trig homework sometimes. I think she might have a crush on me." I went back to scrolling. "Hmm . . . is it—"

"Okay, game over," he announced, walking toward the door. "I have a calculus quiz tomorrow, so I should really start studying."

"That's *so* not fair," I whined. "You have to tell me."

"Some other time. I promise," he said as he led me out of the room.

I said good-bye to Sandy, who was curled up on the couch wiping away tears as she watched a show about lost pets on Animal Planet, and promised her I'd come back for dinner after she finished her Introduction to Persian Cooking class.

"Thanks for having me over," I said to Josh as he walked me out to my car. "And for this," I said, holding up *Manhattan*.

"You're welcome," he said. "Just don't throw it around in that bag of yours so it gets scratched or anything. It's the Millennium edition, so it was pricey."

"I won't," I promised as I got into the car and rolled down the window. "You're not going to tell me who she is, are you?"

"Not tonight," he replied.

"I didn't think so." I sighed. "Tomorrow?"

"Probably not."

I sighed again. "Fine. Be that way. Good night."

"Good night," he replied.

After I rolled up the window, he knocked on it.

"Hey, Dylan?" he said after I rolled it down.

"Yeah?"

He looked at the ground. "Never mind," he said. "Forget it."

"No. Tell me."

It was dark but I could tell he was blushing. "I was just going to say . . . I know you're only doing this because your dad's making you, but . . . it's been fun hanging out with you. Even though you obviously think I have horrible taste in girls."

"Hey, if you like hanging out with me, you have *excellent* taste in girls," I teased. "But seriously—I've been having a good time, too. Like I said, I've realized you're actually not that geeky. I mean, obviously there's room for improvement—like getting you off the inhaler—but you're definitely not as bad as I originally thought."

"Thanks. I guess," he replied.

"Good night," I said, rolling up the window.

He knocked on it again.

"Yes, Josh?" I said, after I rolled it back down.

"Maybe you're right about the inhaler," he admitted. "Maybe it's a little bit of a nervous habit. I'm going to try and use it less often."

"Sounds good," I agreed.

"Well, good night," he said.

"Good night," I said.

As I drove away, I thought about how weird guys were. I mean, what was the *point* of having a crush if you didn't tell someone who you were crushing on?

chapter eight: josh

I really did mean it when I told Dylan that I liked hanging out with her. Sure, she had this way of thinking that the entire world revolved around her, but she had a good heart. Not only that, but she was willing to use the limited skills that she *did* have to help out her close friends. Of which, I discovered the following week, I had become one.

It was Sunday afternoon and I was reading the latest issue of *Fade In* magazine that I had stuck in *PC World* while Raymond explained to a woman who looked like an extra in *Night of the Living Dead* because she had triplets hanging off her that, yes, the Play-Doh that her toddler had stuck in the CD-ROM drive of her laptop might explain why it wasn't working, when I got a text from Dylan.

What time do you get off?

Fifteen minutes, I typed back.

Meet me at Abercrombie then.

I had spent enough time with her by this point to

know that saying no wasn't an option when shopping was involved, even though, for the life of me, I had no idea what she could have wanted. She had finally stopped sighing audibly whenever she took in my standard uniform of T-shirt and jeans, but I highly doubted she was going to ask me for fashion advice.

"What's up?" I asked when I found her in the guys' department of Abercrombie with an armful of T-shirts and cargo pants. "I thought you were going to that tribal belly-dancing class with Lola at the gym?"

She held up a red T-shirt to my chest. "Nope. I decided it was time for me to get started on my new hobby."

My right eyebrow shot up. "What's your new hobby?"

"Makeovers for the less fortunate," she replied.

I tried to avoid looking at the pierced belly button of the Cameron Diaz look-alike salesgirl who was folding sweaters ten feet in front of us, but since almost her entire stomach was bare, it was hard. Amy Loubalu would never dress so cheesily. "So who are we making over here?" I asked.

"You, silly." She smiled.

Uh-oh.

"Where's your camera?" she asked.

"It's at home. I didn't think we were shooting today."

"Oh," she said, disappointed. "That's too bad. This would've been great for the documentary. You could've done a whole, what's it called, *montage* sequence. I *love* makeover montages—they're so much fun."

She held a blue T-shirt up to me. "Even though you still refuse to tell me who you have a crush on, I figured I'd still help you out," she explained.

I gave her a doubtful look.

"Believe me, I've worked on cases that were a lot tougher than you. You know Robert Hughes?"

Of course I knew Robert Hughes. Everyone knew Robert Hughes. He was second-in-command in the Popularity Police after Asher.

"Do you remember what he looked like when he was still going by 'Bobby' back in freshman year?"

In my mind I flipped back the pages of my virtual Castle Heights yearbook. "And people call *me* a geek?"

"Exactly."

"You were responsible for that?"

She nodded proudly. "Yup."

"Wow. I have to admit—that's pretty impressive."

"And I'm going to do the same for you, *mi amigo*," she said as she pushed me toward the dressing room.

"Okay, so she's not a cheerleader," I heard Dylan yell from outside the dressing room as I checked myself out in the three-way mirror in a pair of black cargo pants and a green T-shirt that said PHYS EDU. I didn't think Dylan was aware of the irony of that because, well, Dylan wasn't exactly an ironic kind of gal, but since I had a computer file of various gym excuses that I had been rotating since eighth grade, I thought it was pretty funny.

"Nope. Not a cheerleader," I yelled back. I couldn't decide if I looked cool, or like I should be valet-parking cars at one of those hotels that was so hip it didn't even have a sign.

"And she's not on any sports teams, or on the Student Council?" she announced.

Ever since I had made the stupid mistake of telling Dylan there was someone I had a crush on, she had refused to drop the subject. I had to admit that her tenacity was pretty impressive. If she had put half of that energy toward her physics homework (which, over the last few weeks, I had found myself doing most of), MIT would be banging down her door with a full scholarship.

"Nope. No sports teams or Student Council," I replied as I opened the door and walked out. Since barely anyone at Castle Heights other than me and Amy worked after school, I knew I was coming dangerously close to revealing her identity, but our twenty-questions game had turned into seventy-five questions, and like a captured soldier undergoing Chinese water torture, I was almost ready to crack.

As I stood there like a contestant on one of those reality shows about models, Dylan walked around, examining me from various angles.

I started scratching at my arm. "I think I'm allergic to this material," I announced.

"It's *cotton*," she replied. "Just like your other T-shirts. It's just nicer cotton. Okay, now walk over to that mannequin wearing the tank top and miniskirt and back," she ordered.

I started to walk.

"*No*—the one wearing a *tank* top. That's a *tube* top."

I changed course and did as I was told.

"Those pants are very slimming on you," she finally said.

She sounded like my mom. At least she didn't call them slacks.

As I stood in front of her she examined me from every angle. "It's official," she announced.

"What?"

"There's only a *touch* of geekiness left." She took my glasses off. "Which will be almost entirely gone once you get rid of these." She ruffled my hair. "And when we get your hair cut and lose the soft-rock eighties feathered thing you've got going on? You might even be moving into hottie territory."

I squinted at myself in the mirror. "Really?" I asked. I knew Amy Loubalu wasn't shallow enough to care about whether she was dating a hottie or not, but moving up the scale certainly wouldn't hurt my chances.

I could barely make out my reflection and grabbed for

my glasses. "Sorry, but I'll have to be a little more geek-ish," I said.

"Contacts?" Dylan asked as she placed them back on my face.

I shook my head. "I'm allergic to the plastic. It makes my eyes swell up and I look like a giant bug."

She sighed. "I'm surprised you don't live in a bubble," she said.

I shrugged. "It's probably because I was—"

"—born three weeks early and have an underdeveloped immune system. I know. Okay, Rule number 796? When talking to your crush, skip that stuff. Way too much TMI."

I nodded. "Got it." I had heard that Amy Loubalu used to volunteer at a nursing home, so I bet she would be very understanding of medical issues.

Dylan moved my face to the right, and then to the left. "At least let me take you to l.a.Eyeworks so we can get you a pair of Pradas. I'm thinking *very* chunky black frames. They're the best when it comes to the whole nerd-chic thing."

"You know, Dylan, I really appreciate all this, but I don't have that kind of money—"

"You don't need it." She held up her platinum American Express card. "It's my treat."

I shook my head. "That's really nice of you, but I can't. Absolutely not."

She pushed me back toward the dressing room. "Yes. You can. And you will. I'm a little lazy when it comes to recycling and stuff like that, so think of it as my way of helping the environment."

Her logic didn't quite flow, but by now I knew better than to try to argue with her. "Well, thanks . . . I really appreciate it."

"You're welcome. And while you have the salesgirl cut off the price tags, I'm going to go get you those pants in a few more colors." A few steps later, she turned back. "I saw Julia Miller in front of Whole Foods with a Greenpeace T-shirt last week trying to get signatures. Does that count as an after-school job?" she asked.

A shoo-in for valedictorian, Julia Miller had already gotten early acceptance to Brown and Wellesley. She also had more facial hair than I did. "It's not Julia Miller," I replied.

Forget MIT—the CIA or FBI should hire Dylan to interrogate people. She'd definitely get them to fold.

After stops for jeans and button-down shirts we decided to refuel at Du-par's. No wonder Dylan was so skinny—shopping was exhausting.

"Your new look's working for you—did you see those girls in front of the Hot Dog on a Stick cart checking you out?" she asked as we shared a double order of fries.

"Dylan, they were about *thirteen*," I replied.

She shrugged. "So. Attention is attention. You're *really* not going to tell me who it is, are you?"

"Who what is?"

She rolled her eyes. "Your crush!"

"Oh. Nope," I replied, rearranging the napkin I had tucked into my T-shirt to protect it from any ketchup incidents.

"Guys are so much better at keeping secrets than girls." She sighed. "So are you going to ask her to Fall Fling?"

"The answer to that would be no. I haven't talked to her for more than two minutes at a time, so I think that might be pushing it," I replied.

She reached for another fry. "But you look so good now!" she exclaimed. "Thanks to me, that is. Does she work at a place where you can hang out and not seem like a total stalker?"

"Yeah." I started to reach for a fry, but then thought better of it. If I *did* decide to try to talk to Amy, it wouldn't hurt to lay off the junk food. Not that Amy cared about looks or anything like that.

"So do it." She shrugged. "Have a few conversations with her, then ask for her e-mail address, then her phone number, then start texting, and then ask. But don't ask her through a text. That would be rude. Plus you run the risk that she'll forward it to everyone in her address book, which could be unfortunate, especially if you're a bad speller. Not that you have that problem. Like, you know, *Asher* does.

But, Josh, you need to get going on this—you're already running the risk of offending her by asking her so late in the game. I mean, it *is* only three weeks away."

"I am?"

"Well, yeah. I mean, how much in advance did you ask your date for the prom last year?"

"I didn't go to the prom last year," I replied.

"Oh. Okay, well, then what about Spring Fling sophomore year?"

"I didn't go to Spring Fling, either," I said, my cheeks turning red.

"Wait a sec—are you telling me you've never been to any sort of school dance or a prom?" Dylan demanded loudly.

I slumped down in the booth and shook my head. It was a good thing most of the people in Du-par's wore hearing aids or else my cheeks would've shot up in flames.

For the first time I saw what looked like real compassion on Dylan's face. Even more than when we had passed the cart at the mall that sold fake purses and a little girl was in tears because her mother wouldn't buy her one. "Wow. That's so sad," she said quietly. "That's beyond sad . . . that's like tragedy-size sad. I mean, I've been going to the prom since I was a *freshman*."

"Yeah, well, you know us geeks . . . we're allergic to bad cover bands and punch bowls," I joked.

"No, seriously, Josh—proms and dances and stuff are

like . . . I don't know . . . on the must-haves list for the high-school experience. You have to go to at least *one* in your life. Otherwise the post-traumatic stress might end up making you go postal in a McDonald's or something when you're forty."

I shrugged. "They just seem dumb to me."

She rolled her eyes. "Why do you have to be so bah-humbug? Where's your school spirit?"

"I have school spirit," I shot back. "I'm in the Film Society. *And* the Russian Club."

"Okay, Rule number 549: leave the Russian Club part out when talking to the Crush, okay?"

I nodded.

"What about if you ever make a movie about a prom or a school dance?" she asked. "I mean, it'll be a lot more—what's the word?—*authentic* if you've actually gone to one."

She did have a point. I slumped in my seat and sighed. "Even if I *did* ask her, she'll never go with me."

"Why not?"

The more I thought about it, the more I realized Dylan might have a point. If I had learned anything by hanging out with her and her friends, it was that once you got up close to people, you realized that everyone—no matter how popular he or she might be—was just a living, breathing human being complete with zits and bad breath and ketchup stains on their shirts and all that other stuff that makes them human. While Amy was gorgeous, from the limited interaction we *had* had, she was also nice, so even if she ended up saying no, at least I'd be able to cross off "Never got up the nerve to ask Amy Loubalu out" off my regrets list.

"'Why not' is right!" I said, getting more and more excited about the prospect as I squeezed my fry so hard that potato leaked out onto my fingers. "I'm going to do it. I'm going to ask her!"

"You are?" asked Dylan, just as excited.

I slumped down in my seat again. "I don't know. Can we just go with maybe at this point?"

"Okay, what about just starting with stalking her where she works," Dylan suggested. "Then, if it goes well, you can ask her if she's planning on going to Lisa Eaton's party this weekend. And if *that* goes well, you can think about asking her out."

"You mean on a date?"

She nodded.

I grabbed a fry. "Just me and her? Alone?"

She rolled her eyes. "Yeah, Josh. That's usually what happens when you go on a date with someone."

"Oh."

She scowled. "Unless, of course, you're Asher. Then you just ask your girlfriend to stupid Ultimate Fighting events with your stupid friends," she said bitterly. "Not that I'm bitter or anything."

"Right. Of course not." As Dylan herself would say . . . *Not.*

"And if the date goes well, maybe you'll think about Fall Fling," she continued. "Does that sound like a plan?"

I nodded as I took out my inhaler. Just *thinking* about asking Amy Loubalu made my lungs constrict.

She held out her hand. "Rule number 857? No inhalers when talking to the Crush."

I handed it over with a sigh. This was going to be harder than I thought.

If I've learned anything in my seventeen years, it's that life isn't easy all the time. Parents get divorced, guinea pigs explode under your watch, and you can't get up the guts to talk to a girl you have a crush on. That being said, what I've also learned is that huge dramatic changes can happen overnight. Like, say, the fact that when you catch a glance of yourself in the bathroom mirror the morning after you've been made over, you don't recognize yourself because your new haircut makes you look like a human being rather than a Chia Pet. Or that a new style of glasses can change the shape of your face. I had always considered myself a major player in the film-geek world, but as I put on one of the new outfits that Dylan had picked out for me, I understood what it felt like to feel cool in the real world.

"Just one more picture!" Mom pleaded as I tried to get

out the door after gulping down some oatmeal and orange juice because I had been so busy staring at myself in the mirror.

"Mom, I don't know what you're making such a big deal about—I'm still me," I said, grabbing my knapsack. I was, right? I checked to make sure my inhaler was in there. I had a feeling that, with this dramatic change of events, I might need to use it once or twice today.

"I know, honey, but you look so *handsome*," she replied, snapping away. "I can't wait to e-mail this to Grandma. And maybe I'll send it to my friend Sharon, the one from Introduction to Belly Dancing—I can't remember if I told you, but her daughter is a junior at Harvard Westlake . . ."

"Nuh-uh—no pimping me out," I said, giving her a kiss on the cheek. If everything went according to plan, I'd soon be dating Amy Loubalu. Or at least talking to her.

That day, I discovered firsthand the power of the second glance. After third period, as I walked from Russian to English, senior girls who hadn't ever looked at me let alone talked to me over the last four years did a double take. Then, after fourth period, as I walked to lunch, Ashley Turner actually said *hello* to me. And I knew it was me because she said "Hey, Josh" rather than just "Hey," which could've meant that she was talking to Dinshaw Muzbar, who was right beside me. With her clonelike looks, Ashley wasn't my type, but still. Premakeover, the only interaction

I had had with her was when she snapped, "Hey, watch it!" when I almost smacked her in the nose with the door as I was coming out of the nurse's office one afternoon because I had forgotten my inhaler and thought the dizzy spells I was having might have been early-warning signs of a brain tumor.

"Wow, Dylan, you weren't kidding," said Lola as I walked up onto The Ramp with the guys and our gear.

"Weren't kidding about what?" I asked as we started unpacking our equipment.

"About the fact that you're actually *cute*," said Hannah with amazement. Realizing what had just come out of her mouth, she reached out and patted my shoulder. "Not that you looked, you know, bad before," she said quickly. During the time I had been filming the girls, I had come to realize that while Hannah was first-tier popular, she—unlike Dylan or Lola—wanted to be liked by everyone, even us nonpopular folk.

Lola snorted as she took out her mirror to do a hair-and-makeup check. She, on the other hand, didn't care if *anyone* liked her. "Yeah, anyway, you look good." She pointed at my stomach. "And if you started going to the gym, you'd look even better."

Steven patted his own extra poundage. "You know, Lola, some chicks dig a guy with a little extra junk in the trunk. More of us to love."

Lola stopped applying lip gloss and cringed, but I could

see the slightest smile on her lips. Strangely enough, she seemed to have a soft spot for Steven, of all people. She acted like she couldn't stand him, but ever since the frat party she'd been laughing at his jokes more and more. "Okay, that joke wasn't funny the first time around, so I don't know why you'd think it was funny now."

He shrugged and started unwrapping a Milky Way.

Dylan finished brushing her hair and flipped her head back up, looking like a poster girl for a shampoo commercial. "Didn't I do a great job?" she asked the girls.

Hannah nodded and pointed at Ari, who was in the corner trying to untangle himself from the power cords he had managed to wrap around his legs. "Maybe you could do a makeover on Ari, too," she whispered. "He's got no muscles, and he'll probably be bald by the time he's twenty-five, and he slouches, but other than that, I've been thinking he's got some potential. Plus, he's got a really nice singing voice. We sang some show tunes together at the frat party."

Steven and I looked at each other and raised our eyebrows. Maybe this documentary wouldn't just get me into film school—maybe it could also get Ari a girlfriend as well.

Dylan cringed as Ari tripped on the cable and fell flat on his face. "I'll think about it." She looked over at me. "Are we ready?"

I looked over at Ari, who was feeling around on the

ground for his glasses. "Yeah, let's just start," I said, picking up the camera. "So, I was thinking . . . maybe today you could tell us a bit about the perils of popularity. The dark side."

Lola rolled her eyes. "You sound like a promo for one of those TV newsmagazine shows."

Dylan shook her head. "Hmm . . . let's see . . . well, because you're on everyone's radar, there's the fact that you can't really afford to repeat outfits that often."

"Hey, Josh," said Lisa Eaton as she walked by, flashing me a smile. "You're coming to my party on Friday night, right?"

I put down the camera. "Oh, hey, Lisa. Yeah, I'll be there."

"Cool," she said, her smile broadening. "See you then."

I brought the camera back up to my face. "Okay, so that's one bad thing. What else?"

"Well, there's the fact that—" Dylan started to say.

"Hey, Josh," Shannon Hall called as she walked by. "I love your new glasses. Very nerd chic," she said with a wink.

I put the camera down. "Thanks, Shannon," I said with a smile. I had to admit, it was pretty cool getting this kind of attention. Who knew that a new T-shirt, glasses, and a haircut could do wonders for your social life?

I brought the camera back up to my face, but after ten

more minutes of being interrupted by "Hey, Josh"s, Dylan had had it.

"Okay, I'm done for today," she said, gathering up her stuff.

"But we barely got anything!" I replied.

"That's because you're so busy chit-chatting with every girl that walks by!"

"Someone sounds a little jealous," said Steven under his breath.

"As if," she replied. "This has nothing to do with being jealous. I'm just trying to be a professional here and he's, like, not paying any attention to me—I mean to the movie—which is so not like him." She stood up. "Come on, girls, let's go."

"I think I'm going to hang," said Lola, who was huddled with Steven over his iPod, going through his music library.

"Fine. Come on, Hannah."

Hannah looked up from where she was sitting with Ari, running lines with him from the *Macbeth* musical he was auditioning for. "I think I'm going to stay, too. That is, if it's okay," she said anxiously.

I zoomed in on Dylan's face. She looked like she had just been told they were out of fries at Du-par's. "Suit yourself," she said, walking away. "I'm going to go hang out with Asher."

Except that when she walked over to Asher's table and tried to nuzzle up to him, he ignored her and just kept talking to his buddies. I put the camera down. I had no idea what to do. This makeover was Dylan's idea, but it was like she was mad at me that it had worked. Should I try to talk to her about it? Or should I just let her calm down?

Unfortunately, I realized that *she* was the person who I'd probably ask for advice on this kind of thing.

As I watched her walk down The Ramp, I saw Amy Loubalu. And then I saw her smile. And then I saw her wave.

After looking over my shoulder to make sure it was meant for me, I waved back.

Wow. This makeover thing *was* powerful.

I was waiting for Dylan by her locker when she got out of her last-period French class.

"Hey," I said.

"Hey," she said as she opened it. The top shelf looked like something out of a beauty-supply store—cans of hair stuff, makeup, nail-polish remover, cotton balls. She had also hung up a small rod across the width so she could hang some clothes.

"Look, about what happened at lunch," I began.

"What about it?" she said, changing her red shoes that I had discovered were called ballet flats to the same pair in black.

"I'm sorry if I did anything to upset you," I said. Steven had told me that his dad used that line all the time with his mom and it always worked.

"You didn't do anything to upset me," she huffed,

sounding very much like I had done something to upset her, as she slammed her locker and started walking toward the exit.

I followed her. I could see we weren't getting anywhere. "Okay, you know how there's always that scene in movies where the two main characters get into a fight and then the one main character goes to apologize, and the other one says 'What? You have nothing to apologize for,' but, really, you can tell on their face that actually, the other main character has *a lot* to apologize for, but the thing is, he or she doesn't know what it is because the other main character won't tell him? Or her. Sometimes it's a her, but usually it's a him."

As we got outside, I took out my new Ray-Ban sunglasses she had bought for me and put them on. "And then the next act of the movie is all about the tension of the two of them pretending everything's fine, but it's really not?"

She shrugged as she walked toward her car. "Yeah? So?"

I put my hand on her shoulder to stop her. "Well, I don't want that to be a scene in this movie. I mean, I don't want that to happen with us." I fiddled with the inhaler in my coat pocket. "Because you've been really great to me, and if I did anything this afternoon to upset you, I'm sorry."

She looked at me and a small smile came over her face. "Thanks. I appreciate that." She fiddled with her keys. "See, it's just that I've seen situations where people have these huge transformations and suddenly become popular overnight and totally dis their friends." She looked up. "And it's really not cool."

I nodded. "I agree. I'd never do anything like that."

She smiled. "I didn't think you would. Now, don't you have to go stalk your crush?" she asked.

I patted my pocket for the inhaler again. And then there was the scene in the movie where the hero was forced to summon up his courage and face the dragon. Granted, Amy Loubalu was a beautiful dragon, but still, this wasn't going to be easy.

If you show up where someone works, it's a good idea to actually talk to them, because if not, like Dylan said, you come off like a stalker. Which is what I was starting to look like after my third straight afternoon at Mani's Bakery.

Mani's was very healthy—sugar-free, fruit-juice-sweetened cookies, wheat-free cakes, that kind of stuff. And judging by all the yoga-mat bags and laptops, it was a big hangout for yoga people and screenwriters. But then again, anyplace in L.A. that was on the cheap side and offered free coffee refills was a hangout for screenwriters.

As I walked in, I saw her behind the counter, wearing her gray Mani's T-shirt, which on anyone else would've looked drab and ugly but, on her, managed to make her violet eyes even more gorgeous. As nonchalantly as possible, I took a hit off my inhaler before jamming it back into my pocket and making my way to what I liked to think had become "my" table and throwing my backpack down on a chair.

"Oh, *hey,* Amy," I said as I sat down, as if seeing her here was the weirdest coincidence in the world. "How are you?"

"I'm fine. How are you?" she asked as she put down a pot of tea next to a woman in her twenties with dreadlocks wearing a T-shirt that said REALITY'S OVERRATED.

"I'm good. Just thought I'd get a coffee and get a little work done on my English paper."

"Two-percent-vanilla latte?" she asked.

I smiled. "Yeah. Thanks." I couldn't believe she remembered. That had to be a good sign.

"So are you not working at Good Buys anymore?" she asked as she brought my latte over. Amy had come in there once about a year ago with her mother and Raymond and I had spent a good fifteen minutes explaining all the different kinds of USB cables to them even though it technically wasn't in our jurisdiction, which made Carl, whose jurisdiction it *was* in, very ticked off.

"No. I am. Why?" I looked at the latte. Just like she had the other two times I had been there that week, she had made a heart with the foam.

She shrugged. "It's just that you've been here the last few afternoons."

"Oh. They switched my schedule around." Or rather

I had asked them to switch my schedule around so that instead of coming in at four, I came in at five so I could go to Mani's and stalk. "And, uh, I have to work on this English paper. It's a very hard English paper."

"I'll let you concentrate on it, then," she said as she took a sugar container from the next table where a guy with a goatee was writing poetry in a Moleskine notebook—really *bad* poetry from what I could tell because he was saying it out loud as he wrote—and put it on mine.

"Oh. Okay," I mumbled.

Which, of course, was impossible. Not when the most beautiful girl in the world was less than five feet from me at all times, her smile lighting up the room as she joked with the Rastafarian at the table across the room, and played peekaboo with the baby to my right. All I could do was read the same paragraph of *Madame Bovary* over and over. For all I knew, it was in the original French.

"Hey, did you get a haircut?" she asked later as she brought me over my third latte.

"Me? Oh, um, yeah," I mumbled, trying to get my leg to stop shaking. I didn't know if it was nerves or restless leg syndrome, something I had recently read about on WebMD. After shopping and Du-par's, Dylan had dragged me to a fancy salon over in Beverly Hills where an Italian guy named Miki had gone on for a good two minutes about how Supercuts had ruined America before taking his scissors to my head.

"It looks good. You can really see your eyes now," she said with a smile.

I felt like my heart was going to ricochet right out of my chest and land in the plate of brown rice and veggies that the yogini in front of me was eating.

"And that green hoodie really brings out the green in them," she added.

She knew I had green eyes! Knowing what color someone's eyes were *had* to be a good sign. It meant she was actually paying attention when she looked at me. I wondered if there were any documented cases of people throwing up from happiness. "AreyougoingtoLisaEaton's-partythisSaturday?" I blurted out.

"What?"

I took a deep breath and arranged myself into what I hoped was a cool-looking slouch. "Are you, um, planning on going to Lisa Eaton's Halloween party this Saturday night?"

"No, I'm not friends with her, so I wasn't invited," Amy replied as she started filling the cinnamon container.

"I don't think it's an invitation thing," I said. "I heard it's going to be a big blowout, so it sounds like pretty much *any*one can go. Not like you're just *any*one . . . I mean, you're definitely *some*one . . . " I willed myself to shut up but my mouth just kept moving. "You know, someone in an anyone kind of way . . . " What did that even *mean*?

"Are you going?" she asked, waving good-bye to what

could only be a screenwriter due to his misbuttoned oxford, laptop, and the look on his face of a mole who had been forced out into daylight.

I nodded. "Yeah. For the documentary."

"I keep meaning to ask you how that's going."

"I think I've gotten some great stuff," I replied. "It seems to have become focused primarily on Dylan, which wasn't my original intention, but every day my vision for it becomes clearer. It's almost like watching a Polaroid develop—you know how at first it's all hazy, but as time goes by, the picture gets sharper?"

She nodded.

It felt incredible to be understood. I started to relax. "Well, it's kind of like that." Talking about my work was no problem. Talking about social stuff, especially with a beautiful girl involved—big problem.

"It seems like you and Dylan have become really close," she said.

Uh-oh. Knowing that Amy was Dylan's archenemy, as least from Dylan's point of view, this was a tough one. "Well, she's definitely got strong opinions about things. But she's not as bad as I thought."

"Uh-huh," Amy said. What did *that* mean? Was it uh-huh-you're-so-kidding-yourself or uh-huh-because-I'm-so-nice-I'm-going-to-let-that-slide? It was hard trying to decipher every word and facial expression when you were talking to someone you liked.

She shrugged. "Maybe I will go."

"Cool," I said. I tried to look like I didn't care one way or another what she did, but if I had been a theater nerd like Ari, I would've broken out into song and started dancing around the room. "And, uh, if you go, I guess that means I'll probably see you there." Okay, could I be any *more* of a geek?

"Probably," she replied.

My Sidekick beeped. I looked down to see a text from Raymond: *911 at Mrs. S's house ASAP.* "Not again," I said with a sigh.

"What?"

"Just a work thing. I should go," I said, gathering my stuff up and throwing some money down on the table. "See you at school."

"Do you want your latte to go?" she called after me.

"No, that's okay," I called back. Who needed caffeine when you were energized by love?

"Okay. See you later," she replied, giving me one last high-wattage smile.

The thrill of semiconvincing Amy to go to the party was quickly replaced by panic as I walked out to my car. What was I *doing* asking her to go to somewhere where I knew I'd be?! And if she did come, she'd probably expect me to at least say hello to her if not have a conversation with her. Which, of course, as evidenced by what had just happened, would be a disaster.

I took out my inhaler and squirted. I know I had promised Dylan I'd ease up, but now was not the time.

When it was time for my next review at work, I was asking for a raise if only because of how much time I had spent with Mrs. Spivakovsky. Mrs. S called every other week to say her soft drive—which I was constantly reminding her was called a hard drive—was broken again. In the ten service calls I had made to her house over the last year, not once had it been broken—every time it turned out to just not have been turned on. It wasn't that Mrs. Spivakovsky was an idiot—in fact, back in Russia she had been a physicist—she was just lonely and wanted company. Her husband had died six months earlier and now it was just her and Gorky, her twelve-year-old Chihuahua who had cataracts in one eye. Not that she and Mr. Spivakovsky had communicated all that much. Every time I had been there when he was alive, he was watching chess matches on the Russian community cable station and ignoring her constant stream of chatter. I usually didn't mind going, though, especially because she always had homemade baklava waiting.

As I was parking the Geekmobile, my phone rang. "Hey, Dylan. What's up?" I asked.

"Nothing. I'm bored," she replied with a sigh. Over the last few weeks I had become Dylan's go-to person when she was bored, which, from the number of calls I received, was twice an hour. I could tell by the sound of Elton John's "Candle in the Wind" blending with the hiss of water in the background that she was at The Dell in front of the fountain.

"So go buy something," I suggested.

"I already did. I bought a new bag. A brown one for late fall. It's so cute—it's got little silver—"

"I'm sure it's great but I'm about to go into a house call," I said as I walked up the steps to Mrs. Spivakovsky's duplex. I had quickly learned that if given the chance, Dylan could go on for hours about a bag or a pair of shoes. "Can I call you afterward?"

"Fine." She sighed.

I rang the bell and a moment later Mrs. S opened the door wearing one of her many housecoats (this one had hearts on it) and a pair of the dead Mr. S's fake leather slippers. "Joshie! You come save the day!" she said as she let me in. The Spivakovskys had lived in the same apartment since they arrived from Russia in the 1960s. And it *looked* like something from the sixties—daisy wallpaper in the Formica kitchen, green shag carpeting, a long wood console that, in addition to holding a TV, also housed a record player.

She hugged me to her, and I immediately broke out into a sneezing fit due to all the perfume she wore. "Hi, Mrs. Spivakovsky," I said, grabbing for a tissue from a cat-shaped tissue box. There was a serious animal motif going

216

on in the apartment—cats, dogs, pigs, cows. The thing was, she had told me in one of our many talks over baklava that other than Gorky, she was terrified of animals. Apparently, back in Russia there had been an incident with a goat.

"Gorky!" she yelled. "Come look who's here to see you—it's your best friend Joshie!" Maybe it was because Gorky was so small, but somehow he didn't trigger my animal phobia.

Gorky came trotting into the room wearing a cone on his head and started barking nonstop. He *always* barked nonstop when I was around.

"His allergies are that bad, huh?" I asked. Like me, Gorky had allergies. Unlike me, they affected his eyes instead of his lungs and he spent all day swiping at them.

She nodded. "Unfortunately, yes. He still keep trying to scratch his eye. I think the cone makes him very sad because now he can't play tug-of-war with you and the stocking."

"Yeah, that's too bad," I replied. *Not.* Usually Gorky would come out with one of Mrs. S's nylon knee-high stockings in his mouth and drop it at my feet. There's nothing more disgusting than a nylon stocking covered with dog drool. "So what's the problem today, Mrs. S?" I asked, as if I didn't already know.

She clucked her tongue and led me to the dining room, pushing me down into a chair that was still covered with plastic. "Always working, Joshie. First we visit, *then* you work!" she said, pushing the plate of baklava toward me.

I picked up a piece and popped it in my mouth. "Mmm . . . delicious."

"But no eat too much," she said as she patted my stomach. "Girls your age like two liters."

"Huh?"

She smacked my stomach. "Two liters. *Muscles.*"

"You mean six-packs?"

"Yes, yes. Women my age, no so much care. We just want them not drop dead like Mr. Spivakovsky did, God rest his soul. Soooo . . . Joshie . . . what's going on with the girls?"

I shrugged. "Nothing."

She sighed. "My only wish before I join Mr. Spivakovsky is to see you with a nice girl. Did you call my friend Mena's granddaughter?"

"The one with the body brace for her scoliosis? No, I think I lost her number." I got up and started to make my way toward the desk that was set up in the corner of the living room. "I think I need to make another stop after this, so we should probably look at the computer now. I found the problem," I called out to her. This was our usual routine.

"Already? You so good at this, Joshie. What is it?"

"You need to turn the power button on," I announced.

She came waddling over and squinted at the now-glowing button. "I thought I did."

Just then my phone rang and I looked down at the screen to see that it was Dylan again.

"Hey, I'm still here," I said when I picked up. "Can I call you in a few minutes?"

"Okay, I'm rethinking the bag now. If you were me, would you go with a bag that was in the brown family, or something that was more . . . I don't know . . . *tan*? Because I'm so blonde, I think the brown is a more dramatic contrast, but then again—"

"Um, Dylan? I'm still working. Can we talk about this later?"

"I guess so." She sighed. "Hey, do you want to go to Du-par's for dinner?"

"Sure. I'll meet you there at seven," I said as I hung up.

"Joshie, not that I was overlistening or nothing," said Mrs. S, even though she had been, "but I couldn't help but notice that was a *girl* you just talk to."

"Yup. You're right. It was," I replied.

"So?" she said, with her hands on her hips.

"It was this girl Dylan that's in my documentary."

Her eyes narrowed. "She a movie star? Does she have drug problem?"

"No, Dylan's not a movie star. Sometimes she *acts* like she's one, but she's just a girl in my school," I replied, making my way over to the glass of milk Mrs. S had set out for me.

"And she your girlfriend? Or just girl who is friend?"

"Just girl who is friend."

"Why not make her girlfriend, then?" she asked. "Is she pretty?"

"Yeah, she's really pretty."

"And nice? Is she nice?"

"I didn't think so at first, but, yeah, she's nice. In her own special way. And generous. Very generous."

Mrs. S looked confused. "So she's pretty, nice, generous—what's problem, then?"

"Other than the fact that she has a boyfriend?"

She sighed and put her hand to her head. "Oy. You don't tell me that part, Joshie. That part not so good."

"I was going to say other than the fact that she has a boyfriend, there's another girl I like better."

"This girl have boyfriend?"

"Nope. No boyfriend."

"So what's problem, then?"

"The problem is . . . well, there is no problem. The problem is me, I guess. I'm just too scared to ask her out."

Mrs. S took my hand in both of hers, which were as soft as tissue paper. "Joshie, life go very fast. You must ask her out. It's no fun being alone—believe me, I know." She pointed at Gorky, who was bumping into things as he made his way around the room with his cone. "Yes, I have Gorky, but he's no match for Mr. Spivakovsky. I know it seem like all he did was watch chess on TV, but we had good life together. And now he's gone." Her faded blue eyes started to fill with tears. "Joshie, please, like sneaker commercial used to say—'Just go for it.'"

"You mean 'Just do it'?"

She nodded. "Yes. Just do it."

I don't know if it was that in that moment I realized that like Mr. S, Mrs. S wasn't going to be around forever, or if it was that I was sick and tired of being a wimp, but I was suddenly filled with the same kind of motivation I had felt the night I had put together my proposal for the documentary for USC. Mrs. S was right—it was time to just do it. And I *would* just do it. At Lisa Eaton's party. That is, if Amy showed up. And if she didn't show up . . . well, then I was off the hook and I could go back to being the Guy Who Never Takes a Chance When It Comes to Girls.

chapter nine: *dylan*

It was good that someone—i.e., Josh—was getting attention from the opposite sex, because I sure wasn't. Ever since Asher had called that day that I was getting ready to go to Josh's for dinner, things had officially gotten weird between us. Like I said, after two years together, I was well aware of the fact that life wasn't going to be one continuous magic movie moment, but he was taking longer and longer to return my texts. Plus, on the rare occasions over the last few months that we *did* get together, it was almost as if he'd do anything not to be alone with me. In the beginning, all he had *wanted* was to be alone with me making out, and it was me who had to keep insisting we go do activities where we could talk and get to know each other, like shopping and eating. Call it woman's intuition or whatever, but I just knew that something was up, which was why I had sent him a text the night before saying we needed to talk. But when I asked him at lunch that day why he hadn't responded, he said he never got it. I was willing to buy that, since Mercury had recently gone retrograde, which, according to all the astrology sites, means that all sorts of mix-ups happen in terms of communication and electronics. But then I overheard him talking to Brandon Moglen about a text that he had gotten from *him* last night. Which made my woman's intuition say, "Okay, something *very* fishy is going on here" even louder inside my brain.

But what freaked me out even more was the fact that when I really thought about it, I wasn't sure that I even wanted to be with Asher anymore. Granted, he was gorgeous; and, sure, we were a no-brainer since he was the most popular guy and I was the most popular girl, but over the last month, being blown off all the time and the fact that we never talked about anything important had seriously started to bother me. I might not be the smartest person at Castle Heights (that was Ashima Patel, whose entire family had gone to Harvard) but that didn't mean I didn't read at least the headlines of the top news stories on the Yahoo home page and like to discuss them at length (especially the ones that had to do with the stars that were in rehab). That's one of the things I liked best about Josh—he was interested in my opinions. Even if he tended to talk about movies way too much, he wanted to know what I thought about them. Sure, I hadn't seen most of the ones he brought up because a lot of them had subtitles and were in black and white, but, still, it was nice to be asked for my thoughts.

The problem was that if I broke up with Asher, not only would I not have a date for Fall Fling, which was in three weeks, but seeing as it was already the middle of fall, every guy worth going with to the prom in May was already taken as well. I guess if I wanted to, I could have gotten a boyfriend at another school—maybe I could have even tracked down Michael Rosenberg, who hadn't seen me since I had become a blonde and got my deviated septum fixed—but dating someone at a different school was almost like being in a long-distance relationship. I knew that those were *so* hard from having watched Lola get her heart broken by a guy in New York she had met on Facebook.

My woman's intuition had also told me that french fries would help me stop obsessing about what I should do, and since Lola and Hannah don't eat carbs, that left Josh. I was compulsively checking my Sidekick to see if Asher had returned my *We really do need to talk* text when Josh arrived. Every time I had seen him over the last few days I had to take a moment to congratulate myself at how talented I was at this makeover stuff. It would be a lie to say that he was hot, but as I watched him make his way across the restaurant, stopping to say hello to some of the regulars, he could definitely pass for middle-of-the-cafeteria cool now.

"I'm so glad we got you that green hoodie," I said as he sat down. "It really brings out the color of your eyes."

He smiled. "That's funny—someone else just said the same thing."

"Who?"

"Just . . . someone," he replied, starting to blush.

"Are you going to tell me who?" I asked.

He picked up the menu and hid behind it. "There's so much to choose from—do you know what you're going to get?"

I pushed the menu down. "I guess that's a no."

"It's no one you know . . . anymore," he said.

"Fine," I huffed. I was glad that my ability to highlight people's highlights wasn't going unnoticed, but I couldn't help but feel a little left out. If he was going to get compliments, I should be able to share in them. It was *my* doing, after all. If my own boyfriend wasn't going to give me compliments, I needed to get my fill of them somewhere else—even if they weren't necessarily about me. Compliments once removed are still compliments.

"So what's going on with your crush?" I asked a few minutes later as he ate his burger and I picked at my salad with balsamic vinaigrette—I had convinced Du-par's to start offering it to those of us customers who were calorie-conscious. Mimi, our waitress who looked like she had probably been working there since the place opened in 1939, gave me a look when I asked for a double order of french fries, but whatever. I liked to think that contradicting myself like that was part of my appeal. "Did you see her today?"

He nodded as he dipped a fry in the yummy ketchup/mayonnaise combination he always put together.

"And did you talk to her?" I asked, dipping my own while stealing a glance at my phone. No text.

He nodded again.

"And did you ask her if she was going to the party?" I asked, grabbing a handful.

Another nod. When it came to movies and computers, Josh could talk for days, but when it came to talking about this mystery girl? Forget it—he turned into a mute.

"Well, is she?" I asked, looking at the phone. Still nothing.

"She doesn't know. Maybe."

"Well, did you say something like, 'You should go—it would be nice to get to know you better'?"

He turned so pale you would've thought I had suggested that they go to Vegas that weekend and get married at one of those drive-thru chapels. "No. I said that if she did end up going, I'd probably see her there."

"Okay," I said, "obviously we're going to have to do a crash course in how to talk to girls because at this rate you're not going to get a date until you're forty." As Mimi waddled by, I grabbed her arm. "Mimi, we need your help. Sit with us for a second."

Mimi wasn't big on working hard, so I didn't have to ask her twice. "Ahh . . . that feels good," she said as she plopped down next to me in the booth. "My bunions are killing me."

"Now, Josh, I want you to pretend that Mimi here is your crush and I want you to have a conversation with her."

"Awww—I like that. No one's had a crush on me in a long time," Mimi said.

Maybe it was the wart on the right side of her nose, or the fact that up close, her white beehive had a bluish tint to it, but Josh looked like he had just swallowed an under-cooked fry.

"Go on," I said. "You're an artist—you're supposed to have a good imagination."

"I'm not sure what the point of this is," he replied.

That was the thing about guys—they always had to be able to see the point of something. It drove me nuts. "The point is that this way I'll be able to coach you."

"I'm assuming that you're not going to let Mimi get back to work until I agree to do this." He sighed.

"That's okay—I got time. It's almost time for my break anyway," said Mimi, who I could have sworn had just come back from her break since she reeked of cigarette smoke.

"Just give it a try," I said, shaking my phone in case something was wrong with the vibrating thingie that was preventing me from getting any texts.

Josh sat up straight in his seat. "Hi, Mimi," he mumbled.

"Okay, Rule number 432: *no mumbling*," I said. "You want to project *confidence* when you talk to a girl—like you have no doubt that she's been waiting her entire life to be asked out by you. Plus, you don't want her to think you're doing it just so she'll lean forward so you can look down her shirt. Oh, and try to throw in a compliment right away if you can."

"Hi, Mimi," he said loudly, as if he were the worst actor on earth. "You look very nice today. I like that pig brooch you're wearing. The rhinestones make it very elegant."

Mimi and I looked at each other. "You've got your work cut out for you, kid," she said.

"Tell me about it." I sighed.

As the manager walked by, he gave Mimi a dirty look. "I think I gotta get back to work," she muttered.

"Thanks for your help," I replied as she walked away. I turned to Josh. "Okay, Rule number 512: assume that the person you're talking to isn't hard of hearing and that English is their first language. Just try to be *natural*." Maybe *I* should become a director. Or better yet, maybe I could become a makeover/dating coach and write a best-selling book and end up on *Oprah* and then teach a course at the Learning Annex. Forget just focusing on Castle Heights— geeks all over the world should be given the opportunity to take advantage of my knowledge!

"Okay, okay, natural, be natural. I can do that," he said

as he sat up straighter. He was close to hopeless with this stuff, but the way he was trying was really sweet. Geeky, but sweet.

To help him out, I gave him a big smile, the kind I usually reserved for the rare occasions when Asher and I were hanging out alone.

"You have a really great smile," he said quietly, responding with one of his own.

I could feel my face getting warm. I hadn't realized that when Josh looked at someone, he really *looked* at someone. Asher, on the other hand, was usually looking at his phone or the television when he looked at me. "Thanks," I said. "Dr. Fleischman, my orthodontist, was voted Best Orthodontist three years in a row by *Los Angeles* magazine."

"How was that?" he said.

"Huh?"

"The compliment. It didn't come off too smarmy, did it?" he asked, a worried look on his face.

I felt like someone had dumped a glass of ice water on me. So he had been *acting*. Of course. I knew that. "Oh. No. It was good," I said. "Very believable-sounding."

"Cool," he said, relieved. "So what do I do after that?"

I sat up straight and fluffed my hair. "Well, then you just . . . keep being natural. Be yourself."

"That's it? *That's* the secret to talking to girls? Just act natural and be myself?" he asked doubtfully.

"Well, yeah." I shrugged. "But be your *real* self—the

self you are when we're hanging out and you're talking about Woody Allen or Quentin Tarantula—"

"Tarantino," he corrected.

"Whatever. Him. Be *that* guy—the guy who, even though he's really nice, also knows that he deserves to take up space on the planet just as much as the next person." By this time he had taken out a pad and pen was taking notes. "And—"

"Hold on a second, let me finish," he said.

"Josh, you don't need to write this down."

He looked up. "Oh. Sorry."

"And don't say sorry all the time."

He looked down at his sneakers.

"And don't be the guy who looks down at his sneakers all the time because that's totally not sexy," I continued. "Sexy is telling a girl she's got a great smile and having it come out like you really mean it rather than just a line." Until that came out of my mouth, I hadn't realized how true that was. The more I thought about it, the more I realized that everything that came out of Asher's mouth sounded like a line. And not even *well-written* lines.

Josh flipped up his hoodie hood and started pulling the strings so hard I worried he was going to strangle himself. "I don't want you to think . . . I mean, you *do* have a great smile . . ." he mumbled as his face disappeared. "But, you know, with Asher and all, I didn't want you to think I was being, you know, inappropriate by saying something like that . . ." All I could see now were his eyes. "So I . . . you know what? I'm just going to shut up now," he mumbled, slumping down even farther in the booth.

"No. I get it," I said, mumbling myself. Why was I so flustered? It wasn't like I *liked* Josh or anything. I mean, yes, I *liked* him, but I didn't *like him* like him. I liked Asher. I was in *love* with Asher. Well, I was in love with the Asher from sophomore year when we started going out, back when he treated me like a girlfriend rather than one of those impulse accessory buys from a cheesy store at the mall that ends up in the back of your closet after one wearing.

My phone buzzed. *Yeah, wee need to talk,* it said. Like I said, Asher wasn't much on spelling. I could feel my stomach tighten. I pointed at Josh's plate. "If you're done, I should probably get going," I said.

"Sure," he replied, throwing down some cash and taking off his hood. "Thanks for the tutoring."

"You're welcome," I replied with a smile that I knew was fake-looking, but I couldn't help it. For some reason the last few minutes had weirded me out. "I have a feeling you'll do just fine."

And as a group of freshmen-age girls gave Josh not just a second look, but a third and a fourth one as well, as we walked toward the parking lot, I knew I was so right.

When I got into the car and called Asher, he said that he wanted to talk in person rather than on the phone. Asking me to meet him at the Pinkberry on Beverly Drive, I knew, due to my heightened woman's intuition, was *not* a good sign. You only met in public places if you were afraid someone was going to freak out on you.

Like always, Pinkberry was packed with postworkout women and nannies with screaming kids in strollers. And Asher, reading a text on his Treo with his lips moving.

"Hey, babe," I said, wrapping my arms around him. The fact that he was so cute made it really hard to remember all the bad things about him.

"Hey," he said, unwrapping them and moving away from me as if I had a 103-degree fever and had just sneezed in his face.

I pointed at his yogurt, which was covered with crushed Oreos. "That looks good," I said.

He took a big spoonful as a little blonde girl wearing a princess costume at the table next to us smacked her baby brother on the head with her plastic wand and her exhausted-looking mother typed away on her BlackBerry. "It is," Asher said as he took another spoonful.

I waited for him to offer to buy me one, or at least give me a bite, but he didn't. Instead he picked up his Treo again.

I sighed. "So you said you wanted to talk to me about something?"

"Yeah. Hold on one sec, though," he said as he texted. After he was done, he put the phone down and took a crumpled and smudged piece of paper out of his pocket and put it on the table. "Okay, so listen," he said, glancing down at it and smoothing it out, "I've been doing a lot of"—he squinted—"*thinking*. And while you're a great girl, and you're pretty, and you've got a hot body—"

"Thanks, babe," I said, smiling as I reached over and started stroking his arm. Asher may have had trouble communicating, but when he wanted to, he could be very sweet.

"—but I think it's oven," he said, looking down at the paper.

"Huh?"

He squinted. "Sorry—I mean over. I think it's over."

"What's over?" I asked, snuggling closer to him.

As he scooted his chair away from me, my arm slipped and my elbow landed in his yogurt.

"Oh great," he grumbled. "There goes half my yogurt. And I was starved."

"What's over?" I asked again, wiping my elbow with a napkin.

He looked at me. "We are."

The lightbulb went on in my head. "Excuse me, but are you *breaking up* with me?" I fumed. The little blonde girl stared at me with her mouth open.

"Yeah. We've only got a few more months of school left and I just want to play the field, see what else is out there." He glanced down at his cheat sheet. "I'm feeling too tied down."

"Okay. A) It's only the fall so we've got like a million

more months of school left, and Two) How can you feel tied down?" I cried. "We barely even text, let alone hang out together anymore! Ever since the documentary started we haven't hung out together *once!*"

He ate a spoonful of yogurt. "Yeah, but it's like even when you're not there, you're always there. In my space, mon. It's like I can't breathe. Look how close to me you are right now!"

I scooted my chair back. "Fine. Is that better?"

He scooted his own chair back and picked up the Treo and checked the screen.

I yanked the phone out of his hand. "But what about Fall Fling?"

"What about it?"

"It's only three weeks away!"

He shrugged. "You still have some time to find another date. Hey, can I have my phone back, please?"

Dazed, I put it down on the table. "But . . . you're my *boyfriend.* And the plan was to go to college, and then after graduating from college, we were going to move in together, and then three years after that you were going to propose, and then a year after that we were going to get married at the Hotel Bel-Air, and then two years later we'd have our first kid—a boy, hopefully—and then two years after that we'd have our second kid, a girl, and then forty-six years later we'd celebrate our fiftieth wedding anniversary with a huge party at the Hotel Bel-Air again!"

He looked at me like I was insane. "What are you *talking* about?"

"That was the plan!" I cried. "You're screwing up the plan!"

"I want a plan," the little blonde girl whined.

He stood up. "*You're* the one who's screwed up. I don't even know where I'm going to college yet, let alone if I want to be married to someone for fifty years." He patted me on the arm. "Look, you're a great girl—you'll find someone else in no time. I know—why don't you go out with that Josh guy? He's not looking so bad lately."

"I don't *want* to go out with Josh!" I yelled. "I want to go out with *you*! And what about Lisa Eaton's Halloween party? Now I can't go as a nurse."

"Why not?"

"Because you were going to be a doctor. Doctor and nurse go together, Asher," I hissed.

"I want to be a nurse," the girl whined, starting to cry, while her mother yakked away on her cell phone.

I whipped my head around and glared at her. "You're already a princess," I snapped.

Asher gathered up his wallet and keys, and crumpled up his pathetic breakup script. "So you'll go as something else. Wear your cheerleader uniform from last year. You always looked way hot in that."

"I want to be a cheerleader," the girl screamed while her mother continued to talk on the phone.

"I'm not going as a cheerleader," I fumed. "That's so . . . *predictable*."

He shook his head. "You know, I gotta tell you, Dyl, maybe if you spent less time worrying about what you were going to wear to things, this could have worked out."

I couldn't believe the *nerve* of him. Not only was he criticizing me for wanting to sit in the same zip code as him, but now he was all up in my grill about my interest in fashion? "Fine," I said as I stood up. "It's over, then. Oh, and by the way? I'll have you know that *I've* been spending a lot of time questioning whether this was working, too." Yanking his phone out of his hand, I shoved it in the half-full yogurt container. "So I'd like to go on record that *I* broke up with *you* first. Even if it was only in my own mind!"

I stomped to the door and turned back to look at him, but he was more concerned about cleaning his phone than about the bombshell I had just dropped on him. However, the little girl was staring at me.

And then she stuck out her tongue at me.

So I did what any mature high-school senior who had just been publicly humiliated in a yogurt store would do— before sailing through the door, I stuck mine out at her.

As far as I'm concerned there are three situations where a girl is allowed to eat whatever she wants: when she's PMSing, after the series finale of a television show that changed the course of history such as *The O.C.*, and when she's been broken up with. And if the breakup happens only three short weeks before a major school social event? Then she gets to eat whatever she wants times a hundred, especially because chances are she'll be staying home that night so it doesn't matter how much weight she'll gain from pigging out.

Well, not me, of course—*I* wasn't going to be staying home. Since I was a senior and there were only a few more opportunities for me to get dressed up and be crowned with a rhinestone tiara, there was no way I was going to miss Fall Fling. While I wasn't allowed to pig out times a hundred, I *was* allowed to do it times twenty-five. So on my way home, I stopped at Sprinkles for cupcakes, Whole Foods for Nutty Chocolate Surprise trail mix, and the Pinkberry in Westwood for a large green-tea-flavored yogurt with chocolate chips and coconut.

"I know!" I said to Lola and Hannah an hour later as the three of us sat in my bedroom and I licked the white buttercream icing off a cupcake. "I'll tell Nima that *he* can take me." Nima Ghedami had had a crush on me since sixth grade, even back when I looked like Jewish Ugly Betty. For a while he was putting poems in my locker by poets with weird names like Rumi and Hafiz who used the word *soul* twenty times a poem. Maybe Nima was a little strange, but with his dark hair and dark eyes, he was so the opposite of Asher, who looked like a Ken: The Surfer Version doll, that it would allow me to make a very dramatic statement at the dance about the fact that I wasn't kidding when I said I was over him. Fall Fling problem solved, I threw the icingless cupcake in the garbage as I no longer needed to pig out.

Lola shook her head as she took a swig of the tea she carried around with her that her mother's acupuncturist had said would make her boobs grow. "Too late. I heard this morning that he's going with Asie Khohadiffin."

Calling on the five-second rule, I fished the cupcake out of the garbage. "Oh," I said as I finished it. "That's okay. I should probably go with someone who's removed from the whole Ramp crowd anyway." I grabbed another cupcake out of the box and started in on the icing. "I'm sick of these dumb high-school guys—I need an older man. Like someone in college."

"I bet my cousin Ira would take you," said Hannah. "Technically, he's not in college at the moment because he had to take a leave of absence from San Diego State when he had his nervous breakdown, but my mom told me the other day that he's doing so well that they're now giving him weekend passes off the psych ward."

Lola shot her a look like *she,* and not Ira, was the crazy one.

"Well, he *is* nineteen," Hannah said defensively. "That's older."

I took another bite of the cupcake. "Hannah, I love you, but I'm so not in the mood for jokes at the moment." I should have started doing squats to try to burn off the calories, but I was too depressed. Instead I flopped back on my bed. "Seriously, what am I going to do?" I said to the ceiling.

"You could go with Josh," suggested Lola.

I sat up and looked at her. "Um, hello? Did I not just say this wasn't the time for jokes?"

"I'm not joking," she said. "He's totally your friend boy."

"Omigod, he's *so* not!" I squealed. A "friend boy" was someone with whom there was no physical stuff, but it was obvious you were on the path to becoming a couple. "He's definitely just a brofriend," I insisted. That was someone with whom there was no chance of it ever going past the friend stage.

"Whatever it is," said Hannah, "you guys are together like twenty-four/seven."

"I told you—that's because we're *working* together. It's *business*."

Both of them gave me a skeptical look.

"And you made him over," said Lola.

"Okay, fine, so he's become one of my very close friends," I admitted.

"But he's not one of your closest close friends, right?" Hannah asked anxiously.

"Of course not," I assured her. "Anyway, I can't go to a social event with him where there's physical contact involved. He may look a lot better postmakeover, but he's still, you know, *Josh*."

"I think he's cool," said Lola with a shrug.

I looked at her with disbelief. "Um, hi, but weren't you the one who sat there at the nail salon and told me I needed to be careful or else I'd be branded with a scarlet G for 'geek'?"

She shrugged and got up and went to my closet. "I changed my mind," she said as she started going through my things for stuff to borrow. "Geeks are the new jocks. I just read it in *Seventeen*." She looked away. "And his friends aren't as bad as I thought, either."

I threw the now-empty cupcake wrapper away. "Omigod—I *knew* it!" I squealed. "You totally have a crush on Steven."

Lola turned around. "Ew! I do not!" she squealed.

"You so do," I said, reaching for my Sidekick to see if news had spread yet about the breakup. "You should go with him to Fall Fling—not the Guz."

"That's *so* not happening," she replied.

"Ari's not that bad, either," added Hannah. "Do you know that he knows every single word of every single song in *Grease*? Isn't that amazing?"

"Fascinating," I replied. *Not.* "Anyway, even if I did want to go with Josh to Fall Fling, he's asking someone else," I announced.

"Who?" asked Hannah.

"I don't know. He won't tell me."

"Huh. Good for him," Lola replied, coming back to the bed with my favorite jeans and a cute cardigan I had borrowed from Hannah a few months ago. "I hope whoever she is, she says yes. He deserves to be happy."

I looked up from my Sidekick. She looked totally sincere.

My phone buzzed. As I looked at the screen, one condolence text after another started to appear. I couldn't tell if the reason my heart was beating so fast was because of all the sugar I had eaten in the last hour, or because I realized that if I didn't get moving, I was going to be the only one without a date for Fall Fling.

Like I said, for whatever reason, I seem to be a crisis magnet. Maybe it's because the Universe knows I'm super strong and can handle whatever comes my way. At any rate, over the next few days I had to deal with *two* crises: finding a date for Fall Fling *and* finding a costume for Lisa Eaton's party.

By the time I arrived at school the next morning, the halls were buzzing with the fact that I was back to being just Dylan instead of Dylan-and-Asher. Not wanting to get a reputation as one of those girls who trashes her exes, I refused to comment on the situation as I made my way to English class. No one actually *asked* me for a comment, but still, if they had, I wouldn't have given one.

Did u bring your camera? I texted Josh during class while Mrs. Collett droned on about *The Great Gatsby*. Frankly, I didn't know what all the big fuss was about—that lady Daisy in it was so annoying. Talk about a drama queen.

Yeah. Why? he texted back.

B/c I was thinking it might be fun to film me during lunch today now that I'm single . . . u know, when all the guys start hitting me up for Fall Fling, I typed back.

"Okay, so today we have a very special episode of the documentary," I said into the camera later as I sat on The Ramp during lunch. Thankfully Asher was nowhere to be found. Lola said it was because he and his friends had gotten permission from Coach Shelburn to leave campus during lunch to go to McDonald's because they had just won their seventh straight soccer game in a row, but I think it was because he was too emotionally devastated to have to see me. "As everyone now knows, Asher and I are no longer 'Asher and I,'" I continued as Lola filed her nails and Hannah prepped her for SATs even though she had already gotten 2300 on them last time around. "Which means that I am now free to go to Fall Fling with another guy. As you can imagine, being the most popular girl in school, I'm sure I'm going to be flooded with invites by guys who have been wanting to go out with me for years but haven't been able to because I was taken. So I thought that would be nice to get on camera."

"What would be nice to get on camera?" Steven asked.

"Me being asked out!" I replied.

"Oh. Okay," he said.

"So now we'll just sit here and see who comes up to me," I announced, looking around The Ramp. There was Rob Rosen—he'd definitely come up. And so would Brandon Moglen—he'd had a crush on me for ages. And Huck Hirsch would, too, even though there was some buzz that he might be gay.

"Got it," Josh said.

We sat there for a minute, but no one came up.

"Hey, do you think this is going to take long?" Steven asked. "Because I think my blood sugar's falling and if we're going to be here a while I should probably get some protein in me."

"You'll be fine," I assured him. "Everyone's still eating. Once they're done they'll come up."

The guys nodded.

Ten minutes later, everyone was done eating—even Hannah, who's the slowest eater on the planet—and still no one had come up.

"They're obviously a little intimidated," I explained to the camera.

"Yeah, that sounds good," Lola said, without looking up from her magazine.

I turned to her. "What? They are. They're just getting their nerve up." I got up and walked close to the camera. "Sometimes it takes guys a while to talk to girls they like. RIGHT, JOSH?"

He backed up, knocking into Ari, who tripped on one of the cords and went down.

"Omigod, Ari, are you all right?" asked Hannah as she rushed over to him.

"I think so," Ari replied.

Just then Drew Anderson got up from his seat. "Look, there's Drew—he's been crushing on me forever. Hey, Drew!" I called out, waving my hands.

He turned and looked at me. "Oh, hey, Dylan."

"Come here for a second," I ordered.

He walked over, looking at the camera warily like it was going to tackle him to the ground. Drew wasn't the sharpest knife in the drawer—having been on the varsity football team since he was a freshman, he had been hit in the head a few times—but he was cute. In fact, in the right light (like not a lot of light) he was even cuter than Asher.

I twirled a lock of hair around my finger and smiled at him. "So Fall Fling is coming up," I said.

He nodded. "Yeah, it's in a few weeks."

I gave the camera a smile before turning back to him. "So do you have a date?" I asked.

"Well, I was going with Jenny Frankel, but once she heard I had only asked her because Paula Lyons said no, she dumped me for Mark Roberts."

244

"How interesting." I moved a little closer to him. "So you may have heard—Asher and I broke up yesterday."

He moved back a step. "You did?"

"Um, *yeah*," I replied. "It's only, like, *the* biggest thing everyone's talking about today."

"Oh. Not in remedial reading they weren't. They were talking about that sophomore Jackson Posner who announced he wants to get a sex-change operation after college," Drew said.

"Yeah, well, anyway, so because Asher and I broke up, he's no longer my date," I said.

"Oh. Sorry to hear that. You must be bummed. Asher's a rad guy."

I turned to Josh. "You can edit that line out later." Turning back to Drew, I smiled. "Soooo . . . if *you* don't have a date . . . and *I* don't have a date—"

He looked very confused. "Wait, is this a word problem? Because I'm not very good at those 'cause of my dyslexia."

"Never mind." I sighed. "Well, it was nice talking to you," I said, pushing him off to the side.

I looked around the cafeteria. "Okay, who else is there?"

It turned out there wasn't anyone.

I could not believe that I, Dylan Schoenfield, the most popular girl at Castle Heights High School, could not find *one* guy in the senior class to go with to Fall Fling. I must

245

have been even more intimidating than I thought. Not only that, but it used to be that when I walked down the hall from one class to another, people would clear a path. They still did that for Asher, but now I got jostled just like everyone else. Which is beyond rude because I bruise very easily.

But that wasn't even the worst part.

The *worst* part was that all the girls in school were treating me different. Instead of kissing my butt, which is what they had been doing ever since Asher and I started dating, they started treating me like I was normal or something. Like one of the crowd. Instead of "Dylan! Hiiiii!" which is what most of them used to do, now I just got "Oh, hey."

Maybe it was just because, now that I was single, they felt more threatened by me than usual, but for someone who's as sensitive as I am, being treated like that was hard to take.

At least I could count on Lola and Hannah.

"So what are we doing after school?" I asked the next afternoon after lunch as we stood in front of the bathroom mirrors doing our daily postlunch makeup reapplications.

The two of them looked at each other. "Oh. I have plans," said Lola guiltily.

"Me, too," added Hannah, even more guiltily.

I stopped applying my eye shadow. "Plans doing what?" I asked. "We never make plans without running it by each other."

"Dentist," said Lola.

"Doctor," said Hannah.

I put my eyelash curler down on the sink. "Okay, what's going on here?"

Lola stopped applying her eyeliner and sighed. "Okay, we were planning on going over to Montana Avenue to go Fall Fling dress shopping."

"Without me?" I cried.

Lola shrugged. "You already bought three dresses."

"And you don't even have a date," Hannah added.

Talk about stabbing someone with a fork and twisting it.

"*Yet*," I corrected, jabbing the curler at her reflection in the mirror. "I don't have a date *yet*. But I will. Very soon. Anyway, it's shopping—we never go shopping by ourselves! That's, like, prime bonding time!"

"You can come if you want," Hannah said, brushing her straight bob so it was even straighter. "We just thought you might feel left out, seeing that you don't have a date and all."

I dug into my bag for my brush and started brushing my hair with long, hard strokes. "Thanks for the news flash, Hannah, but I heard you the first time you mentioned it."

"So do you want to come?' asked Lola.

"I can't," I said, flipping my head upside down and brushing harder. "I have plans."

"But you just asked what we were doing," said Hannah.

I flipped my head up and shrugged. "I know. But I just remembered I have to be somewhere."

"Where?" asked Lola.

I shoved everything in my bag. "Somewhere." I shrugged. "See you around," I said as I walked out.

I ended up going to The Dell for a little retail therapy, but frankly, I was so depressed that I couldn't even find anything to buy. As I wandered around aimlessly, I thought about how, before I met Amy Loubalu, I used to spend lots of time by myself, mostly sitting too close to the television vegging out on *telenovas*, which are soap operas in Spanish. Not only was being by yourself boring, it was also very lonely.

As I was walking back to the parking lot, I ran into Ashley and Britney Turner.

"Hi, guys," I said.

"Oh, hey, Dylan," Ashley said, barely even looking up from her Sidekick.

"How are you?" I asked.

"Good," they replied in unison.

"Hey, I'm super hungry. Any interest in going over to Du-par's?"

They looked at me like I was crazy. "You mean that pancake place in the Farmers Market?" asked Britney.

I nodded. "Yeah. They have lots of other stuff, too. And amazing fries."

Ashley patted her flat stomach. "Thanks, but I don't want to risk not being able to fit into my Fall Fling dress."

"Oh. Right. I totally get it," I said, mustering a smile.

"We're here to find shoes for Fall Fling," said Britney. "See you at school."

"Yeah. See you at school," I said as they walked away.

I couldn't believe it—these were the same girls that just a week ago would've died to watch me get a cavity filled. But now that I no longer had Asher, or a date to Fall Fling, I was a leopard or something!

Who knew that people could be so shallow?

At least I had three more weeks to work on getting a date— I only had three *days* to get a costume for the Halloween party, so on my way home I stopped at Costumes R Us. Sadly, I quickly discovered that the best ones were pairs, like Romeo and Juliet, Doctor and Nurse, and Fork and Spoon. Not only were all the single ones beyond lame (who on earth wants to go to a party dressed like a cockroach?) but they were super itchy and smelled like mothballs. When I texted Josh to ask if he wanted to pair up costume-wise (unlike Fall Fling, this was just a Halloween party, so it would be okay due to the fact that there was no slow dancing involved), he wrote back that he and Steven and Ari had already gotten their *Star Wars* costumes. Although he did offer to let me join them as Princess Leia, there was no way I was going to wear my hair in two buns on the side of my head because that was just *wrong*. He was going to pick me up, though, so he could film me beforehand and give viewers some insight into what goes into getting ready for a party.

Even though blue is more my color because of my eyes, I finally settled on Little Red Riding Hood. Unfortunately, as I was getting dressed on Friday night, I realized that I had mistakenly grabbed the R-rated rather than PG version of the costume. Unless I wanted to wear leggings underneath my skirt so that my butt didn't show (which would've been almost as much of a fashion faux pas as the Princess Leia hair), I was out of luck.

"Give me two minutes!" I screamed down to Josh, who was listening to a Neil Diamond bootleg with Daddy in the family room. The good news about being the most popular girl in school meant that even though I wouldn't be winning Best Original Costume that night, I was able to whip up a princess costume in moments by pairing the big poufy pink prom dress I had worn when I was a sophomore and went to the senior prom with Jace Gardner (right before Asher and I started dating) with the silver strappy sandals I had worn to last year's homecoming dance and my May Day queen tiara. Unfortunately it was so heavy that it wouldn't stay on and kept falling off to the side.

"So? How do I look?" I asked, straightening my tiara as I click-clacked into the family room, where Josh was holding his Chewbacca head while he and Daddy ate Mallomar cookies.

"Look at you!" Daddy exclaimed. "You look gorgeous, sweetie! Doesn't she look gorgeous, Josh?"

"Mmh-hmh." He nodded with a mouth full of Mallomars.

"You don't think the dress is *too* pink, do you?" I asked them.

"What do you mean 'too pink'?" Daddy asked. "It's pink. Pink is pink."

"Pink is not just pink," I explained. "There are many different shades of pink. There's pale pink, and hot pink, and—"

"So you're going as a May Day queen?" Josh asked.

"No. I'm just your run-of-the-mill princess." I sighed, straightening the tiara again.

"But your crown says 'May Day Queen,'" he said.

"It's not a crown—it's a tiara. And just ignore that part. Like I said, I'm a princess."

He shrugged. "Okay."

I looked at my reflection in the TV screen. "Wait—you think everyone is going to think I'm a May Day queen?" I asked.

"It *does* say that on the crown," Daddy replied.

Guys took everything so *literally*. "It's a tiara," I corrected again as I straightened it.

"Believe me, they'll know you're a princess," said Daddy.

"And if they don't, I have the credit-card bills to prove it. Honey, you look gorgeous. Just get your stuff so you can go. Poor Josh is *schvitzing* to death in that costume."

Josh wiped the sweat off his forehead. "It *is* a little warm." He started scratching at his neck. "Plus, I don't do well with synthetic materials. I hope I don't break into hives."

"Fine." I sighed. "Let's go."

Usually, from the moment I made my entrance at a party, I couldn't catch my breath. *Omigod—Dylan's here! Omigod— Dylan, come sit next to me! Omigod—Dylan, I have to tell you what just happened!* It was like everyone wanted a piece of me. But when we walked into Lisa's, it was like no one even wanted a *crumb* of me, let alone an entire slice. As soon as everyone looked up to see who arrived and saw that it was me, they just went back to their conversations. As if I were just anyone rather than someone. They were probably just intimidated by what an awesome costume I had put together on such short notice, but still, I can't deny that it really hurt.

Glancing around the living room for Lola and Hannah, I finally spotted them near the fireplace. I couldn't see who they were talking to, but from the way they kept throwing their heads back and laughing and the way Lola kept trying to flip her hair (but couldn't because she was dressed as a Chinese princess and her hair was pulled back in a bun with chopsticks holding it in place), I knew it had to be a guy. And imagine my surprise when I walked over there and discovered that it wasn't just "a" guy but *Asher*, of all people.

"Excuse me, but can I talk to the two of you over in the corner, please?" I demanded as they threw back their heads and giggled some more as he told them the story about the time he was an extra in a skateboard movie. I couldn't *believe* he had the nerve to come dressed as a surfer. I mean, talk about wanting to flaunt your hot body to get back at your ex.

They turned and looked at me. "Oh, hi, Dylan," said Lola in the same bored tone she used with her mom.

"Oh, how cute," Hannah said. "You decided to go as a May Day queen." She was wearing one of the long black robes that the girl who played Hermione had worn in one of the *Harry Potter* movies because her uncle worked at the studio that produced it.

"No I'm not. I'm a princess," I corrected.

"But your tiara says 'May Day Queen,'" Asher said, confused.

"Not that I'm talking to you or anything, but I'm well aware of that fact, thankyouverymuch," I snapped. "Girls? Over here, please," I said, marching them over to the corner.

"What's the problem?" Lola asked, not taking her eyes off Asher.

"Um, hi, Rule number 532? No talking to best friend's ex-boyfriend ever?"

She continued staring at him. "How come you never told us he had such awesome pecs?"

"Hello?! Rule number 612: no bringing up his hotness. Plus, he's so just doing that to make me jealous. Especially since he always wears a wet suit when he surfs."

"Hey, Dylan? Can we get some tape?" said a muffled voice.

I turned around to see Josh, now wearing his Chewbacca head, aiming his video camera at me while Ari as C-3PO and Steven as R2-D2 stood nearby.

"Oh. Uh, sure," I said. "Just give me a sec." As I flipped my head over to give my hair some body, my tiara fell off and was promptly stepped on by Deb Eiseman as she walked by in her ski boots. "My tiara!" I cried.

As Josh leaned down to help me pick it up, the weight of his Chewbacca costume pushed him off balance, which made him pitch forward, which made him spill his Coke on my dress, which then made him step on the hem, which, when I stepped back as he moved forward to swipe at it with his Chewy paw, made it rip.

"Whoops," he said. Because of the mask, it sounded more like "Moops."

"My dress!" I cried, grabbing for some napkins and trying to blot out the stain.

He took off his mask. "Sorry about that," he said, grabbing more napkins and blotting as well.

By the time we were done, it looked like I had peed in my pants. Or, rather, my dress.

"I can't believe this!" I said, trying to fit the pieces of my tiara back together. Some girls walked by and snickered. "This is so embarrassing."

"If you want, I think I have some fake blood in my trunk," said Steven. "We could do a *Prom Queen Massacre*-type look."

I gave him a look.

"Or not," Josh said.

I grabbed Hannah and Lola's arms. "Come sit on the couch with me," I demanded.

Lola disengaged herself from my hand and started walking back to the fireplace. "We'll be there in a few minutes. I want to hear the end of Asher's story."

I couldn't believe it—my best friend was ditching me for my ex-boyfriend.

"Fine. Be that way. Come on, Hannah," I said to my *real* best best friend.

She gave me the same guilty look she gave her cat when she was about to push him off her lap and took my hand off her arm. "In a sec. I promise," she said as she turned around and followed Lola.

I turned to Josh and the guys and adjusted my broken tiara. "Can you go film some other people? I'm not really in the mood."

The three of them looked at me with something that looked like pity but I'm sure wasn't because the idea of me being pitied by a group of geeks was as believable as the idea of snow in L.A. "Sure," Josh said. He turned to Steven and Ari. "Why don't you guys go get some footage while I hang out with Dylan on the couch for a while?"

It was nice to know I could still depend on *some* people.

As the two of us sat there watching the crowd, I got to experience what it felt like to be invisible. At first I tried to engage people in conversation, but after the fifth bored-sounding "Oh, hi, Dylan," I stopped trying.

Talk about a fun way to spend a night.

"So is your crush here?" I asked Josh.

He nodded.

"Have you talked to her?"

He shook his head.

"Listen, if I've learned anything in this week of drama, it's that life can change in an instant. I mean, look at me—I went from being the most popular, best-dressed girl at Castle Heights to"—I looked down at the ripped, Coke-stained, tiara-and-friend-less mess I had become—"this. So I really think that you need to go up to her and ask her to the dance."

"You do?"

"Yeah."

"But what about you?"

I stared at him.

Oh. My. God. How could I have been so *dumb* all this time?

How could I have not figured out that the girl that Josh was crushing on was . . . *me*?

Suddenly the movie of the last few weeks with Josh started running through my mind. The way he got all flustered whenever I questioned him about his crush. How, that night I went over to his house for dinner, he was so nervous when he made me roll down the window to tell me that he liked hanging out with me. The way he complimented my smile when I was teaching him to flirt at Du-par's and then pretended that he was just saying it as part of the pretending. The way he shared his fries with me all the time.

Everything clicked into place. Of *course* he was in love with me. Why wouldn't he be? And I, in turn, thought he was a fantastic guy. He just wasn't *my* guy. This was one crisis I just could not handle right now. I took a deep breath and reached for his hand. "Josh, look, I know we got off to a rocky start, but as I've gotten to know you over the last month, I think you're amazing and I now consider you one of my closest friends."

"Thanks," he said, looking confused.

"But as much as I love our conversations, and the way that you never complain while I shop, and all your other great qualities, it's just not there for me."

"What's not there?" he asked, even more confused.

"You know, the physical-attraction thing. I mean, since I made you over, you've definitely become a cutie, but for now I just think that we should stay friends."

The confused look was still there, but I knew it was just to cover up his heartbreak. "Who knows," I continued. "Maybe down the line that'll change"—although I *so* couldn't see that happening—"but for now I don't think so." I patted his hand. "I hope I haven't just completely smashed your heart into pieces." God, it felt good to clear the air. To deal with a problem in the moment instead of letting it turn into a big old elephant in the middle of the room. I could feel my entire body relax. Even my feet, which were killing me because they were stuffed like sausages into my heels.

He scratched at his neck, which was all blotchy from the synthetic fur. "Uh, when I said, 'What about you?' I meant, 'Will you be okay if I leave you here on the couch while I go talk to her?'."

Now I was the one who was confused. "Talk to who?"

"My crush."

"Wait—*I'm* not your crush?"

He shook his head.

I wished I was the one wearing a mask. Between my costume being ruined and being rejected by someone I had just rejected, it hadn't been one of my better nights. "Oh. Well, that's good," I said. "Because if I had been, then, well, we would've had a problem."

"But thanks for saying all that," he added. "Because

I feel the same way. About you being one of my closest friends."

"Thanks," I replied glumly. I guess I had been expecting him to put up a little bit of a fight when I told him I wasn't interested. Any guy would have killed to go out with me. Okay, well, maybe not Asher. And apparently not any of the Fall Fling–dateless guys at my school, but other than them, there were *tons* of guys who I knew would be asking me out soon enough. I waited for Josh to use his debating skills to convince me why I should give him a chance, but he didn't. Instead he reached for a handful of pretzels on the coffee table.

"You're welcome," he said, after he had swallowed. "I have to admit, in the beginning I thought you were just a spoiled rich Beverly Hills girl, but you're not. You're actually very open-minded. Especially when it comes to trying new restaurants."

"Thanks," I replied. I really *was* grateful to have Josh as a friend, especially since it felt like all my other friendships were disappearing as quickly as a killer bargain on a pair of shoes at a Bloomingdale's sale, but for some reason I also felt disappointed. The more I thought about it, the more I realized that Josh was the kind of boyfriend I'd want to have if he wasn't . . . well, *Josh*. I mean, if he were a non-geek. "So I guess that's that."

He looked relieved. "You'll be okay if I leave you here and go talk to her?" he asked, putting his mask back on.

I nodded, reaching for a handful of M&M's. If having

my social status crumble over the last few days wasn't an opportunity to binge, I don't know what was.

"Luck," I said halfheartedly as I reached for more M&M's with my other hand. "But you might want to take the mask off when you get to the asking part."

He nodded. "Mask off when asking. Got it." He reached into the pocket of his costume, I'm sure to make sure he had his inhaler. "I know if it were up to you, I'd leave this behind, but I just can't risk having a full-blown asthma attack in front of her."

I shrugged. "Don't worry about it. Use it all you want." Who was I to be giving anyone dating pointers?

"You're sure you'll be okay here?"

I nodded.

"Thanks, Dylan," he said. "For everything."

I mustered up a smile. "You're welcome."

As I watched him lumber off toward the kitchen, I suddenly felt very much alone. Like it was the first day of fifth grade again and I had just gotten my lunch and was standing at the edge of the cafeteria with no idea where to sit.

I made sure to swipe at the tears that started to fall out of my eyes before anyone could see them.

chapter ten: *josh*

After that weird exchange with Dylan, I needed a little alone time to regroup before I could stand in front of Amy Loubalu without my mask and have her risk laughing in my face when I asked her to go with me to Fall Fling. From what I had seen in movies, people always seemed to gather in the kitchen at parties, but this one was empty, making it the perfect hideout.

I chugged a Red Bull and did some deep breathing in order to lessen my chances of having to take out the inhaler when talking to Amy. I was glad Dylan and I had had that conversation, as it seemed to be something that was weighing on her mind, but I was confused about the way that she had seemed a little disappointed when I told her I didn't like her "that" way.

After my heart rate was close to normal, I tried to do what Mom had learned in her Intro to Manifestation class: fill my brain with visions of Amy and me dancing at Fall

Fling. Or maybe not dancing—maybe just hanging out in the corner talking, which required a lot less coordination and physical effort.

"Hey, Josh," a voice said as I was picturing Amy laughing at one of my jokes.

The manifestation stuff worked because when I turned around, there she was, wearing a pair of black yoga pants and a light blue top that made her eyes sparkle even more than usual.

"Amy. Wow. You're here. Hi," I babbled, holding on to my Chewy head like it was a football helmet. I reached into my pocket for my inhaler, but it wasn't there. I shifted my mask to my other arm and checked the other pocket. Nothing.

My worst fear had come true—I had lost my inhaler.

"Hi." She smiled as she made her way over to the stash of bottled water. "I like your costume."

"Thanks. And I like yours. What are you supposed to be anyway?" I asked, trying to keep the panic out of my voice as I patted my pocket again. It was *just* there a minute ago. It must have fallen out on my way in from the living room. Obviously I couldn't excuse myself and go crawl around on the ground looking for it, but how was I going to talk to Amy if I couldn't breathe? And how was I going to breathe if all I could think about was that there was a chance that I might stop breathing because I didn't have my inhaler?

"A yoga teacher," she replied.

"A yoga teacher! That's so great! Really, really original!" I exclaimed. I cringed when I realized how much I sounded like Fast Eddie, the owner of Good Buys, in his TV commercials that ran on the local cable-access channel.

"Actually, there're three others here tonight," she said.

"Oh," I said, willing myself to keep the exclamation points out of my voice. "I hadn't seen them. But I bet you're the best-looking one. I mean, the best-*dressed* one."

She laughed. "That's very sweet. Thanks, Josh."

"You're welcome," I replied. I tried to think of something to say after that—stupid or unstupid—but nothing came to mind. If I couldn't think of anything stupid or unstupid to say to Amy when we were hanging out in a kitchen, how on earth was I going to be able to take her on a date? And how was I going to take her out on a date without my inhaler, especially since it was most likely being stepped on and crushed into pieces at this very moment? Panicking, I did the only logical thing I could think of: whipped off my glasses, put my Chewy head back on, and stood by the window and watched Mark Berger try to throw Katri Wood into the pool.

"Isn't it hard to breathe with that thing on?" Amy asked.

Ha. If she had any idea of how difficult it was at that moment to breathe *period*.

I turned around. "It's not so bad," I replied as I nervously pulled at the cord on the shade over the window.

"Plus, I thought it would be good for me to practice being in costume so that when I'm a director, I can sympathize with the actors," I explained as I yanked too hard and the shade came tumbling down. "Whoops."

"Here, let me help you," she said, rushing over to help me pick it up.

I couldn't believe I was this close to the girl of my dreams. The two of us squatted on the floor, me trying not to hit her in the face with my paw, and tried to pick up the shade. Even through my mask I could smell her perfume, a delicious combination of vanilla and coconut. Unfortunately I was severely allergic to coconut—a fact that my allergist could vouch for—which is why I started having a sneezing attack.

"Are you okay?" Amy asked after I had sneezed six times in a row.

It was either take off my mask or suffocate to death. As I yanked it off, I prayed to God I didn't have snot running down my face.

"Josh?" I heard her say as I blinked to adjust to the light.

I could feel my lungs constricting from her beauty. "Yeah, I'm fine," I replied with a wheeze, reaching into my pocket for my glasses. Most people, close up, are less attractive because you can see every little mark on their face, but Amy was even *more* beautiful. Her eyes were even more violet than they appeared from far away, and her teeth were as white as a toothpaste commercial. There was even a little pimple, right near her left ear. This made me like her even more, probably because I'm so into gritty realism.

"Good," she said with a smile, taking the shade from me and standing up.

"Oh—I'll do it," I said, standing up so fast I got a head rush from the lack of oxygen in my lungs and had to steady myself against the windowsill until it passed.

"It's okay," she replied, trying to fit the shade back into the grooves.

"No, really—I'll do it," I said, yanking it from her. Here was my chance to show Amy how handy I was so that when we bought a house when my first movie was number one at the box office, she'd feel comfortable that I'd be able to fix things. Or at least hang a picture or two.

Except that I wasn't handy. At all. In fact, as hard as I tried, I couldn't fit the shade into the grooves. I turned to her. "I think it's better to just let Lisa's parents deal with it when they get home, don't you?"

"Yeah, you're probably right," she agreed as she started throwing all the empty water bottles and soda cans that were on the counter into the recycling bin. That made me like her even more. Not only was she considerate and neat, but she cared about the environment.

"So are you going to Fall Fling?" she asked as she wiped down the counter with a sponge.

I was so busy trying to force myself to breathe that I almost didn't hear the question. But when it did register, I froze. With those seven words, my whole plan of attack for asking her to the dance had gone up in smoke. Not that I had had much of a plan, or any plan for that matter, but I did know that *I* was supposed to be the one to bring up Fall Fling—not her. On my report card in first grade my teacher had written, *While Josh is a very conscientious student (especially in math) and good about sharing with others, he is prone to fits of anxiety whenever previously announced plans and ways of doing things are altered.* Obviously I hadn't evolved much in eleven years.

"Am I going to Fall Fling," I repeated. "Well, at the moment, uh, no, I'm not. But that could change. If, you know, I asked someone. But I haven't asked anyone. Yet."

She gave me a weird look. "Are you okay?" she asked. "Your face . . . it's really red."

"I'm fine," I replied. "I have asthma."

She nodded. "That's right. I've seen you with your inhaler."

"Yeah, well, I lost it," I said. "The inhaler, I mean." *And my mind*, I wanted to add.

"That's too bad. My sister has asthma, so I know how scary that can be."

I just knew my hunch that she was a compassionate person had been right.

I shrugged. "Well, I try and do my best to get through

it." I went over to the refrigerator and started examining it like I was on an archaeological dig and had never seen one before in my life. "So, uh, you going to Fall Fling?"

She started examining the stove. "No," she replied. "I haven't been asked."

I couldn't have asked for a better opening, so I turned to her. After taking a moment to smooth my mask-head (like hat-head, but worse), I cleared my throat. "Well, there's still three weeks. I'm sure someone will ask you." The minute the words left my mouth I wanted to crawl into the dishwasher. "I mean, you're smart, and nice . . . and . . . *pretty* . . . " I trailed off.

It was probably my imagination, but I thought I saw her face fall. "Thanks, Josh. I appreciate that."

"You're welcome." I couldn't believe I had wimped out like that. I bet if I had had my inhaler, I wouldn't have.

"I think I should go find Whitney," she said.

"Oh. Okay. It was nice talking to you."

"You, too," she said as she left the kitchen.

I put my mask back on before I started banging my head against the wall in order to cushion the blow, but it didn't stop me from thinking that I was the biggest idiot not only in all of Los Angeles, but also California, the United States, and possibly the entire galaxy.

If Dylan found out that I had blown my chance like that, I'd never hear the end of it, so I spent the next ten minutes slumped in a corner of the laundry room drowning my sorrows in a box of Cinnamon Life cereal that I had found in the pantry.

"There you are," said an out-of-breath Steven. "Dude, I've been looking everywhere for you. What are you *doing* in here?"

I held up the cereal box.

He looked into the almost-empty box. "Trying to commit suicide by ODing on fiber?" he asked.

"Something like that," I said miserably.

He grabbed me by my furry arm. "You gotta hurry, bro. Dylan's totally freaking out and keeps asking for you. Lola and Hannah are trying to calm her down, but she says she won't talk to anyone but you. I went ahead and took the camera out and Ari's shooting it now."

I struggled to my feet. "What happened?"

"I don't know. The most I could make out was that it's something about Fall Fling," he said as we ran into the living room after we got Steven unjammed from the doorway.

Sitting on the couch where I had left her, stuffing her face with M&M's, Dylan looked like the star of *Prom Queen Massacre*. The half of her tiara that was left was tangled in her hair and swinging back and forth as big mascara-gloppy black tears fell down her face.

"There you are," she said with her mouth full between hiccupy sobs.

"What happened?" I asked as I glanced around at the pockets of people staring at her and whispering.

She held out the dish of M&M's. "Do . . . you . . . want . . . some?" she hiccuped.

"I think I'm good," I answered.

She grabbed another handful and shoved them in her mouth. "Can . . . we . . . go . . . now?"

"Sure," I said. I turned to Ari, who had the camera rolling. "Put that down," I hissed.

"Dude, but this is *awesome*," Steven whispered back. "This is exactly what we need to give this thing some life. Otherwise it's yawn city." When it came to movies, Steven was all about gross-out scenes and car crashes.

"No—keep it going," Dylan ordered as she stood up and stepped out into the middle of the room. "I've given my *life* to this high school," she said, reaching down the front of her dress to snake out part of her tiara, "and to now be pushed aside like a carton of soy milk with an expired date? *That's* the thanks I get for being such a great role model?" she yelled.

"That's what you get for being so snobby," someone called out.

It was so quiet you could've heard a DVD drop.

She whipped around. "Who said that?" she snapped.

A bunch of masked faces stared back at her, many of them trying not to laugh.

"We go to one of the best schools in the city," she continued. "You would've thought that kids here would have been taught some manners. But no!"

"Dylan, are you okay?" I asked.

269

"Of *course* I'm okay!" she yelled with as much dignity as someone wearing a ripped, Coke-stained prom dress and half of a broken tiara could muster.

I grabbed the camera from Ari. "Come on, Dylan," I said, leading her toward the front door. As we walked, she clutched my hand so hard my circulation was cut off. No one said anything, but I could feel a hundred eyeballs on my back. At that moment I really wished I had had my inhaler. Not for me, but to give to Dylan. Although I'm sure she would have thought that was disgusting.

Right before we got to the door, I heard her dress rip even more. "I think I have a pair of sweats in the car," I whispered.

She squeezed my hand ever harder. "Thanks," she whispered back. You had to give the girl some credit— even though everyone was looking at her and trying not to laugh, she managed to keep her head high.

The minute we got outside she plopped down on the porch swing and began crying again.

"Are you going to tell me what happened?" I asked.

She nodded, but didn't say anything.

"Are you thinking of telling me now, or do you want to wait until next week?"

She wiped her nose with her dress. "Asher just asked someone to Fall Fling," she hiccuped.

Ouch. That was a bummer. I could only imagine how I would've felt if I had found out that Amy had gotten asked.

Then again, it *was* Asher. And he *was* the most popular guy in school—of course he was going to snag a date. Unlike, say, me. "I'm sure that must suck, but didn't you sort of expect that was going to happen?" I asked gently.

She turned to me and burst into tears again. "I didn't expect him to ask Amy Loubalu!" she wailed.

My heart stopped. I didn't have to wonder how I'd feel if Amy got asked—the answer was devastated. "He asked Amy Loubalu?"

"*Yessss,*" she cried, rubbing her face on my shoulder to wipe away her tears and leaving black skid marks.

I patted her on the arm. I felt like the scene in the movie *About Last Night* starring Rob Lowe and Demi Moore where Demi Moore's roommate, played by Elizabeth Perkins, sits there consoling her after Rob Lowe breaks up with her. Except Dylan and I weren't roommates, and I wasn't a girl.

I *did* know what it felt like to have your heart broken, though.

She looked up at me. "You're such a good friend." She sniffled.

"I am?" I asked, still mechanically patting her arm.

"Yeah. You look like *you're* going to start crying, too, to support me."

"Oh. Well, it's a real bummer," I replied. A *real* bummer. Like the worst-possible-thing-I-could-have-ever-imagined-happened-level bummer.

Du-par's is good for your everyday run-of-the-mill burgers, but for special occasions—happy or sad—then a trip
to The Apple Pan is worth the drive.

Not surprisingly, Dylan had never been to The Apple
Pan. From the outside it wasn't much to look at—it looked
like a ramshackle shack. And with its scratched wood
floors and ripped vinyl seats it wasn't much to look at
inside either, but so what? It had incredible hickory burgers
with barbeque sauce and the world's best banana-cream
pie. That was the problem with this city—everyone judged
people, places, and things by their outsides rather than
their insides. I was under the impression that Amy was
different, but if she was going to Fall Fling with Asher, obviously she wasn't. Sure, she may have thought I had nice
eyes, or good taste in movies, but at the end of the day
she was probably just like every other girl who had grown
up reading fairy tales and wanted to go off into the sunset
with a Surfer Ken doll–looking prince rather than a four-
eyed film geek. It didn't matter that I could list the title
and year of every Woody Allen movie or the soundtrack
listings of Quentin Tarantino's films. Living in L.A., I was
always going to come up short next to guys like Asher.

"The first movie I make when I get out of film school
as part of my three-picture deal with Warner is going to be
an *anti*-fairy tale," I announced as I dragged a fry through
some barbeque sauce. I was so depressed I couldn't

muster up enough energy to make one of my special dipping concoctions.

"What are you talking about?" asked Dylan as she wiped barbeque sauce off her still-dangling tiara. Most of the UCLA students who were chowing down around us were also dressed for costume parties, so we didn't look too out of place. We were, however, the only morbidly depressed ones.

"Nothing. Never mind," I said glumly.

"I can't believe that out of all the girls at Castle Heights, Asher had to ask Amy," she said for what had to be the third time in five minutes.

"Tell me about it," I said with a sigh.

"I mean, he *knows* how I feel about her—"

"Yeah, how *do* you feel about her?" I asked, dragging another fry through the sauce.

She put her burger down. "Well, I hate her."

"Yeah, that part I know. But what exactly happened with you guys?"

As she tipped her chocolate milk shake back, a glop of ice cream fell on her dress, but by this time she was such a mess that she didn't even try to wipe it off. Instead she just picked the glop up and put it in her mouth. "Michael Rosenberg is what happened with us."

I shifted in the booth so that the couple dressed in salt-and-pepper costumes two booths away making out weren't in my sightline. It was too depressing to see people who were in love at the moment. "Who's Michael Rosenberg?"

"A guy who goes to Buckley," Dylan explained, attempting to use her straw as a fork and now eating her shake. "She stole him away from me in eighth grade."

"What happened?" Salt and Pepper were now going at it big-time, so I angled myself in my seat again.

"What happened was that after talking to him for fifteen minutes at Kate Lieberstein's bat mitzvah, I fell madly in love with him and became obsessed with getting him to be my boyfriend," she replied. She hid her face in her hands and opened her fingers so one eye was peeking out. "I can't believe I'm admitting this, but I even used Daddy's credit card to buy an e-book called *Love Spells by Larissa* on Amazon."

"*Love Spells by Larissa*?" I repeated, trying not to laugh.

She smiled. "Don't laugh."

"I'm not laughing," I said, almost laughing.

"But you're about to laugh," she said.

"No I'm not," I lied, about to laugh.

"Well, obviously it didn't work, because instead of asking *me* out, he asked *her* out. Total waste of twenty-two ninety-five."

At that, I let myself laugh. "Did she say yes?"

"Oh yeah. And they dated all spring and summer until the beginning of freshman year. It wasn't like they saw each other in person a lot because Michael spent the summer on a teen tour in Israel, but still—everyone knew they were together."

Salt and Pepper were now almost lying down in the booth. I wanted to scream *Get a room!* but I didn't. "Did she know that you had liked him?"

Dylan started in on my fries. "Did she know?! She was the one who made me download the e-book!"

"Oh." This didn't sound like the Amy I knew, but I guess everyone had their dark side. "Well, did you try and talk to her about it?"

She starting mixing the barbeque sauce with some mayonnaise and nodded. I was glad one of us was able to still function. "Yup. And she told me that because I had only talked to him for fifteen minutes, it wasn't like he and I had been in a relationship or anything and that I was over-reacting. But here's the thing: when you've met your soul mate, it doesn't matter if you talk to them for fifteen or fif-teen *hundred* minutes—you just immediately know."

I sighed. That's how it had been in the kitchen that night—within five seconds of our conversation, I had just *known* that Amy was the girl I was supposed to spend my life with. "But you always used to say that Asher was your soul mate," I said. "In fact, I think I have it on tape a few times."

"Yeah, well, we won't be using that footage." She shrugged. "He was—at least until he broke up with me the other day—but that's only because Amy had stolen

275

Michael away from me. If she hadn't, then Michael would've been my soul mate and I wouldn't have had to settle for Asher."

Salt and Pepper finally got up to leave. Salt's lipstick was smeared to the point where she looked like ketchup had exploded on her. "Is that how it works?" I asked. "Soul mates are based on availability? Like back before Netflix, when you still had to go to Blockbuster and if they were out of *Godfather II*, then you'd just have to settle for *Herbie Rides Again*?"

She took another handful of my fries. "Kind of. Omigod—with my crisis, I didn't even get a chance to ask you what happened with your crush! So did you ask her?"

I shook my head.

"How come?"

"I . . . didn't get a chance." Not *entirely* a lie. If Amy hadn't walked away and we had stood there for another ten days, maybe I would've screwed up the courage to go through with it.

"That's too bad. Are you going to do it on Monday?"

"I think she might already be going with someone else," I replied.

"You *think* she's going with someone else, or you *know*?"

"I think I know."

She shook her head. "That's not good enough. You have to find out for sure." She reached for my hand. "You have to do it, Josh. You have to take a risk. I may have just been betrayed and humiliated in front of the entire senior class because I took a chance on love and then lost everything in the breakup, but that doesn't have to be your story." She squeezed my hand. "You're a *great* guy and any girl would be lucky to be your date for Fall Fling. I mean, I'd go with you, but like we talked about earlier, I just don't think of you like that."

I slumped down in the booth. "I don't know—the more I think about it, the more I wonder if I even want to go. It's just a stupid school dance. Plus, I think I remember reading that *Rocky*'s playing at the New Beverly that night—"

She shook her head. "I just don't get it. When it comes to movies, and going after your dreams, you're totally fearless. But when it comes to girls? Total wimp."

I slumped down farther. She wasn't wrong.

"Seriously, Josh. Don't be such a geek—just ask her out already."

"But I am a geek," I corrected.

She shook her head. "No—you *were* a geek, once upon a time, but now you're not. Okay, remember that scene in *Say Anything* when John Cusack calls the girl up and asks her out?"

"You've seen *Say Anything*?" I asked, shocked.

She rolled her eyes. "Of course I've seen *Say Anything*. Everyone's seen it. It's only on HBO like every other hour."

"Cameron Crowe is one of the greats." I sighed. It was obvious from the raw authenticity of all his movies—from *Say Anything* to *Almost Famous* and everything in between—that he had intimate knowledge of what it was like to pine away for girls and be rejected.

"Yeah, whatever. Anyway, be him—be John Cusack and just do it," she pleaded. "I can't know for sure, because you won't tell me who it is, but I have a feeling that because of your good judge of character, whoever this girl is, she's probably really nice and sweet and would love to go with you."

If she only knew. I couldn't even begin to imagine what she'd do to me if she found out I was in love with the enemy.

The next week at school I went to any length to avoid Amy, even ducking into the janitor's closet on Wednesday between fourth and fifth period. I hadn't had a chance to replace my inhaler yet, but steering clear of Amy had drastically lessened any risk of asthma attacks.

Maybe I *was* a wimp. But so what? I was an artist—I was allowed to be wimpy, and moody, and stuff like that. I didn't need to have different life experiences, like dates and school dances and girlfriends, in order to make my art—reading about it would be enough.

But on Thursday I was forced to have a life experience.

"Pizza or turkey pot pie?" demanded Harriet, the lunch lady with the three stray hairs on her chin, when I stood in line in the cafeteria debating between pizza that looked like it had been run over by a truck and left under hot lights for three days and something that looked like cream-of-mushroom soup.

"I'm still deciding," I replied.

"Hey, Josh?"

I turned and felt the blood drain from my face. Amy was standing there with her grilled cheese sandwich and carrots.

"Hey, Amy," I mumbled, unconsciously patting my pocket for my phantom inhaler. "How are you?" It was like that scene in *Annie Hall* that had made Dylan cry—the one when Alvy and Annie ran into each other at the movie theater; that horrible feeling of seeing someone you had once loved who no longer loved you.

"I'm good. I haven't seen you at Mani's recently."

I continued staring at my lunch choices. "Yeah, I've been kind of busy with . . . stuff and other stuff," I said to the pizza. "You know, stuff like that." With a vocabulary like that, Dylan was right: I should stick to directing other people's scripts rather than writing my own.

She nodded. "Well, I was just going to say, if you had a sec I wanted to talk to you about something."

I looked at Amy like she had just told me she was pregnant and I was the baby daddy. What could she possibly have to say to me? "Hi, Josh, I just wanted to tell you that, unlike you, Asher isn't a wuss and has the guts to ask someone to a dance, which is why I'm going to Fall Fling with him and not you"?

279

"C'mon, kid, it's not an SAT question—pizza or turkey pot pie?" demanded Harriet again.

I ignored Harriet "Uh, yeah, sure, but can we do it some other time?" I said to Amy. "I need to eat and then . . . go set up the chairs for the mock revolution we're having in Russian class." It was a good thing I was in the make-believe business and could therefore come up with such an authentic-sounding excuse on the spot.

Again, it was probably my imagination, but like that night in the kitchen at Lisa's party, her face fell and some of the glow dimmed. "Yeah, seeing that, you know, we both go to school here, I'm sure we'll run into each other at some point," I said.

"I'm going to make your decision for you," said Harriet. "You want pizza."

I stopped and turned to see not only Harriet looking annoyed, but a line full of hungry students. "Okay," I said meekly before turning back to Amy.

"So maybe I'll see you around," Amy said. "Or maybe not."

"Yeah. Maybe." I tried to think of something else to say, but I had obviously used up all my words. When I got home I was going to check on WebMD to see if there was a name for the syndrome where you rambled on and on when you were nervous.

"Bye, Josh."

"Bye, Amy."

As she walked away, Harriet slid my pizza toward me, clucking her tongue. "Maybe next time, Romeo," she said.

Yeah, maybe. But probably not.

"Dude, what's your problem?" Steven asked on Saturday afternoon. We were sitting in my living room getting ready to watch the rough cut that he had edited together of the footage we had so far. "Just go up to her and see what she wants. Maybe she's heard how awesome the doc is and wants to invest in our next one so she can get a producer credit and come to the Sundance Film Festival with us."

"I just feel so stupid," I admitted. "I just keep wondering what would have happened if I had asked her before Asher did . . . "

Steven held up the DVD. "Listen, my friend, once you see this, you're going to forget all that and instead just focus on your career and the fact that DreamWorks and Paramount and every other studio in town will be *begging* you to leave USC early and come make movies for them."

I sighed. Maybe Steven was right—if I swore off love now and made the decision to put all my energy into my career now, not only would it save me a lot of heartache, but it would probably earn me a few extra Oscars. Plus, I felt like I had been neglecting the documentary the last few days because I had been too busy replaying the scene with Amy in the kitchen at the party over and over in my head, wondering what I could have done differently so that she would be going to Fall Fling with me and not Asher.

After we watched the cut, I was silent.

"Awesome, right?" he said, shoveling sunflower seeds into his mouth. "So awesome that you're speechless."

"No, I'm speechless because it's so . . . *wrong.*" He had made Dylan out to be a completely self-involved, spoiled brat. In almost every scene she was yelling at someone, or fixing her makeup, or checking out her hair in the mirror. Granted she did do that stuff more than your average person, but it wasn't *all* she did. "What do you think we're doing here?" I demanded angrily.

He sat back and let out a huge burp. "What do you mean?"

I opened up the disk drive and yanked out the DVD so hard it almost went flying across the room. "This isn't supposed to be the Beverly Hills version of *Cops,*" I said angrily. "This is supposed to be a fair and balanced documentary."

He rolled his eyes. "Yeah, but, dude, that's so *boring.* Listen, I sat here and watched all the footage, and frankly, it was like watching paint dry. People don't want to see that the most popular girl in school is actually a decent human being—they want to see drama, and backstabbing, and meltdowns. That's what *sells.* Have you never seen reality TV?"

"But I'm not trying to sell this—I'm using it to get into college."

"Yeah, but come on, given the choice, USC would rather admit students who are going to graduate and go on to make blockbusters—not do-good documentaries that play at some small film festival in Washington state to an audience of seven. The blockbuster people are the ones that'll give them big donations later on in life. Like to build indoor swimming pools and stuff."

"I don't *care* about having a stupid swimming pool in my name!" I retorted.

He shrugged. "If you make enough blockbusters, maybe you could build an entire gym."

"Okay, that is so off point!" I yelled. "And what about the stuff from the ZBT party after she threw up—how did you get that? And why does it look like it was taken from five miles away?"

He smiled proudly. "I know—isn't it great? I had Ari do it when you were running around looking for paper towels. Listen, I know this is your movie and all, but I also knew that you'd be seriously bummed later on if we passed that stuff up. Because I'm your co-executive producer, I did you a huge favor."

"But you make her out to be a total diva!"

He shrugged. "Hey, there's some do-good stuff in there that shows her in a decent light," he said defensively.

"Like what?"

"Like . . . that shot where she's petting the puppy on Robertson Boulevard while she's holding all those shopping bags? Audiences *love* watching people be nice to animals—especially puppies. *Huge* crowd-pleaser. And when she gave the homeless guy at The Dell a dollar? Talk about giving back to the world."

"Yeah, but what about that shot of her I got when I was leaving her house that night after the UCLA party?" I asked. "The one where she's standing at the front door waving and the way that the moonlight hits her makes her look so small and frail and sad, like a character out of a French film? I can't believe you left that out."

"Bo-ring," said Steven.

I put the DVD in its case. "Look, I know Dylan can be a little . . . difficult at times—"

"Like that day she freaked out on me when we were shooting her at the nail place and she asked me to bring her a bottle that was pale pink and it turned out there were about seventy-five pale pinks to choose from, so I grabbed five of them and none of them were the right one?" he replied. "Dude, you're so lucky I restrained myself from including that in the cut because, I'm telling you, people would so despise her if they saw that—"

"Come on, give her a break—she had major PMS that day."

He laughed. "Hey, Mr. Fair and Balanced Documentary Filmmaker, what happened to telling the truth? *That's* the truth. Just like the puppy part is the truth."

Maybe I had lost my objectivity over the course of filming. But I had found that this popularity thing and, more importantly, Dylan, wasn't black and white. It was gray. I knew that underneath the shiny blonde hair and designer clothes and brand-new BMW was a girl who still thought of herself as that curly-haired, metal-mouthed fifth grader who wore the wrong jeans and carried the wrong back-pack and had a poster of a kitten hanging from a tree that said HANG IN THERE on her bedroom wall. I knew that when she was stressed out, she ate a lot, and that she hated to be left alone in her house. I knew that Indian food made her burp a ton, and that she hummed sappy love songs, like the kind you'd hear at the dentist, while she ate, always off-key. I knew that part of why she was putting off doing her college essays was that she had no clue as to what she wanted to be when she grew up. And that her biggest fear was that she wasn't good at anything other than shopping. And that she was just as confused as the rest of us when it came to muddling through Life 101. That's what I wanted to show with this documentary—that at the end of the day, there really *wasn't* all that much difference between prom queens and film geeks. That we were all just people.

I stood up and pointed toward the door. "Okay, I'm the director here—not you. So can you please leave so I can get to work?"

He shrugged. "Fine," he said as he stood up. "Be that way." He walked to the door. "Maybe me and Ari will just do our *own* documentary."

I didn't even reply. I just sat down at my desk, cracked my neck, and pulled up iMovie on my computer so I could get to work. I just knew there was a way to strike a balance in this documentary. Kind of like Annie in *Annie Hall*—sure, she was neurotic and annoying, but she was also funny and cute. Dylan was my Annie, and I would work day and night if needed to show the world how deep and multi-layered she was. Okay, maybe deep and multilayered was pushing it. I could at least show that while she had her moments, she wasn't a drama-queen diva 24/7.

chapter eleven: *dylan*

That Saturday night was the first one since eighth grade when I didn't have plans. Ever since the Halloween party Lola and Hannah had been calling me less and less often and whenever I asked them what they were doing I'd get a guilty-sounding "Uh . . . nothing." It was like overnight it had gone from DylanLolaandHannah to just LolaandHannah. I was still sitting on The Ramp with them, but just last night I had had a horrible nightmare where I was physically removed from our table by members of the football team and Amy Loubalu took my place.

Rather than sit at home, morbidly depressed, I decided to be productive and go through all the photos I had of me and Asher, as well as the pictures of me in my various princess and queen crowns, and think back on how things used to be before tragedy had struck my life.

After a half hour of sniffling and wiping my nose on the sleeve of Daddy's Northwestern sweatshirt while flipping through pictures of what I had *thought* were good times, but now realized weren't (like me standing on the beach in Malibu rubbing my head after Asher had inadvertently hit me on the head with his surfboard, or me with a big smile on my face hugging him from behind while he leaned away from me and sent a text, or me sitting on his lap next to Lola's pool while he stared at Lola's sister in her bikini), I wiped my nose for the last time and turned off the "Dylan-N-Asher 4ever" playlist I had going on my iPod.

"What am I doing?" I said aloud. "Asher's a loser."

I had seen too many movies about how you were supposed to act after a breakup. The truth was, I wasn't that broken up about it. He *was* a loser, and it was time to stop wallowing. No more moping for me—I was moving on.

I picked up the phone and dialed.

"Hey, Josh," I said.

"Hey. What's up?"

"Where are you?" I asked. Wherever he was, it was super loud.

"Outside the New Beverly with Raymond getting tickets for the Spielberg double feature."

"That sounds . . . fun," I said. I started cutting out Asher's face from the previously framed pictures of the two of us that had been all around my bedroom.

"What are you doing?"

"Nothing." I sighed. "Just hanging out. Alone. By myself."

"Oh."

I waited for him to say something else but he didn't. "Well, I'll let you get back to having fun with Raymond," I finally said. "While I just sit here and hang out. Alone. By myself."

I thought I heard him sigh, but I'm sure it was just my imagination. "Do you want to come meet us?" he finally asked.

"That would be great," I said brightly. "Hey, what movies are they showing?" Not even bothering to change out of my sweats, I shoved my feet into my sneakers and grabbed my bag. Ever since the Halloween party, my interest in fashion had dropped drastically, which, according to most magazines, was a telltale sign of depression. I did, however, grab a baseball cap from the top of my closet since I hadn't washed my hair in two days.

"*Jaws* and *Duel*," he replied.

"Never heard of them. Do you think I'll like them?"

"No," he said doubtfully.

"Oh. Well, are there any cute boys there?"

"I'm pretty sure the answer to that is negative," he replied.

"That's okay. I should probably take a break from guys for a while anyway," I said, switching handbags to match my sweats. I may have been depressed, but I wasn't suicidal.

"That sounds like a good idea. I'll see you in a little while."

"Hey, Josh?"

"Yeah?"

"Thanks for inviting me to join you," I said. "You're a really good friend."

"Not a problem."

Before I walked out the door, I stopped in front of the mirror in the hall and readjusted my hat. Even though Josh said there probably wouldn't be any cute guys, you never knew.

However, in this case, he was one hundred percent right. Even premakeover Josh would have been considered Calvin Klein underwear model–hot compared to these guys. In addition to rumpled khakis and Mom jeans, everyone there was wearing either a T-shirt with the name of a movie I had never heard of before in my life (a bunch of them seemed to like something called *Taxi Driver,* whatever that was) or one with a *Lord of the Rings* character. Maybe if I had been in the right frame of mind I would've looked at it as a way to work on my hobby, but I just found the whole thing depressing. Not because they were so fashion-challenged, but because I no longer felt like I fit in anywhere.

"Hey, guys," I said after I made my way through the Eau de Seventeen-Year-Old Sweaty Boy crowd.

"Hey, Dylan. You remember Raymond, right?" asked Josh.

"Well, hello there, Dylan," the guy I had met when I went to pick up Josh at work said in a smooth-jazz-radio-station-sounding voice as he planted a slimy kiss on my hand. "Aren't you looking lovely this evening."

"Thanks," I said as I wiped my hand on my sweats.

Josh gave me a weird look.

"What?" I asked.

"Nothing. I've just never seen you so . . . "

"Dressed down?" I suggested.

"I guess that's one way of looking at it," he replied.

Raymond took a step toward me and sniffed the air loudly. "That's a lovely scent you're wearing. I seem to detect notes of tuberose and gardenia, a combination that seems to work quite well with your particular body chemistry."

"Really? It must be leftover perfume because I haven't showered since Thursday," I said.

He leaned in so close I could smell his own cologne, which resembled a combination of Lysol and cinnamon. "I'd even go as far as to say that for someone who just got pink-slipped in the love department, you look positively ravishing."

"Thanks. I think," I replied.

Josh started steering me toward the entrance. "Okay, time to go in," he said.

It turned out he was right—I didn't like the movies. One was about a giant shark that terrorizes a beach community and the other was about a giant truck that terrorizes a guy driving a car. I'm sorry, but why these movies were considered classics was beyond me. I mean, *The Devil Wears Prada* and *The Nanny Diaries* were *so* much better. At least they were based on reality.

After the movie, we went to Du-par's. It was strange to see it filled with pimply teenage guys instead of senior citizens and their walkers. "So, Dylan, I heard about the unfortunate turn of events in regards to that intramural school social event that's coming up," said Raymond, chewing his tuna sandwich with the crusts cut off.

"Huh?"

"The Fall Foliage dance."

"Fall Fling?"

"Correct," said Raymond as he carefully lined up his fries on his plate.

"Hey, Raymond, why don't we talk about something else?" Josh suggested. "I'm sure Dylan would like to hear all about the horror script about the killer clowns that you've been working on for years—"

"No thank you," I said as I shoved a bunch of fries into my own mouth.

"Josh, I find it rude to talk about myself and my achievements on the first date," Raymond said.

I may have been desperate, but I wasn't *that* desperate. "This isn't a date," I chimed in.

"Technically you're right—it's not," he replied. "But I'm feeling as if we're on our way to one," he said with a wink.

At least I *think* he was trying to wink, but it looked more like he was having a seizure.

"Is he for real?" I whispered to Josh.

"Unfortunately, yes," he said, sliding down in the booth.

"Dylan, forgive me for being so bold here," said Raymond, "but what's your stance on May-December romances?"

"May what?"

"Relationships where one partner is significantly older than the other. Listen, I'm not one of those people who beats around the bush. You can ask anyone at Good Buys—when something's on my mind, I have no problem saying it. And the fact of the matter is that I'm very attracted to you, Dylan, and I'd say that from what I've observed in your body language this evening and from that time you came by the store, the feeling is mutual. Therefore, even though I'm twenty-three, I'd very much like to escort you to your upcoming dance."

I turned to Josh and gave him a panicked look, but he didn't see it because his head was in his hands.

"Obviously, a few heads may turn because of the age difference between us," Raymond continued, "but you strike me as a trailblazer and someone who doesn't buckle under the weight of social conformity, so I'm thinking you can handle what might be viewed as a potential scandal." He grabbed my hand across the table. "So what do you think? Are you up for it? Are you ready to take another chance on love so soon?"

I knew life could change in an instant, but is *this* what mine had come to? That the only date I could get for Fall Fling was a twenty-three-year-old guy with adult acne who used more SAT words than I could remember even learning in SAT review class? How had this happened? Maybe my karma really *had* gotten screwed up in some previous lifetime.

"Uh—" I began.

"She'd love to, but she and I already have plans to hang out that night. We're going to have a Woody Allen film festival. Right, Dylan?"

I turned to him and smiled with relief. "Right." So maybe it wasn't the Fall Fling evening I had been dreaming about, and obviously I wouldn't be adding to my crown collection, but, hey, I'd be with my best friend rather than stuck at home by myself. Not to mention that it took the pressure off having to decide between the three dresses I had bought for the occasion.

"So you really want to hang out the night of Fall Fling?" I asked Josh later on the phone as I continued going through photos. After dumping the ones of me and Asher in the garbage, I started organizing the ones of me by school dance. I held up one of me surrounded by May Day court. I couldn't believe there was a time I had been so happy.

"Sure. Why not?" he replied. "I mean, you know, if *you* do."

"Yeah. Sure. That is, if *you* do," I said. Something was weighing on my mind but I didn't know exactly how to bring it up. "Okay, so I need to ask you something," I finally said.

"What?"

"I know we already talked about this at the Halloween party, but I just want to make sure it's not going to be . . . a *date* or anything like that," I confessed. "I mean, I've seen a lot of movies where after getting dumped, someone hooks up with his or her best friend of the opposite sex, but if you think about it, it's always really awkward afterward, you know?"

"You mean like in *When Harry Met Sally*?"

"Exactly," I replied. I held up a picture of me being crowned Private School Princess. Everyone in the audience looked so proud to know me.

"Yeah, I know what you mean, but honestly I was just trying to save you from Raymond and I figured that you probably wouldn't want to be alone that night."

"Right. That's what I thought," I said. "But I just wanted to check and make sure."

"Got it." I could hear him yawn. "I think I'm going to get to bed. I want to get some editing done on the doc tomorrow before work."

"Okay. Well, thanks for letting me come with you tonight," I said.

"You're welcome."

There was yet *another* thing weighing on my mind and I knew I'd have trouble sleeping if I didn't put it to rest. Having things weighing on your mind made it really heavy. "Hey, Josh, can I ask you one last thing?"

He yawned again. "Sure."

"You agree with me that going out with Raymond is probably a bad idea, right?"

"What?! He's, like, a bigger film geek than me, Ari, and Steven put together."

"That's what I thought but I was just making sure."

"Believe me, you don't want to go out with him," he replied before yawning again. "Are we done now?

"I think so. Good night. Thanks again."

"You're welcome. I'll talk to you tomorrow."

"Oh, hey, Josh?"

"Yeah, Dylan." He sighed.

"How's the documentary going?" I asked.

"It's good."

"You're happy with it?"

"Getting there," he said, yawning again.

As I picked up our junior-class photo taken at a beach in Malibu with me standing smack in the front, I got one of my brilliant ideas. "Wait. Stop the presses. I just got *such* a brilliant idea!" I announced.

"Is there any way we can talk about it in the morning?" he asked.

"No, because it has to do with you," I replied. "I'm going to have a party to screen your documentary."

"Dylan, I don't know—"

"It'll be great," I promised. "Not only will people get to see how talented you are, but it'll also help to remind them that even though I'm no longer dating Asher, I'm still a great example and role model of a popular teenage girl." I clapped my hands. "Ooh, it's been forever since I've had a party! I'm so excited. Omigod—I have so much to do. I totally don't have time to be talking right now. Bye," I said, hanging up.

If I could make Josh over, why couldn't I make myself over back into the most popular girl in school?

chapter twelve: *josh*

After Steven had shown me his cut of the documentary, I had spent every free moment I had holed up in my bedroom (aka the editing room) with iMovie. Soon it even looked like an actual editing room, with soda cans and fast-food wrappers strewn about. I'm normally pretty neat, but you have to be willing to throw that out the window when you're in the thick of creating a masterpiece.

That Tuesday I was trying to edit together a montage of Dylan, Lola, and Hannah walking down the halls of school like they were Charlie's Angels when there was a knock at the door.

"Come in," I called out.

Mom entered with a basket full of laundry and started unloading it on my bed. "So how's it going?" she asked. Out of the corner of my eye I could see her trying to peek over my shoulder.

"Good. But it's not done yet," I said, covering the

screen. She had been badgering me to show her some of it, but like any artist, I was very protective of my work until I felt it was in decent enough shape.

"Honey, it's never going to be done," she said, rolling my socks into balls.

I turned to her. "What are you talking about? It has to be done by Friday! That's when Dylan's party is!"

She shook her head. "That's not when I mean. You know that quote I have over my computer?"

"Which one? There's, like, fifty of them." Mom was big on quotes. In fact, she had taken a Learning Annex course entirely devoted to inspirational quotes.

"The one that says 'A poem is never finished—it's merely abandoned.' The same thing can be said for a movie. You can sit there polishing it and polishing it, but at some point you have to put it out in the world."

"I guess you're right." I sighed. But I bet Woody didn't release anything into the world until he felt it was good and ready.

"So can I see just a little bit?" she asked. "Please?"

I scooted my chair over. "Okay. But you have to remember that it's still really rough," I warned.

She dragged another chair over. "I know. I know." She kissed me on the forehead. "But I already know it's brilliant."

I shook my head. As my mom, what else was she going to say?

I cued up the scene in the car after the UCLA fraternity party.

"I don't know," Dylan was saying on-screen, "sometimes it's like . . . when people see you a certain way, they don't *want* you to change. They just want you to keep being *that* girl—the popular girl."

I had intercut this with Dylan walking down the hall, as everyone yelled out hellos to her.

"Believe me, if I were to chuck it all and go all boho hippy and stop shaving my legs, people would freak out," her voice continued. Here, I had cut in some footage of the boho hippies sitting outside school smoking clove cigarettes. "Not just because it would be disgusting, but because they expect me to be . . . well, *me*," came the voice again. At this point I had cut back to the footage in the car, close on her face. "I've been this for so long I wouldn't even know how to go be someone else," she said quietly.

I loved the look on her face when she said that.

"Oh, Josh—it's wonderful," Mom whispered, squeezing my shoulder.

"You think?" I said anxiously.

She nodded. "It's like you managed to capture the vulnerability that all teens feel, but try so hard to hide. And the fact that it's coming from the most popular girl in school? Well, that alone is going to make people feel so much better. Everyone thinks that the grass is always greener on the other side, but, really, it's not. Believe me, I know—I used to live in Brentwood and shop at Saks and now I can't even afford to get my hair colored there."

"That's exactly what I was going for!" I said excitedly. After I sat down and watched all the footage, I had realized that while an inside look at the popular kids of Castle Heights would be interesting, what would be even *more* interesting would be to look at the pressures of popularity and how lonely it could be when you were that popular— like those princesses in fairy tales who live in castles and do nothing all day other than play with a golden ball only to find themselves in real trouble when they drop it down a well and have to ask a frog to retrieve it for them.

By the time the party rolled around on Friday, I had made Dylan so human—so vulnerable—that once people saw this, even the biggest Dylan hater would turn into a Dylan lover. I'm not the kind of guy to use the word *genius* lightly, but sometimes that's the only one that works. Even though the documentary focused primarily on Dylan, I think I had managed to tell a universal story that hit on everything audiences like to see—love, greed, ambition, popularity, heartbreak, betrayal. All stuff that Shakespeare wrote about in his plays.

Not only did I hope the USC admissions committee would like the documentary as much as Mom did, but I was hoping it would help get Dylan back on solid ground in terms of her social status. Although I'm all for a character getting payback in order for the audience to feel satisfied (one of the first things Quentin talked about when he spoke to the Film Society), I couldn't help feeling bad for her and the way that everyone had been treating her since she and Asher broke up. Instead of falling all over her, they were just tolerating her. Sort of like how on the news you saw people being nice to ex-presidents as if they'd get arrested if they weren't.

It wasn't a huge bash—more of a small get-together of twelve or so of the A-minus/B-plus crowd as well as me, Steven, and Ari. According to Dylan, the party was her way of telling the world that even though Asher had dumped her for Amy Loubalu, she was a survivor. She may have survived the breakup, but judging from how no one was paying attention to her at the party, she might not survive the fallout of no longer being the girlfriend of the most popular guy in school. I had always thought that Dylan was just as popular as Asher, but judging from the way that people were now treating her, that didn't seem to be the case. Not only was she no longer royalty, but some of them didn't even try to hide their yawns when she went on about the top thirty reasons why her life was already better since the breakup. To be honest, number fourteen— "I now get to wear the color green whenever I want because I had stopped wearing it because Asher didn't like it"—felt like it was stretching it a bit.

"Well, should we screen it now?" Dylan asked. I was sitting next to her on the couch feeling nauseous from all the sushi I had just scarfed down. It was one of the foods on the "Things That I Never Got to Eat When I Was Going Out with Asher Because He Didn't Like Them" menu that she had served, some of the others being egg salad (which no one was interested in) and beet salad (ditto). "I'm afraid if we wait until after everyone starts in on the black-and-whites, they'll go into a sugar coma and fall asleep."

"That's a good point," I said. I could feel my stomach start to jump.

"Want to do a little breathing first?" she asked.

I nodded.

"Okay, and breathe in," she instructed.

We both took a deep breath in.

"And out," she said as we started to exhale.

"Excellent! And again," she said.

I still hadn't replaced my inhaler, and every time I said I was going to, Dylan convinced me to go one more day without it. The breathing really helped. Who knew? Maybe one day I'd be off the inhaler forever.

After we were done with the breathing, she turned to me. "How's that?"

I gave her a thumbs-up.

She gave me a hug. "I'm so proud of you!" she squealed. "I *knew* you didn't really need that thing."

"Maybe I outgrew my asthma," I said as I stood up.

"Maybe you never even *had* it. Maybe it was all just stress-related," she replied.

"Okay, everyone—it's time!" she yelled, clapping her

hands and running around the living room. "Everyone in the family room so we can screen my—I mean, Josh's—movie!" When no one moved, she put her fingers in her mouth and gave an ear-shattering whistle. "Let's move it, people!" she bellowed.

Soon enough everyone was settled in the family room, with Dylan standing in front of the big-screen television. She cleared her throat. "Okay, so before we start, I just want to say that as many of you know, when Josh first brought up the idea of doing a movie about me, I wasn't all that interested—"

Lola rolled her eyes. "It's not a movie just about *you*—it's a documentary about the inner workings of the in crowd of Castle Heights, which means it's about *all* of us, right, Josh?"

"Ah . . . yeah, well, kind of," I stuttered as I scratched at my neck.

"Yeah, but seeing that *I'm*, like, the central figure in the movie, that kind of makes me the star. Right, Josh?"

I scratched at my neck some more before giving a combination shrug/nod that I hoped would make each girl feel that I was in agreement with her. I could already tell I was going to hate the politics of filmmaking.

"So as I was saying," Dylan continued, "when Josh first started filming, I was a little worried that this was just some warped way for him to take out his frustration because he wasn't popular." She smiled at me. "But over the last month, not only have I gotten to see that Josh is so *not* warped in any way—unlike, you know, *some* people who shall remain nameless who go out with a girl for two years and then dump her three weeks before a major social event—but he's also not a geek even though he may have looked like one before I gave him a makeover. In fact, not only is he so *not* a geek, but he's probably the nicest person I've ever met and I feel incredibly honored to be the star of his first movie"—with this, Lola rolled her eyes again—"in what I know will be a supersuccessful career with tons of hit movies and television shows. And with that, I'd like to introduce my dear friend Josh Rosen."

As everyone started to clap, I gave my neck one more good scratch before making my way up to where she was standing. Looking out at the group of kids who, a little more than a month ago, didn't even know my name and were now giving me what looked to be genuine smiles, I started to relax. Sure, the first eleven years and one month of my school career had been tough, but hey, it happens. As far as I was concerned, all that was water under the bridge. Finally I felt a part of something other than the Film Society and the Russian Club, and I had to say, it felt amazing.

"Thanks, Dylan," I said. I looked out at the crowd and remembered to stand up straight. "I'm really excited that you're all here for the world premiere of *The View from the Top of Castle Heights*. Not only was it a very rewarding experience creatively, but I also got the opportunity to make some great new friends. I don't want to say any more, because I'd rather let the documentary speak for itself, but I just want to thank all of you for being so generous with the access you gave me and Steven and Ari into your lives. And, uh, with that, I hope you enjoy *The View from the Top of Castle Heights*."

I started to sit down, but then stopped and faced the crowd. "Oh, and there'll be a brief question-and-answer period after the film. Thanks," I said, with a slight bow.

Once Steven killed the lights, I waited until I saw A FILM BY JOSH ROSEN appear on the screen before making my way to the kitchen. From every interview I had read, no director who was really good ever stayed for a screening of the film. Instead they went to some bar and knocked back a couple of shots of Jack Daniel's or stood outside and chain-smoked and paced until it was time to come back for the Q&A. Part of being a director was pretending you didn't care what the audience thought, even if you did. Because I didn't smoke or drink, I figured I could calm my nerves with food but still be close enough to be able to hear the laughs and sounds of amazement from the audience.

I was in the process of putting together an Everything-but-the-Kitchen-Sink Special when I heard the scream.

"Josh, GET IN HERE! *NOW!*" I heard Dylan yell.

There was something about the tone of her voice that made me think she wasn't calling me in to tell me how brilliant I was.

As I walked into the family room, on-screen was Dylan sitting on The Ramp one day during lunch. She was sitting in between Hannah and Lola, with their arms folded, the three of them looking down at the rest of the cafeteria like they were the judges for *Project Runway: Castle Heights.* "Um, hello, but could that girl's outfit *be* more hi-I-live-in-Seattle-and-therefore-I-have-no-fashion-sense?" Dylan was saying on film.

I could hear a nervous giggle from somewhere in the room, but otherwise it was quiet. Except for the sound of my very loud gulp.

"Asher and I pretty much *have* to date," she said to the camera in the next scene as a sea of kids parted to give her room to walk. "It's not like I could be dating someone like, I don't know, *you* or him," she said, pointing to someone offscreen, which, from the look of distaste on her face, meant that it was probably Steven. "That would be like . . . a giraffe ending up with a tiger or something. It's just not physically possible, you know?"

As I watched the screen, my mouth fell open so wide I actually *could* have fit the kitchen sink in it.

I had grabbed the wrong DVD before I left the house that night.

Instead of bringing the version that showed Dylan as a multilayered, three-dimensional character, I had picked up the one Steven had put together.

As Dylan liked to say . . . *Oh. My. God.*

I immediately ran over to the DVD player.

"No, leave it," she ordered. She sounded so mad I almost expected her head to go around in circles like Linda Blair's in *The Exorcist*.

"I know a lot of kids do things like volunteer at nursing homes or stuff like that," she was saying on-screen, "but I feel like I can do a lot more good just by being around kids my own age and showing them what's new in fashion, you know?"

Not the type of footage that was going to have Oprah's people banging down Dylan's front door to have her on the show for an episode about "Inspirational Teenage Role Models."

"Dylan, I can explain—" I stammered.

There was a shot of Lola and Hannah being cooed over by two gay guys at a little French bakery on Westwood Boulevard. "I have gay friends, too," said Dylan on-screen, "but not naming names or anything, I feel like *some* people rely on them for attention. Especially if they feel like they're being overshadowed by their best friend."

At that line, Lola and Hannah gasped in stereo on the couch.

"Catfight," someone called out.

"Now you can turn it off," Dylan said quietly.

Someone turned the lights on. "Dylan, I can explain—" I began as I felt every eye in the room staring at me.

If I had really wanted to show Dylan in a sympathetic, vulnerable light, I should have had my camera with me, because the look on her face at that moment was heart-breaking. Instead of looking like the beautiful, put-together popular girl who had intimidated hundreds of less popular kids in the halls of Castle Heights, she looked like her fifth-grade self in that picture that was in her dad's office. The glasses and braces were gone, but the emotional gawkiness was there.

She looked like I had felt all these years up until I had met her.

"So this is what you think of me?" she asked softly. Even from across the room I could see the tears that were brewing in her blue eyes.

"No! What happened was—"

"You know, maybe I'm not Shari Chase or Debra Wellington"—two girls in school who were always organizing do-good events such as food drives for Feed the Homeless of War-Torn Countries and Take an Elderly Neighbor to School Day—"and maybe I like to go shopping and maybe I know a lot about nail polish, but that doesn't mean I'm a bad person—"

"Of course not," I agreed. "You're not a bad person at all. You're a *great* person—"

"I mean, would a bad person help someone who she considered a *friend* change their look?" she asked, her voice rising.

"Please—just let me explain—"

"And would a bad person give that quote-unquote

friend tips on how to talk to the girl he had a crush on?" she asked, the tears now falling down her face.

"I'm telling you, it's all just a misunderstanding—"

"And would a bad person let someone follow them around with a camera for weeks, and sing Neil Diamond songs with them in the car, and make sure that they didn't go to sleep without calling or texting to say good night?" she said as her nose started running.

"No," I said quietly.

"I didn't think so," she said, wiping her face with her sleeve. Gone was the perfectly put-together girl from that day in front of the fountain. "You know, I'm thinking this might be a good time for you to leave."

"But if you just give me a minute to explain—"

"A *really* good time," she shouted.

It was so quiet I'm sure you could hear my stress-induced wheezing all the way across the room. Everyone was staring at the floor. Finally Steven spoke up.

"Dylan, I'm the one you should be—"

She held up her hand. "And I want you and him," she said, pointing at Ari, "to leave, too."

I pointed at the DVD player. "I'll just take that DVD back—"

She grabbed it out of the machine and threw it at me.

"Thanks," I said, picking it up off the floor. I pointed at the machine. "If I could just get the sleeve for it—"

The laser beams of hate she was shooting through her eyes would have been enough to scare the biggest action hero away. "On second thought, I don't really need it," I mumbled. As the three of us made our way toward the hall, Steven stopped and grabbed a handful of popcorn.

"What are you doing?" I hissed.

He shrugged. "Humiliation makes me hungry," he whispered defensively.

"*Everything* makes you hungry," whispered Ari.

"So sue me," Steven whispered back.

Once we were on the front steps, I heard the click of the dead bolt on the door behind us. I plopped down and put my head in my hands. "I can't believe this," I moaned.

"If you ask me, she's overreacting a little," said Steven.

The two of us looked at him like he was crazy.

He shrugged as he reached into his pocket and took out a handful of the Hershey's Kisses that he had stockpiled from the dishes that had been laid out around the family room. "What? People make mistakes."

"Yeah, but usually when they're going to screen a movie before an audience, they check to see if it's the right one," said Ari.

"Still, you have to admit, *my* cut looked great up there on the screen," Steven went on. "The pacing was awesome."

I sighed as I rubbed my arms in an attempt to get

warm. For a few weeks I had been granted entrance into the inner sanctum of Castle Heights society, but that was now a fading memory. Once again I had been thrust back out into the cold. Or at least as cold at it got during an unseasonably warm November in Southern California.

chapter thirteen: *dylan*

Thanks to Josh—my *ex*-best friend—it turned out my wish had been granted: the documentary *was* like a real-life *Laguna Beach*. Except that he had cast me in the role of the bitch.

After I locked the door behind him and his stupid geek friends, I stood in the foyer and forced myself to breathe. At that moment I wished *I* had an inhaler. To say I felt betrayed and humiliated didn't come close to describing how I felt. No—it was as if I was *beyond* betrayed and humiliated.

As I slowly walked back to the family room, I prayed that when I got there I'd discover that this so wasn't a big deal. Wasn't Lola always telling me I tended to overreact? And back when we had been going out, Asher had said that all the time, like when I got all mad when he had called fifteen minutes before he was supposed to meet Daddy and me at the country club for dinner and said he couldn't make it because he had just scored a ticket off Craigslist for an Ultimate Fighting match.

Before I walked in, I took a deep breath. "Keep it together," I whispered to myself. As I walked into the room, everyone immediately shut up. "Hey, does anyone want to watch a *real* movie?" I asked, trying to sound like what had happened was no big deal. "Something fun and uplifting, like a John Hughes one?"

No one answered. Instead they just stared at me like I was one of those actresses that kept showing up on the cover of the tabloids because of public freak-outs.

Okay, so maybe it was a bigger deal than I had thought.

I sat down and picked up a container of Twizzlers. "Don't tell me you guys haven't figured out that what Josh put together was just his way of taking out all his anger and frustration on us popular people because he's such a geek."

"What do you mean 'us'?" asked Lola. "We look fine. *You're* the one who comes off as a bitch."

I shoved a stick of licorice into my mouth as fast as I could. "Well, that's just because he's secretly in love with me and he finally got it through his thick head that I was never going to feel that way about him," I replied with my mouth full.

"You always think everyone's in love with you," said Hannah accusingly. "But they're so not. I mean, look at

Asher—you keep saying how you guys were going out for two years but the truth is you barely ever saw him."

Even though it was full of licorice, I couldn't stop my mouth from opening, which meant some of it fell out. I couldn't believe of all people, Hannah—the person who was always nagging me about whether we were best friends or best best friends—would talk to me like that.

"Yeah," agreed Lola. "And if we're being really honest here, the only reason you were—note the past tense, please—the most popular girl in school is because you happened to be dating the most popular guy in school."

I picked the licorice off my shirt and put it in a napkin. "That's so not true!" I cried. I looked around at everyone. "Right?"

No one would look me in the eye.

"Right?" I asked again.

All I got in response were some coughs.

"I can't believe you guys are going to let some total geek control you like this," I said.

"Maybe he's not a geek," said Lola. "Maybe *you're* the geek."

If I hadn't had such good manners, I would've punched her in the nose right in front of everyone. Or at least ripped her new blouse.

"At least he doesn't sit there and pass judgment on people for what they're wearing, and who they date, and what kind of car they drive," added Hannah.

What had gotten into her? "Okay, well, then if I'm so horrible, what are all you guys doing here?" I demanded.

"Because you always serve good party food?" asked Robbie Shapiro, who could've stood to lose a pound or ten.

"And because there was nothing else going on tonight?" suggested Lisa Eaton.

I stared out at the people who, until ten minutes ago, I had considered my friends. I couldn't believe they could just turn on a dime like that. "So what are you saying?" I asked, my voice shaking. "That you guys think I'm as hideous as the documentary makes me out to be? That none of you want to be my friend anymore?" I bit the inside of my cheek. Even though I hadn't been able to control myself earlier, there was no way I was going to start crying again.

Instead of everyone quickly saying "What are you talking about—of *course* not! Of *course* we're your friends!" which is what you would've thought they would've said to the most popular girl in school, they were all quiet.

Except for Lola. "The camera doesn't lie," she said with a shrug.

So much for not crying, I thought as the tears started rolling down my face. "Well, then maybe you should all leave," I managed to get out.

I didn't have to ask twice. They got up so fast and started for the door you would've thought the In-N-Out burger party truck had just pulled up outside.

Hannah and Lola hung back. Thank God they had come to their senses and remembered they were my best friends. As I turned to them, for the first time in what felt like forever, I allowed myself to smile.

They, however, *weren't* smiling. "You know, after seeing Josh's documentary, it makes me wonder what *else* you've said about us when we're not around," said Hannah. I hadn't seen her this PO'd since her father's secretary had forgotten to mail her Princeton application and she missed the early-admission cut-off date.

"And I don't know who died and made you in charge of everything," said Lola. "Listening to you up there, you'd think that we were just your dumb backup singers or something."

"You know, if it weren't for Amy taking pity on you all those years ago, you'd still be wearing ugly clothes and eating lunch by yourself," said Hannah.

"And instead of spending your time shopping, you'd be . . . volunteering at cat shelters," added Lola.

"Sometimes I wonder if Lola and I made the right decision when we chose sides that day," said Hannah. "Amy may have her issues, but somehow I doubt stabbing her so-called best friends in the back on film is one of them. Come on, Lola, let's go."

As the two of them stomped out of my house, I sank down into the couch and began to *really* cry, but not before grabbing every half-filled bowl of popcorn, chips, and pretzels to keep me company now that I was officially friendless.

I didn't stop crying all weekend, except for the fifty or so times I called Lola and Hannah to apologize, but it didn't even matter because they didn't pick up. The only person who called or e-mailed me was Josh, but I just deleted all of his messages without listening to or reading them. I couldn't believe I had been such a fool for thinking we were friends—all he cared about was getting into USC and it didn't matter who he hurt in the process. In fact, he'd probably do really well in Hollywood for that very reason. What made me even madder about the situation was that I found myself missing him. Hannah was right—even though Josh wasn't my boyfriend, I had spent more time with him in the last month than I had with Asher in the last year.

But how could you miss someone you hated? Because I did hate Josh Rosen. More than anything.

And yet I also really missed talking to him on the phone, singing Neil Diamond songs with him and eating his fries.

The whole situation was so confusing that I had to stay in bed all weekend. The only time I felt better was when I was lying down with the covers over my head. Daddy was in Napa Valley on a wine-country tour with Amber and I was all alone anyway, so I didn't have to deal with anyone asking me what was wrong. When Monday rolled around, I still wasn't ready to face people, so I told Daddy I was sick and needed to stay home from school. As he had a big meeting that morning, he was too busy to check and see if I was lying when I said I had a 105-degree fever, so I spent the day researching boarding schools online.

But on Tuesday I knew I couldn't put off the inevitable anymore.

Usually the week before a major school social event, all conversation centers around dresses and after-parties. Except when the most popular girl in school has been thrown off her throne and kicked to the curb. Then it's about her. Or, rather, me.

No one said anything to my face, but I could hear the whispers and giggles as I walked the halls between classes. Not even Ashley and Britney Turner would talk to me. I didn't even bother going into the cafeteria during lunch. Instead I went to the girls' bathroom. Luckily there was a nice, big handicapped stall for me to hang out in as I ate my protein bar and read through all the boarding-school info I had printed out.

Maybe all this time alone is a good thing, I thought as I read about the Bradberry School for Girls in the boonies of Massachusetts. Back when I was popular and everyone wanted to hang out with me 24/7, I was always annoyed that I never had any downtime. Now that I had no one to hang out with, this was the perfect opportunity to really get to *know* myself. To catch up on all the classics that had been collecting dust on my bookshelf, like Jackie Collins's *Hollywood Wives,* because I was busy spending my time reading magazines to figure what to wear to all the parties I used to go to. To find a hobby that I could do alone since I no longer had any geeks in my life to fix up. Maybe I would follow in Josh's mom's footsteps and look into something at the Learning Annex. I could even teach my own class and call it "How to Go On After Your Entire Life Has Been Blown to Bits and You're Officially a Loser Again." Plus, with all this extra time, I could work on my college essays since there was no way I would submit the documentary.

As I studied a photo of a bunch of pasty girls playing field hockey and tried to imagine myself as one of them (the little plaid skirts *were* pretty cute), I heard the door to the bathroom open. A moment later the smell of spicy vanilla filled the room.

Just when I had thought it couldn't get any worse, it had. I knew that perfume as well as I knew my own: it was Comptoir Sud Pacifique Vanilla Passion Eau de Toilette and I used to smell it on Amy Loubalu's mother when she drove us to the mall. Now it was Amy's signature scent, much like Princess by Vera Wang was mine.

I listened to Amy brush her teeth (she was one of those always-brush-and-floss-after-every-meal people, which drove me bonkers) and wondered how I was going to get out of the bathroom without her seeing me other than crawling through the ceiling like you saw people do in movies.

After the water stopped, I stood up and crept up to the door, where I watched through the crack as she carefully dried her toothbrush before putting it back into its holder. I guess I hadn't locked the door all the way, because a moment later it opened and I went crashing through it and landed on my butt.

To her credit, Amy didn't start laughing like I probably would've done. "Are you okay?" she said as she came over and tried to help me up.

"Yeah, I'm fine," I said, trying to scramble to my feet. I walked over to the mirror and started fixing my hair, as if falling on my butt was part of my lunchtime exercise routine.

She looked at me, then stood in front of the other mirror and started putting on lip gloss. It reminded me of when we'd hang out at Sephora and make ourselves up. Thankfully, as we'd gotten older we'd both gotten a little better at it and no longer looked like circus clowns.

"I heard what happened with the documentary," she finally said.

I stopped applying my own lip gloss and turned to her. "I guess you probably thought I deserved it."

She shrugged. "I don't know. I mean, yeah, as far as I'm concerned you took the Michael Rosenberg thing a little too seriously—"

"You know how difficult it is for me to let things go," I interrupted.

"But, Dylan, that was *eighth grade*. And you never even had the decency to confront me about it. You just stopped talking to me completely."

"You know how much confrontation scares me," I retorted.

"But you were my best best friend," she said.

As I looked at her, all the guilt I had never let myself feel for the way that I had acted came rushing to the surface. "I know," I said quietly. "And you were my mine."

She looked at me like she was waiting for me to tell her I was sorry, which I should've done right then and there, but it was like my mouth had been Krazy Glued shut.

"Anyway, it's too bad that no one got to see the real version," she said.

I turned away from the mirror. "What do you mean 'real version'?"

"Ari told me and Whitney in history yesterday morning that the version you saw was an earlier one that Steven had put together. Apparently, when Josh saw it, he freaked out because he thought it was too much like a bad reality show," Amy explained. "So I guess he did another version, but he brought the old one to the party that night by mistake."

"So in the real one I'm not this evil person who's a spoiled brat?" I asked.

She shrugged. "I don't know. I heard there's a moment when you're yelling at a guy with a cane in a crosswalk that I can't imagine you'd want in there, but other than that, it sounds like Josh made you out to be . . . human. Just like the rest of us." She looked down at the floor. "Even the ones who go out with the guy who their best friend has a crush on because they're going through a desperate-for-attention phase because their dad just told the family that he's moving out," she said softly.

I had forgotten that Amy had been going to therapy ever since seventh grade and always talked like that. "Now that I think about it, holding a grudge for four years over a guy like that seems really dumb," I said. "I mean, if he were someone super hot and cool *maybe*, but seeing that it was Michael Rosenberg—"

"You know, I saw him at the movies recently and he's so *not* as cute as he was back then," she said.

"Really?"

She nodded.

I guess it was a good thing I hadn't spent much time trying to track him down as a potential Fall Fling date. We both went back to fixing our hair and it felt like old times. So much so that I had almost forgotten that she was going to Fall Fling with my ex-boyfriend. Once I remembered, I could feel myself revving up inside to have a fit, but it was like those times when my car wouldn't start: the gears of the engine were turning and turning, but then . . . nothing.

Just some sputtering. It was as if all my drama-queen tendencies had dried up. Especially when I remembered that even though Asher had been my boyfriend, he really hadn't been my boyfriend for about a year.

"I heard you're going to Fall Fling with Asher," I finally said.

I saw her look at me to see whether I was about to freak out.

"That's cool," I continued. "He's a good guy. Most of the time, that is. Not when he's dumping people right before school dances with no warning or explanation, but he's got his moments of niceness."

She shrugged. "He was the only one who asked me and I figured it would be nice to go to one of those things before I graduated."

"Yeah, I never did understand why you're never there," I replied. I had figured that it was because she was dating twenty-five-year-old talent agents and that would look really creepy.

"Because no one ever asks me."

"Really?" I asked as I took out my mascara. I don't know why I was bothering—I had been crying so much over the last few days my eyes were so puffy you couldn't even see them.

She nodded and then reached in her bag for a pack of gum. "Do you want a piece?" she asked, holding it out.

"Thanks," I said. I had also forgotten that when

Amy wasn't stealing people's boyfriends, she was very generous.

"You should be going with Josh, then," I joked as I pulled my hair back into a ponytail. "He's never been to one, either."

She pulled her hair back into a ponytail, too. "That's who I wanted to go with, but he didn't ask."

I glanced over at her to see if she was joking, but the look on her face was dead serious.

"There was a point where he was coming to Mani's every day after school a few weeks ago and I thought he might, but he didn't."

Wait a minute—that week when Josh was going to see his crush every day but couldn't talk to her . . .

It couldn't be.

Could it?

Oh. My. God. It was *Amy* that Josh had had a crush on all this time! No wonder he wouldn't tell me who it was. I couldn't believe that out of everyone at Castle Heights, it was her that Josh was crushing on. Granted, maybe the last few minutes had made it so that she was no longer my archenemy, but back when he and I were friends, he didn't know that. I could only wonder what *else* I'd find out he had done behind my back.

"Anyway, I'm not going with Asher anymore," she said, cleaning out her purse. I had forgotten what a neat freak she was.

"What are you talking about?" I asked.

"He texted me the other night and said that he had just heard that Rebecca Jenkins and Mark Wolcott had broken up, and because he had been wanting to go out with her since freshman year, he wanted to jump on it."

"I can't believe that!" I said. "What a jerk."

She shrugged. "It's okay. I wasn't that into going with him anyway. Since I had already gotten a dress, I called Josh last night to see if he wanted to go. But he said that even though you weren't talking to him at the moment, you guys had made plans to hang out that night and he didn't feel comfortable breaking them until he checked with you. Except that you wouldn't return any of his calls or e-mails."

I couldn't believe it—my best friend had a crush on my ex-best friend, and because he was such a good friend, he would've given up the opportunity to go to Fall Fling with his dream girl and stay home with me watching old movies because I didn't have a date.

Josh wasn't the geek here—*I* was.

"He's a really good guy," Amy said.

"Yeah," I agreed. "He really is."

Too bad I had screwed everything up.

As far as I was concerned, just because I wasn't going to Fall Fling didn't mean I couldn't wear one of the three dresses I'd already bought, even if the only place I was going that night was Pinkberry. Maybe I looked ridiculous ordering a quart of frozen yogurt with raspberries and coconut while wearing a black minidress with fake leopard-fur cuffs and black patent-leather stiletto heels, especially since it was pouring rain, but I liked to think of myself as an example for all the other girls who didn't have dates that night. Even if we didn't have dates, or weren't invited out, that didn't mean we needed to stay home all night in yoga pants and stained sweatshirts feeling sorry for ourselves.

That being said, I had to admit I *was* feeling sorry for myself. Not because of Fall Fling, but because I had called and texted Josh a bunch of times and now *he* was the one who wouldn't return my messages. Given how I had acted, I couldn't say I blamed him, but, still, I really missed him. Eating Everything-but-the-Kitchen-Sink Specials by myself was getting boring, and without Josh's tenor voice, "Song Sung Blue" didn't sound as good with just my soprano one. But most importantly I just missed talking to him. Even if he always had to compare everything to a movie, our conversations had always left me with something to think about. As I turned on Sunset Boulevard to go home, I had resigned myself to the fact that I was destined to finish off my senior year friendless when Neil Diamond's "Cherry, Cherry" came on the radio. At first, hearing it just made me more sad, remembering that night when Josh drove me home from the UCLA party, but as I started singing—softly at first, but soon louder and louder (it really *is* my favorite Neil song)—it filled me with courage.

At the next light I pulled an illegal U-ey and drove toward Hollywood. The Universe really must have supported me in what I was about to do because I had all green lights the entire way, and before I knew it I was in front of Josh's house. Unfortunately the only parking space I could find was two blocks away, so by the time I made it to the house, I looked like a drowned rat. Or, rather, a drowned leopard.

"Whoops," I said, tripping as I made my way up the walkway. I probably could have left the stilettos out of the equation and still made my point about not needing a date to dress up, but it was too late for that. Plus, I never understood why someone would wear something as boring as flats or flip-flops when they could make their legs look even longer with heels.

"Dylan! Come in, come in," said Josh's mom after she answered the door. "You must be freezing to death!"

"No," I said through my chattering teeth. "I'm okay." I stepped inside and tried not to drip too much on the rug. "Is Josh here?"

"Sure. Josh!" she yelled. "Dylan's here!" She turned back to me. "He didn't tell me you were coming by. If I had known I would've saved you some of the stuffed eggplant I made from my Introduction to Turkish Cooking class."

"He's not really expecting me—"

From the surprised look on his face when he walked into the living room, that was definitely the case.

"What are you doing here?" He took in my outfit. "And what are you *wearing*?"

"Sorry to just show up like this, but you didn't respond to any of my voice mails or texts, so I figured this was the only way to talk to you . . . "

"Mrs. Spivakovsky's dog got ahold of my phone on Wednesday when I was over there and dropped it in his water bowl, so I've been phoneless," he replied.

"Oh."

He sniffed. "What's that weird smell?" He turned toward his mother. "Mom, do you think once in a while you could make nonethnic food?"

I held up my arm and sniffed. "I think it's my wet fake fur. So do you think I can talk to you for a second?"

"Sure. Come on back to my room."

As I started to follow him, Sandy did as well.

"Um, Mom?" Josh asked when we got to his bedroom.

She stopped and turned toward her own bedroom. "I'm just going to my room to finish putting away my laundry."

"The laundry's still in the dryer," Josh replied.

"Oh. You're right." She took my hands in hers. "Okay, I'm not going to eavesdrop, but I just want to say that I'm really glad you're here, Dylan, and I just know you kids can work out your problems. I've been setting that as my intention every time I've meditated this week."

"Thanks," I said as I walked into Josh's room while she continued to stand at the door.

"Mom?" Josh said again.

"Okay, okay," she said as she finally walked away.

329

The two of us stood in the middle of the room while I dripped on the rug some more.

Sandy poked her head in. "Dylan, honey, I thought you might be more comfortable in these," she said, holding out a pair of yoga pants and a UCLA sweatshirt.

"Thanks. That would be great," I said, taking them from her.

I went into the bathroom and changed. Okay, so maybe I *was* spending Fall Fling in yoga pants and a sweatshirt, but seeing how the last few weeks had gone, I shouldn't have been too surprised that things weren't working out the way I had planned.

When I came back out, Josh was fiddling with something on his computer, but as I got closer he minimized it before I could see what it was. It felt like more than a week since we'd seen each other. For a second we just stared at each other and said nothing. Actually, we stared at anything *but* each other. I pointed at his desk. "You got a new inhaler," I said.

He nodded. "Yeah, but I haven't had to use it yet," he replied.

"That's great," I said, before we went back to saying nothing. "So I ran into Amy Loubalu the other day when I was hiding out in the bathroom during lunch."

"Oh yeah?" he asked, turning red as he got up from the computer and walked over to his *Star Wars* action figures.

"Yeah."

More silence.

"She told me about the other version of the documentary," I added.

"She did?" he asked, fiddling with Luke's light-wand thingie.

"Yeah," I said.

Even more silence.

"She also told me that she called and asked you to Fall Fling but you said that you had to check with me first because we had had plans."

He fiddled with Luke some more. "Well, we did," he replied.

I took a deep breath. "Okay, so here's the deal: I owe you a huge apology, Josh. I said some really horrible things, and to be honest, I wouldn't blame you if you never forgave me, but I hope you will because you're not a geek— you're . . . my best friend. And I'd be really, really bummed if you weren't in my life anymore. I mean, who else am I going to find to sing Neil Diamond songs with other than my dad? And who's going to give me a play-by-play analysis of every scene of a movie? And who else am I going to meet who knows the contents of WebMD by heart? And who else am I going to call to say 'I'm hungry' or 'I'm cold' and get a thoughtful response like you always give me? And who's going to help me write that 'Best Black-and-White Cookies in L.A.' blog we talked about a few weeks ago? You might be a total geek sometimes, but like a total geek in the best sense of the word, you know? That supernice, supersweet, supersensitive part of geekdom.

And, by the way? *I'm* a total geek, too, sometimes! Like remember when there was that Disney double feature at the New Beverly—the one with *Lady and the Tramp* and *101 Dalmatians*—and I really wanted to go but you said that even you wouldn't be caught dead watching that stuff on the big screen?"

"Yeah, I remember," he replied.

"Well, I didn't tell you this because I was embarrassed, but I went."

"You did?"

I nodded. "Yeah. And I loved it."

"Wow. Alone at a Disney double feature. That really *is* geeky," he said.

"So what I'm saying is I'm beyond sorry," I announced.

"Okay," he said.

"And if there's—wait, that's it? You're accepting my apology?"

He shrugged. "Yeah. Why not?"

I went over and picked up a Harry Potter action figure on a shelf. "Boy. You're easy. See—that's another thing I love about you, Josh: how uncomplicated you are."

"Are you saying I shouldn't accept your apology?" he asked as he walked over and put the figure back in its right spot after I set it back down.

"No. Not at all. I'm just saying that someone who wasn't, you know, as *mature* as you are would make the person suck up to them for a while longer. And that's another thing I love about you—the way that you don't believe in wasting time—"

"You can stop sucking up to me now."

"Okay. Great. Thanks. So we're friends again?"

He nodded. "You know, it was really hard when you just shut me out, and just wouldn't respond to my e-mails and calls. But . . . yeah. We're friends again."

I flopped down on his bed. "Thank God *that* crisis is over." I sighed.

"But, Dylan?"

"Yeah?"

"Can you get off my bed? Or at least not put your head on my pillow? Your hair's still wet and I don't want to catch a cold when I go to sleep."

"I know—because your lungs never fully developed because you were born premature," I said as I stood up. "And now moving on: so Amy's your crush, huh?"

He blushed as he started straightening the covers on his bed.

"I think you two make a cute couple."

He stopped and looked at me. "You do? I thought you hated her."

I shrugged. "She's not so bad." I looked at my watch. It was only nine. "Obviously it's too late to go to Fall Fling—and since those school-dance things are so lame, why would you even want to?—but maybe you should call her and see if she wants to grab a slice of banana-cream pie at The Apple Pan or something."

"Tonight?"

"Yeah, why not?"

From the way his hand hovered over his inhaler, the idea terrified him. "I mean, you talked to her on the phone the other day."

"But I haven't spent time with her *in person*! Doing that would be like . . . a *date* or something!"

I put my hand on his shoulder. "Josh—it's time. You can do it. I know you can."

"You think so?"

I nodded. "I know so. Plus, she's already into you!"

"She is?"

I rolled my eyes. "She called you and asked you to Fall Fling—how many more neon lights do you need?"

"Oh. I guess you have a point."

I reached for his hand. "Seriously, Josh—you're, like, a total . . . *prince*."

"I am?"

"You are."

"Thanks," he said shyly as his face turned as red as the comforter on his bed. He started to reach for his inhaler again, but then thought better of it and stood up straight. It turned out he was pretty tall. "But what are you going to do tonight?" he asked.

"I don't know." I shrugged. "Maybe watch *Hannah and Her Sisters*, if someone will loan it to me."

"I have something even better you might like," Josh said as he walked over to his computer.

"Better than *Hannah and Her Sisters*?" I teased. "I thought you said that was Woody's last great midcareer masterpiece."

He popped a DVD out of his computer and, after carefully placing it in a case, handed it to me. "It is. But this is *my* first early-career masterpiece. It's the documentary. The *real* version."

I took it from him and smiled. "Thanks." I walked over to his closet and picked out a pair of khakis and a sweater from The Gap that not only complemented his eyes but made him look like he had some upper-body strength, and put it down on the bed. "Call me tomorrow and let me know how it goes. Or if you need advice or something in the middle of the date, just call me from the restaurant."

"Okay," he said. "Hey, Dylan?"

"Yeah?" I said before I left the room.

He tossed me the inhaler. "You're my best friend, too."

When I got home, I settled into bed with an Everything-but-the-Kitchen-Sink Special, and in between texting Josh through his first date/inhalerless panic whenever Amy got up to go to the ladies's room, I watched what, in my humble opinion, was an Academy Award–winning documentary. Okay, yes, I had some areas to work on in terms of dealing with people, but hey, nobody's perfect. And, frankly, who *wants* to be? If you ask me, perfection is boring. I'd much rather be one of those girls that guys call "complicated."

Later, as I turned out the light to go to sleep, I thought about how right that guy on *Oprah* had been that day when he said that sometimes a crisis really *is* an opportunity. In this case it had been an opportunity to see that sometimes things weren't what they looked to be—like Asher, and Amy Loubalu, and, most importantly, Josh. I really had meant it when I told him he was a prince. A bit on the geekier side of princehood, maybe, but definitely a prince.

By the next week everyone at Castle Heights knew about the geek prince and his new princess, and instead of comments along the lines of "She's dating *him*?" everyone was genuinely happy for them. Josh and Amy were inseparable. Actually, the *three* of us were inseparable. At first I felt like a fifth wheel, but they seemed to really want me to sit with them outside at lunch (my Ramp days were long gone), and because I didn't have any other friends, it was either that or continue eating in the bathroom. The goofy perma-smiles on their faces may have bordered on nauseating at times, but because they were so sweet (not just to me, but to everyone, because that's the kind of people they were), I was happy for them rather than jealous. It was weird—even though it had been years since Amy and I had been friends, we picked up right where we had left off and it felt like no time at all had passed. I even started becoming friends with Whitney Lewin, who, it turned out, wasn't stuck-up at all—just shy. Having her to hang out with came in handy when Josh and Amy wanted to hang out alone.

Because of an incident at Fall Fling that may or may not have happened concerning Rachel Trebecnik, a bottle of peppermint schnapps she stole from her parents' liquor cabinet, and Mr. Marino, the boys' soccer coach, I soon became old news. At first it was weird to fly so low below the radar, but it was also liberating. I mean, I got to do things I *never* would have done back when I was the most popular girl in school—like wear sweats in public or show up to school with unwashed hair and limited makeup. I only did that twice, because, you know, I'm *me*, but still . . .

One of the best things about just being one of the crowd was that I had the time to really get to know myself because I no longer had people trying to get my attention all the time. For instance, I never would've found out that I liked singing show tunes if I hadn't lost everything and had no social life and therefore had nothing better to do than spend three hours on a Saturday in Ari's car when we all road-tripped down to San Diego to go to the Seventh Annual Ukrainian Film Festival.

Actually, the day of the Ukrainian Film Festival ended up being a really important one for both Josh and me. Not only was it the day that Josh found out he had gotten early acceptance at USC, but when I turned around at the refreshment stand that afternoon after paying for my popcorn, I bumped smack into Roger and spilled it all over him and now he's my boyfriend! He's currently studying molecular biology at UC San Diego, but that's just to make his parents happy. What he really wants to be is a writer/director, which is why he just got a job at a video store. People might say I'm biased, but I happen to think he's *beyond* talented. Like Woody Allen–level talented. The other day he let me read the first ten pages of his new screenplay about a character from a video game who turns into a human and starts killing people, and it's brilliant. He says it's because I'm such a powerful muse, which I think is just beyond romantic. *And* unlike some people, he doesn't move his lips when he reads. The distance makes it hard, but we've been seeing each other every weekend. At the moment he's still geek-hot rather than hot-hot, but when he comes up on Saturday I'm taking him shopping at The Grove.

Not that I don't already adore him just the way he is. But still, you know, I'm *me*.